Never Sit Down in a Hoopskirt

and Other Things I Learned in Southern Belle Hell

CRICKETT RUMLEY

EGMONT

USA

New York

EGMONT

We bring stories to life

First published by Egmont USA, 2011
443 Park Avenue South, Suite 806
New York, NY 10016

This book is a work of fiction. Names, characters, places, and incidents are either the product of the author's imagination or are used fictitiously, and any resemblance to actual persons, living or dead, business establishments, events, or locales is entirely coincidental.

1 3 5 7 9 8 6 4 2

www.egmontusa.com

Library of Congress Cataloging-in-Publication Data
Rumley, Crickett.
Never sit down in a hoopskirt and other things I learned in Southern belle hell / Crickett Rumley.
p. cm.
Summary: After being ousted from yet another elite boarding school, seventeen-year-old Jane returns to her Alabama hometown, where her grandmother persuades her to enter the Magnolia Maid pageant.
ISBN 978-1-60684-131-0 (pbk.) — ISBN 978-1-60684-255-3 (e-book)
[1. Conduct of life—Fiction. 2. Beauty contests—Fiction. 3. Etiquette—Fiction.
4. Grandmothers—Fiction. 5. Fathers and daughters—Fiction. 6. Alabama—Fiction.]
I. Title.
PZ7.R8879Nev 2011
[Fic]—dc22
2010043617

Printed in the United States of America

Book design by Room39b

CPSIA tracking label information:
Printed in April 2011 at Berryville Graphics, Berryville, Virginia

In loving memory of my mother, Franke Kugler Rumley, who lived every day as a work of art and taught me to do the same.

The successful candidate for the Magnolia Court will be an upstanding young citizen of Bienville's fine community, a junior in high school no more than seventeen years of age at the time of her nomination to the Court. She will comport herself with dignity, charm, and grace in all situations, public and private. She will possess a deep love for her native city and be able to converse about its history with knowledge and vivacity. Charity and concern for others shall guide her actions. She will demonstrate an esprit de camaraderie *by allying with her sister Magnolia Maids to promote the high moral values of the Court, thus serving as a model of young Southern womanhood that inspires and uplifts young people throughout our nation and around the world.*

The Magnolia Court Manifesto, 1950

Chapter One

There's a whole chapter in the *Magnolia Court Orientation Handbook* titled "Manners Befitting a Maid Upon Announcement of Selection to the Court." It goes something like this, but not exactly like this because I've added a few flourishes to jack up the entertainment value:

1. DO glide on air across the stage of the Bienville Civic Center, visions dancing in your head of encasing your teeny-tiny size-two body in a giant Scarlett O'Hara dress.

Mallory Ross accomplished this task with panache as she stepped into the Winner's Circle.

2. DO NOT smirk as if there had *ever* been any doubt that you *wouldn't* make it. You may be Ashley LaFleur, perfect little princess with loads of Daddy's

money and Mother's good looks (thank God!), and you may think you rule the universe, which of course is why the judges announced your name first, but still. Arrogant smirks never look good on anyone, especially achievement pageant winners.

3. DO smile humbly and wave into the dark auditorium toward where your family is cheering you on, even if the rest of the audience *is* gaping in stunned silence. Zara Alexander aced this feat, but then she's one hundred percent grace and elegance, so what else would you expect?

4. DO NOT remain frozen solid in Finalists' Row as you scream inside your head, *What?! Me? Whyyyyyyyy??????*

That would be me. I violated that one.

But that was nothing compared to the rules Brandi Lyn Corey broke next:

5. DO NOT let your boyfriend and his redneck buddies from the EZ Lube shout "Who let the dawgs out?" and punctuate it with air-horn blasts.

6. DO NOT play overwhelmed beauty-pageant winner by fluttering your hands in front of your face like a nervous butterfly and staggering in the direction of the Winner's Circle (see previous graceful gliding), and most certainly . . .

7. DO NOT proceed to faint right in front of me, because

I will be scared to death that you're going to knock your teeth out, and I might have to jerk you up by your big blonde hair, accidentally ripping out a patch which will hurt like h-e-double toothpicks *and* take forever to grow back in, but you will forgive me for it because God wants us to forgive (your words, not mine), which is exactly what happened and is exactly what I did . . .

Followed by all hell breaking loose.

I hate to say it, y'all, but I, Ashley Jane Fontaine Ventouras (just call me Jane. Seriously. I did not name myself!), am possibly the world's worst Southern belle: I wouldn't know how to bat my eyelashes at a boy if my life depended on it. There's no way I would look a pair of panty hose in the eye on a hot summer's day, much less put them on, even if it is the civilized thing to do. And I think I just might be the only girl born and raised below the Mason-Dixon Line who is not genetically hardwired to dream of being a beauty queen. The thought of a tuxedo-clad dinosaur singing tribute to my beauty while I parade across a stage in a cleavage-enhancing gown to claim a tiara and a sash that reads, MISS LOCAL BEAUTY CONTEST WINNER—well, I'd be lying if I didn't say it makes me want to, um, *gag*. Oops, what am I saying? If the organizers of the Magnolia Pageant could hear me now, they would have my hide!

They will have you know it's an *achievement* pageant. That the selected girls become our fine city's *ambassadresses* to the world! We don't do tiaras, sashes, or octogenarians singing tribute to our beauty. Our girls are just as *smart and knowledgeable* as they can be!

Still. Never in a million billion trillion years would I have freely chosen to put myself up on any type of pageant stage, especially in front of the good people of Bienville, Alabama, the place of my birth.

But Holy Plastic Tiaras! Grandmother has been all in a tiff about how this is the family's last chance to snatch my childhood from the jaws of tragedy before I go off to college where I will be lost to my own misguided adulthood forever. So, after a prank in April got me expelled from the latest in a long line of "veddy elite, veddy disciplined" boarding schools, she somehow convinced the man who calls himself my father not to stick me in yet another one. Cosmo actually agreed to let me come home to Bienville and finish the year with a tutor so that Grandmother could rehabilitate me into a decent young lady. And I was cool with that, relatively speaking. She had already practically raised me for a good portion of my life, and I love her to death. In fact, I would go so far as to say that she's my favorite living relative. And Lord knows she's tried with me. She really has. It's not her fault I'm so incorrigible.

I will say this, though. I was dubious with a capital *D* about coming back to B'ville. I'd been gone for so long that I wondered if it was even possible for me to fit back in again. Five years and a series of highbrow boarding schools puts a lot of distance between a girl and the people she did seventh-grade cotillion with. I don't want to sound like a snob, but one of the advantages of hopping from boarding school to boarding school and having an international man of business for a daddy is that I've gotten to do some major traveling: New York, DC, Paris, London, Athens. You name it, chances are I've been there. And the kids I've been going to school with are cut from the same cloth, not to mention the fact that many of their parents practically run the planet.

Bienville, on the other hand, is a small town and it's got small-town values: church and family reign supreme. Folks make friends, and enemies, for life. They don't really leave, except maybe to go to college for a few years, then they head on home to settle down and raise a family just like their forebears did. So coming back made me wonder if I even had anything in common with kids who have never been anywhere except maybe on vacation to Disney World. Sure, I was *from* good old B'ville, but did I *belong* here anymore?

Besides, Bienville is so far off the beaten track that nobody even got Internet until last year. Okay, I'm kidding, but it's true that hardly anyone outside the Gulf Coast region had heard of it until the oil spill. And because there's not a lot to do around these parts, the number one source of entertainment in the Bienville area is gossip. At any given moment, the average Bienvillite is either gossiping, doing something to make themselves the subject of gossip, or having something done to them that will make them the subject of gossip. The last thing in the world I wanted to be was the subject of gossip. I could hear it now:

"Did you hear? Jane Fontaine's back in town."

"Cecilia's daughter? Oh, that Poor Little Orphan Girl."

"Losing her mother at such a young age."

"And her father! I heard he hasn't been back to Bienville since Cecilia's funeral . . . ?"

"Tell me that can't be true!"

"Swear to God! Charlotte DeVille and I were talking about it just the other day!"

"Where is Cosmo from again? France? Italy?"

"Greece."

"That's right. I always remember Jane's got a different last name. I just forget what it is. So who in the world is raising that child?"

"I don't know. She's at her grandmother's now."

"Well, that's good."

Rinse and repeat at any church fellowship hall, mall parking lot, beauty salon, ATM line, or gas station in town.

And I was right. The first day I got back into town, the proof that the gossip mill had kicked into overdrive was as obvious as a pimple in the middle of somebody's forehead. I popped into Piggly Wiggly just to pick up a Red Bull and was not able to get out of there without running into some

Old Bienvillite who recognized me because I "was simply the spitting image of my mother," she said (minus the big boobs, I said). Of course, she was just dying to tell me how fondly she remembered Cecilia, what a wonderful woman she was, how much she contributed to the Junior League and the Presbyterian Church and the Arts Council, how everyone still talked about what a vivacious woman she was.

Then a look of pity entered her eyes, and she said, "Tsk tsk, shame, shame, poor little lamb" or some such. All I wanted was an energy drink and instead I'd been blasted back to a past full of tragedy. What was I supposed to say? "Oh, thank you! You're so sweet to remind me! Yes, it was horrible! Yes, I'm permanently scarred! Want to know about my first period? The time I had chicken pox? Oh, and by the way, if you and everybody else in town had really cared about Cecilia, you wouldn't have completely abandoned her when she got sick!" I said nothing, though. Instead, I fiddled nervously with the tab on the Red Bull until it popped open, drenching me in sticky liquid, a fitting match to the tide of grief rising in my throat.

I'll say one good thing about boarding school(s): no one knows about your deep, dark, depressing family secrets unless you tell them. Which I never did. I kept everything behind a carefully constructed wall. The subject of my mother's death? Packed in a box and bricked behind the wall. The pain of my father's abandonment? Ditto. The destruction of my closest friendship in the world at his hands? Well, it would take a jackhammer and a backhoe to dig that thing out.

But since I'd been back, everywhere I went, there was some version of the Piggly Wiggly conversation. I tried to shrug it off, act like it wasn't a big deal, but I'd have to be dead myself for the Poor Little Orphan Girl thing not to get to me. Even Grandmother used it, which is exactly how she roped me into this whole Magnolia Maid business to begin with!

"Sweetness," she said, sneaking up on me all pre-coffee and half asleep at the breakfast room table one morning. "I want you to think about trying out for the Magnolia Maids. Now, I'm not putting any pressure on you," she insisted as I rolled my eyes so far back in my head I'm surprised I didn't need a surgeon to pull them back out. "But it meant so much to your mother when she was a Maid and wouldn't it be *just darling* if you followed in her footsteps?"

With grandmother guilt like that, combined with the fact that okay, maybe, yes, I would like to follow in my mother's footsteps somehow . . . come on! What would you have done? That's right. You, too, would have agreed to repress every grrrrrl-power fiber in your being and try out for this organization that is so old school, it requires you to wear an antebellum dress. Antebellum. Prewar. Pre–*Civil War*. We're talking hoopskirts, parasols, Scarlett O'Hara batting eyelashes at Rhett and proclaiming, "Tomorrow is another day."

Not exactly my style.

But okay, I thought, *Jane, try out. Make your grandmother happy. Just do it. Kinda sorta pretend like you enjoy it and she'll be thrilled. You don't have to actually get on the Court. They'll for sure never pick you anyway.* After all, my application looked more like a juvenile delinquent's rap sheet than a gleaming résumé. And I made sure that I took every precaution to look like the anti-belle. I specifically showed up at orientation looking like Taylor Momsen when everyone else was sporting their sweetest Southern belle style. I did my three-minute-history speech on a topic that was not exactly Bienville-friendly: the last slave ship to arrive in the bay in the 1800s. During my personal interview I even told the judges—all upstanding members of the chamber of commerce—that world peace was about as attainable as a date with Robert Pattinson, so what was the point in bothering?

But despite all of that, I had managed to land myself on the civic center stage, on this sultry spring night in May, following in my mother's footsteps as a Maid. Whether I liked it or not. And I'll be honest, it's so *not* darling to be struggling under the weight of a petite yet surprisingly busty blonde—herself a shocker of a Magnolia Maid choice—while the hundreds of people jam-packing the Bienville Civic Center look on!

"Catch her!" I yelled as Brandi Lyn's hair ripped out and she continued to fall forward. But the three other girls standing in the Winner's Circle were too frozen with disbelief to leap to my aid.

So I lunged, tossing myself between Brandi Lyn and the stage floor. I grunted as her body slammed into me with a force that nearly toppled me. Brandi Lyn's chin hooked over my shoulder, her big blonde hair flew in my face, blinding me, and her giant boobs were two seconds away from suffocating me. "It's okay! I've got her!" I exclaimed.

But then Brandi Lyn's feet started sliding out from under her, forcing even more of her dead weight on me. I heard massive gasps from the audience of Old Bienvillites as I pushed her up to partially standing . . . yet she slid lower. What, was there baby oil on her shoes or something? More gasps. These from the girls in the Winner's Circle. Ashley could barely mask her annoyance, probably more upset that her fancy pageant was being destroyed than that a girl had fainted. Mallory looked like a deer in headlights. Zara, well, she at least moved forward to help as I pushed Brandi Lyn up again. But Brandi Lyn's feet slid out from under her once more and then it was all over. I lost my traction and she plummeted . . . TAKING ME DOWN WITH HER!

Brandi Lyn and I hit the floor with a bang.

"Maid down! We've got a Magnolia Maid down!" Walter Murray Hill, the chamber of commerce guy who heads up the Magnolia Maids, screamed into the auditorium's abyss. "Is there a doctor in the house? Someone please help this little lamb!"

I spit Brandi Lyn's hair out of my mouth and pushed at her deadweight of a body. "Excuse me? Having trouble breathing here! Can you move her off me, please?"

Suddenly, my prayers were answered. A guy in an EZ Lube uniform shirt—the leader of the air-horn brigade, I'm sure—ripped Brandi Lyn off me. "JoeJoe's here, baby, it's all right! Baby? Oh my God, she's dead!" He started some version of CPR that surely he got out of some hospital drama. It didn't look legit at all.

I clambered to a sitting position. "She's not dead." I pointed to Brandi Lyn's chest. "See?" Walter and JoeJoe studied her chest, which was infinitesimally rising and falling with each slow breath.

JoeJoe cradled Brandi Lyn in his arms. "Oh, thank God. Stay with me, baby, stay with me."

"I'm sure she'll be fine, young man." But Walter looked worried, and who could blame him, what with his esteemed pageant being all ruined? "Is there a doctor in the house?" he yelled again.

As I struggled to catch my breath, something flashed before my eyes. Not my entire life, but one specific big thing: Luke Churchville, the best friend I ever had, the boy of my seventh-grade dreams, the one who had been taken away from me . . . he just might be in the audience. Watching this whole insane scene play out.

Yikes. How awkward.

"Well, I think my work here is done," I announced as I picked myself up.

Then I saw what could only be Brandi Lyn's mother (maybe because she cried, "Brandi Lyn! Momma's come for you, chile!") barge onto the stage. As tiny as Brandi

Lyn was, her momma was an Amazon. Giant arms, trunks for legs, even her hair managed to be bigger and blonder than Brandi Lyn's, if that was at all possible. The woman was a tank.

And the tank was heading my way.

I had three choices: Get mowed down. Curl up in a ball and hope for the best. Or get the hell out of the way.

I got the hell out of the way.

I leapfrogged forward like we used to on the playground (which I will tell you is a lot easier when you're five and wearing OshKosh B'gosh, instead of seventeen and constricted by a tight cocktail-dress bodice and four-inch Manolos). My maneuver was possibly the most unladylike, awkwardly bizarre performance that has ever occurred on the Bienville Civic Center stage, but it did the trick. Brandi Lyn's momma's foot stomped mere inches from my face, but I was safe and free. If you call landing face-first in front of hundreds of people, your dignity completely and totally demolished, "safe and free."

Super awkward.

Next thing I knew, not one, not two, but *twenty* doctors ran up onstage. There were so many doctors in the house that night that if somebody elsewhere in Bienville had stubbed a toe, they would have bled to death. While the doctors argued over what was wrong with the girl and peppered Mrs. Corey and JoeJoe with questions, I took the opportunity to park myself backstage behind the rainbow flats for the upcoming production of *The Wizard of Oz* and light up a smoke. Yes, a smoke. Didn't I mention earlier that I was the world's single worst candidate for the Magnolia Court?

"Excuse me, I don't think you're allowed to smoke in here."

I turned to see one of the other finalists—the one I had nicknamed "the Reader" during orientation because she had had her nose stuck in a book the whole time. Now the Reader was hiding deeper in the shadows of backstage than I was. Interesting. I took a deep, lung-poisoning drag and headed her off at the pass: "I KNOW you're not allowed to smoke in here. Hey, aren't you the girl who was trying to sneak offstage earlier?"

The Reader blushed. "Yeah, sorry. Was that distracting?"

"Are you kidding? It was hilarious! But what's up with that? Do you have someplace to go?"

The Reader glanced down at her hands. "I hate being onstage. I thought that if maybe I could just make it to the edge, everyone would forget I was there. I could just disappear into the darkness."

"I take it it's a good thing you didn't get put on the Court then?"

The Reader nodded vigorously. "A very good thing."

"Congratulations, then." I stuck out my hand for a high five. "My name's Jane, by the way."

"I know. Our mothers were on the Friends of the Library

board together." It didn't escape me that she said it matter-of-factly. With none of the usual Poor Little Orphan Girl pity. I took it as a good sign.

"Really? My mother knew yours?" Jeez. Mom died seven years ago, and the Reader remembered her from even before that? I barely remembered what I ate for breakfast. And if the Reader knew who I was, then I should know who she was, but I didn't. Except . . . "Oh! Caroline! But didn't you used to be . . ." I stopped, mortified as I realized I was on the verge of barreling into a faux pas as big as Brandi Lyn's mother.

Caroline supplied the answer. "Thinner."

"No, no, that's not . . . Well, you look great." Caroline shrugged and I felt like a jerk because obviously she didn't look great—she looked great plus fifty pounds. Not that I like to judge people by their weight because I think that's so unfair, but how do you backtrack after that? Talk about the weather?

Caroline went pale. "Oh no, I was afraid of this."

Shoot. "Look. I'm sorry. I didn't mean to offend you. It's just me and my big mouth."

"No, not that. *That*." She pointed toward the wings where I could just barely make out the silhouette of Walter Murray Hill getting berated by a woman I had nicknamed the "Bobbed Monster" in my head.

Caroline sighed. "I knew Mother would be furious."

"Oh, that's right! The Bobbed Monster . . . uh, Mizz

Upton is your mother!" Martha Ellen Upton had introduced herself at orientation as the Official Etiquette Mistress and Head Advisor of the Magnolia Maids. She then immediately launched into a lecture on how "any girl can be a Southern belle, but Magnolia Maids are the most perfect Southern belles of all. And if you're going to be a Magnolia Maid, we *will*, capital W-I-L-L, require perfection."

Wow. No wonder poor Caroline had put on fifty pounds.

"What's she giving old Walter a hard time for?" I asked.

But Caroline was gone. She had scurried deeper into the wings. "Her short list!" she called over her shoulder. "The judges didn't follow her short list!"

"Short list? What's a short list?"

Turns out that Mizz Upton wasn't simply in charge of Magnolia perfection, she was also in charge of compiling a short list of names to recommend to the judges. Interesting. According to Caroline, Mizz Upton's ideal candidate was a definite type. She lived in the kingdom of Old Bienville High Society, attended either First Presbyterian or First Episcopal Church, and was educated at either the St. Andrew's Preparatory Academy or the St. Peter's School for Girls. Her family was historically significant in the community and/or filthy rich, preferably both. Sure, a few girls from more humble beginnings did dare to try out for the organization, and Mizz Upton took a look at them, too, but without the right pedigree it was highly unlikely they would make it far up the Magnolia Maid ladder. Mizz Upton pored over all three hundred–plus applications, evaluating GPAs and extracurricular activities and reading each and every two-page personal statement that each girl wrote extolling her qualifications as a Magnolia Maid. From those, she culled a list of finalists who interviewed with the judges and delivered a three-minute speech on some aspect of Bienville history. Out of all of this she concocted a "short list" of the five most Magnolia-worthy candidates, plus a few recommendations for alternates, and handed it off to the judges. Every year for the past decade, the judges had followed her suggestions as if they had been sent down by God Himself. The new Court always consisted of five new Maids and one alternate that Mizz Upton herself had preapproved.

Until this year.

Three of the five girls the judges had just named to the Court were absolutely, positively NOT on Mizz Upton's list. Which was why she was having a conniption fit over there with Walter Murray Hill.

"Which three? Who wasn't on the list?" I asked.

Caroline looked away.

"Don't worry. You won't hurt my feelings. I know I wasn't anywhere near her top fifty. And I'm thinking that the fainting beauty over there"—I nodded at Brandi Lyn and her tank/mother and her EZ Lube boyfriend—"wasn't exactly A-number-one high, either. But who else?"

Caroline remained silent, as if spilling the family Magnolia Maid secrets would cause her instant death.

"Can you at least tell me who *was* on the superspecial, creamy-delight short list?"

Apparently, answering that question was safer, because after a moment, Caroline pointed across the stage to a group of girls in the midst of a hysteria fit bigger than Mizz Upton's. "They were," she said solemnly.

Chapter Two

Katherine DeVille. Ashley LaFleur. Courtney Lennox. Mallory Ross. The belles of Bienville Place. One of our town's more *prestigious* addresses, Bienville Place was a small court of only four houses. Allegedly, Bienville Place was the spot where the Frenchman Jean-Baptiste Le Moyne, sieur de Bienville, set up his first shack and declared it a village during his pirating and pillaging days. But I guess Bienville was too small even back in the 1700s because old Jean-Baptiste didn't stick around long. He went on to found more notable cities along the Gulf Coast like Mobile and New Orleans. Smart guy.

Anyway, of course Katherine, Ashley, Courtney, and Mallory had all been on Mizz Upton's short list. Those girls had been gunning for Magnolia Maid status practically from birth. Okay, since they were five. Seriously, Ashley and Mallory figured it all out during a rainy afternoon session of dress-up. They were playing in Ashley's mother's closet when Mallory got the idea to put necklaces in their hair to look like tiaras and play beauty queens. Ashley suggested they play Magnolia Maids instead, to which Mallory agreed, and after a very brief argument and a pinching fight that Ashley won, it was determined that she would be queen and Mallory would be first lady-in-waiting. The following year, Courtney and Katherine moved to Bienville Place, and they joined in the pageant game as second and third ladies-in-waiting.

How do I know this? They told me. When I was eight. I was over at Ashley's house—our mothers were on the Junior League together so they were meeting to plan some fund-raiser or charity event—and Ashley informed me that they would let me play M&Ms with them as long as I understood that she was queen, her three little BFFs were ladies-in-waiting, and I was just a maid.

"Why?" I asked.

"'Cause that's the way it is," Ashley replied.

"Well, what if Mallory wants to be queen?"

Mallory chirped up, "Oh no, Ashley's the best choice for queen, Jane. She has it all planned out. She knows what charity we're going to work for and which fund-raiser we're going to throw."

Ashley nodded. "And I have the recipes picked out for the cookbook, too!"

I didn't buy it. "I think we should play rock, paper, scissors, and the winner gets to be queen."

Ashley scowled. "No. We are the belles of Bienville

Place"—yes, one of their fathers nicknamed them that—
"so it's our rules, right, girls?" Her girls all nodded.
Enthusiastically. "So are you in or what?" Ashley had asked
me. Even back then, Ashley was the D-Girl.

Oh, you know. The D-Girl. The Dictator Girl. The one in
charge. The girl who tells everyone else what to do.

But even back then, I wasn't the kind of kid who played
well in a dictatorship. I defied Ashley's orders by skulking off
to read a book. She's been annoyed at me ever since.

And boy, could that girl hold a grudge. Within seconds of running into her at the Magnolia Maid Pageant
Orientation I could tell she still hadn't let it go. The orientation session was held on a Saturday afternoon in late
April. Henry, Grandmother's handyman/butler/chauffeur/
lifesaver, dropped me off and I walked in by myself, wend-
ing my way through the chatting Maid-hopefuls. As I approached each cluster, conversation ceased, then picked up
again with a low whisper after I passed.

"Who is that?"

"She looks so familiar. . . ."

"I remember her! She did cotillion with us."

"Jane Fontaine Ventouras, that's who it is!"

"Oh my God, *she's* back in town?"

"Isn't she the one whose mother died of—"

"I heard she had to leave town because she was pregs."

"No! Really? She would have been sooooooo young!"

"It's what I heard."

"Last *I* heard she was at some boarding school in Texas."

"No, she got kicked out of that one. She's been in Massachusetts, my mom said."

"Why is she here?"

"She's back for senior year."

"Oh my God, what is she wearing?"

I looked down at my black tank top and butt-hugging skinny jeans. They certainly were not anything that could be categorized as "garden party casual."

"My daddy would never let me out of the house in jeans that tight!"

"I can't believe her arms are bare!"

"Sooooooo inappropriate!"

"She has on an inch of eyeliner!"

Normally, I don't give a petunia about looking inappropriate. And at orientation, I was actively trying *not* to be a Magnolia Maid. But I couldn't help that this gauntlet of gossip made me uncomfortable. So I focused on trying to ignore it as I searched for some quiet corner.

One stare was impossible to block out, however. It was so fiery, so strong, that it burned a hole in my back. I knew without looking who it belonged to . . . Miss Ashley LaFleur.

She looked me up. She looked me down. She subtly jutted her chin in my direction, silently pointing me out to the other Bienville belles. "I am soooooooo sorry, Jane," she drawled, "but the tryouts for America's Top Street Walker are down at the docks." Ashley sneered, and her minions laughed.

I sashayed over to the Fab Four and didn't even bother to hide the fact that I was studying them right back. It seemed that Queen Ashley had circulated her own memo about attire, and I suspected it looked something like this:

TO: My Little Minions
FROM: Your Leader
DATE: The First Day of the Best Year of Our Lives
RE: Total and Complete Magnolia Maid Domination

Girls, girls, girls, it's the moment we have all been waiting for since we first played Magnolia Maid dress-up in my mom's closet all those years ago. We are going to be Magnolia Maids for real! To be the part, we must look the part, therefore, the dress code for orientation is as follows:

Dress: simple linen sheath in the pastel color of your choice, to be purchased in the Belle Department at Dillard's. I call pink, so y'all can fight over pukey peach, bleh blue, yucky yellow, and gross green. Choose wisely, girls—when we get elected these will be the colors of our Scarlett O'Hara dresses!

Panty hose: Yes, panty hose. I know it will be ninety degrees outside with eighty-five percent humidity, and that panty hose will raise our internal body temperature to two thousand and five, but our mothers did it, our grandmothers did it, so help us, God, we will do it! Terrifying Taupe by Anne Klein.

Jewelry: I don't think I need to put this in writing, but pearls. Pearls, pearls, and only pearls. If you don't have real ones yet (*Katherine!*), snag from mother or grandmother.

Hair: shoulder-length, flipped up on end. Straight and sleek. Held back with your choice of headband: tortoise shell or linen that perfectly matches your dress. ABSOLUTELY NO CURLS. (Mallory, have Mavis house-call morning of and straighten yours out.)

Accessories: These are the key ingredients in establishing ourselves as a unit! All our accessories must match perfectly!!!!!! So my mom put Burberry plaid pumps on hold at Waldorff's. The dominant color of your shoes will match your dress, but then we will all match with the backup pattern colors: brown, red, and black. Because we'll look like a group, they'll take us as a group, get it? Isn't that genius? Ditto for bags. Burberry clutches that match shoes.

Makeup: No drugstore brands, girls, even if they do look exactly like department store, and I can tell the difference, so don't even try (*Courtney!*). M.A.C. eyeliner and eye shadow that match dress. Pout lip gloss from Smashbox. Brown mascara by Estée Lauder.

Any questions, please see me, but there better not be any questions because this is the perfect plan, so please execute it to a tee. Speaking of executing, any rule breakers will be immediately executed.

Kidding!

Not!

No, I am! You know I love uuuuuuuuuuuuuuuuu all!

Yours in Magnolia love,
Ashley

"Thanks for the info, Ashley," I replied. "I'll have my driver take me there." I unlocked my phone and perused the screen as if I had just gotten a text. "Oh, darn. This is so sad."

The girls looked at me. They were curious even though they never would have admitted it in a court of law.

"It's from the Easter bunny." I pouted for effect. "He wants to know when he can get his eggs back."

I stalked off, grinning as I listened to the confusion that ensued as D-Girl and her minions tried to figure out what in the world I was talking about.

"I don't get it," Mallory said.

"Was she saying we look like Easter eggs?" asked either Katherine or Courtney. I wasn't sure which.

I could almost hear Ashley's blood boiling as she exclaimed, "That bitch!" But she swallowed the "itch" at the last minute when Mizz Upton walked in, so it just sounded like, "That biiiiiiiii . . ."

Alas, Ashley's Operation Easter Egg, brilliant a plan as it was, had just bitten the big bunny. She and her minions now huddled in the center of the pageant stage mourning the fact that while Ashley and Mallory had made it on to the Court, Courtney and Katherine had been passed over in favor of me, Brandi Lyn, and Zara. It was a shocking turn of events.

"It's not fair! Y'all should have made it!"

"No, y'all are so pretty, you deserved it!"

"Don't talk down about yourself. You're as pretty as we are."

"Prettier!"

"But we're has-beens!"

"They've broken us up!!!!!"

"Our lives will never be the same again!"

Snivel, slobber, wail, gnash, hiccup. I'd say it was a six-Kleenex-per-girl meltdown.

"This is one for the history books," I said to Caroline. "Ashley LaFleur not getting her way."

Caroline nodded. "I do feel sorry for Katherine and Courtney, though. They wanted it so badly."

"One of them can have my place."

The girls onstage weren't the only ones upset by the selection of the Maids. Down in the audience, heads were wagging and astonished expressions plastered a majority of the faces. The Lennoxes and the DeVilles were fit to be tied. Mr. and Mrs. Lennox were having a heated discussion with the judges. Mr. DeVille struggled to calm down his wife, who was crying almost as much as her daughter.

Ashley finally managed to extract herself from the pain and wiped off her running Estée Lauder mascara. She glanced across the stage, to where Brandi Lyn was being revived by the sea of doctors. She glared at Zara, who looked decidedly uncomfortable as she lingered at the front of the stage talking to a stylish couple who I thought were probably her parents. Then she pursed her lips, set her jaw, and turned back to her girls. "Wipe your tears and fix your lipstick, girls! I don't know who those, those . . ." She racked her brain for the appropriate insult. ". . . *creatures* think they are, but this is an injustice to the entire city of Bienville and to the legacy of our founding father. They are *not* taking what belongs to us."

It took a few minutes, but Ashley's rich, white, upper-class, well-dressed, landed-gentry minions bucked themselves up and set across the stage to fight for their rights.

"Ooooh, this is going to be good," I said to Caroline. I just couldn't resist. I tossed out my cigarette and followed.

"Uncle Walter? I'm sorry, Mr. Hill?" Ashley called into the wings.

Walter waved Ashley over, looking delighted by the interruption to Mizz Upton's haranguing. He instantly swept Ashley into an affectionate hug. "Ashley, my sweet girl! Congratulations." He glanced at Mizz Upton, who was doing her best to paste a perfect, poised expression on her face but it only made her look like an angry lemon. "Let's get out of this darkness, okay."

Walter Murray Hill is the kind of Southern man who punctuates his sentences with "okay." He's not asking a question, or asking permission. He's saying, "Okay, this is the way things are going to be. Whether you like it or not."

This time he meant that he was moving far, far away from the blustering Mizz Upton and the girls better follow. They did.

"What can I do for you ladies?" Walter Murray Hill asked when they all arrived at the rear corner of the stage.

I lingered close enough to eavesdrop, yet far enough away to appear uninvolved. Ashley beamed. Gone was her righteous indignation. In its place was eyelash-batting sweetness as she played the simpering Southern belle card. What a chameleon in pearls.

"Yes, well, thank you, Uncle, Mr. Hill. Being a Magnolia Maid is such a tremendous honor for me, and you remember my friend Mallory?"

"Geoff Ross's daughter?" Walter shook her hand, squeezing her upper arm with his other hand in the process. "Oh yes. Your grandfather gave me my first job out of college. Fine man. Glad to have you on board."

Mallory nodded her head so hard it nearly flew off. "Yes, sir, it's such an honor to be honored like this. With this honor, I mean."

"Mallory!" Ashley jabbed her in the side.

"Oh, sorry, babbling. I'm just so excited about getting to play a part of Magnolia Maid history. Oh my gosh! I get to wear the dress!"

Walter nodded. "You girls are going to have a big year, yes, you are, being Bienville's ambassadresses to the world."

Ashley clutched at his arm. "Well, that's just it, Mr., oh, whatever, Uncle Walter. We thought, well, it's such a big responsibility. The entire future of Bienville rests on our

27

shoulders, and it's so important that we represent the city well, so that, we, you know, do a good job of recruiting new business and giving our city a beautiful face."

"And what a beautiful face it will be." Walter Murray Hill, swear to God, actually *pinched* her cheek. "And you girls are real important to Bienville these days. You know we're trying to rebuild the economy, what with everything that's gone wrong with the oil spill and all. You beautiful girls are gonna help attract some more business. Get some international factories in here and such. That's what's gonna happen, okay."

"Hush, Uncle, aren't you sweet? But, well. These are our best friends, Courtney Lennox and Katherine DeVille." She gestured at her sniffling friends. "I'm sure you know that Courtney's mother is head of the Junior League and her daddy owns the biggest car dealership in Alabama. And Katherine's mother and daddy own a great deal of downtown's commercial real estate, plus they have a long family history in Bienville, just like me and Mallory. So we think it's only fair that they be on the Court with us, too." Ashley nodded in earnest, as did Mallory and Courtney, plus Katherine.

Walter Murray Hill watched the heads nod nod, nod nod, then he shook his. "I understand you're disappointed here, Ashley. And Courtney and Katherine, you are wonderful girls, just wonderful." He sighed. "And I sure do hate that we've got some hurt feelings here. But I can't help you. The judges, we all decided that, what with our new president and needing to get some new business in here, we've got to keep up with America. We're in the twenty-first century here, girls. Bienville's a diverse city, full of promise, of progress, and our Court should be reflecting that. It's time for a change."

Oh no. He did *not*. But yes, he did. Mr. Walter had just uttered the dirtiest six-letter word in town. *Change.* Southerners tend to have a real hard time with that word. Don't get me wrong, we do appreciate certain kinds of change: bigger Walmarts with grocery stores inside for easy one-stop shopping. Fancy, new subdivisions out in the county, far from those darn city taxes. Modern new churches with rapidly expanding memberships.

But when push comes to shove, if the change is substantial, forget it. People who don't understand us would like to say it's because we're backward or stupid or lazy. But really, it's because of the ancestors. It's as if everybody thinks all our dead ancestors, back to the ones who showed up here from France and Spain to colonize the joint, are sitting up in the afterlife watching our every move, fixing to send hellfire and damnation down on us if we dare deviate from the way they set things up for us. We fear that more than we fear the Supreme Court, the National Guard, and that evil guy from *Saw* all put together. For that very reason it is not uncommon for a young lady to hear things like, "Your great-great-grandfather founded the Presbyterian Church in 1785. No, you cannot take yoga. It's heathen." Or "I know that Granddaddy's old wood rolltop desk doesn't fit in with your new Pottery Barn Caribbean Beach Bungalow bedroom suite, honey, but he built his lumber company on that desk. We can't get rid of it and that's the only place I have for it!" Or "Your mother did cotillion, your sisters did cotillion, your grandmother did cotillion, *you* will do cotillion. And you are not a lesbian and that is final!"

Ashley sped right into resistant-to-change mode. "Well, I am sure that getting modern is a great idea and all, Uncle Walter," Ashley huffed. "But how in the world can you say the girls that got picked represent the city?" She gestured at her minions. "*We* know our Bienville inside and out. *We* were all born and raised here. I'm just worried that some of these other girls aren't going to be able to keep up." She pointed at Brandi Lyn. "She goes to County High, which means she lives outside the city limits. Can she truly represent Bienville? I don't think so!"

Walter shook his head. "The bylaws do allow county girls on the Court."

Planting a hand on her hip, Ashley swiveled her head around until her laser beams landed on me. "And Jane!"

She spat my name out as if it was dirt on grits.

I laughed in her face. "Oh, come on, Ashley. You know I have the pedigree."

Mallory perked up. "That's right! If I'm not mistaken, Divine Causeway and Irving Street are named for your people!"

That was surprising. "Wow. You know that?" I asked.

"I just *love* local history."

"Cool." I turned back to Ashley and ticked names off on my fingers. "I am the granddaughter of Digger Fontaine and Jane Irving. Grandniece of Danielle Renault. Great-granddaughter of Lawrence Divine. B'ville history is in my blood, Ashley."

She pursed her lips. "Well, what does that matter? Where have you been lately, Miss Fontaine Ventouras?"

"Boarding school. Well, a series of them. All of quite the highest caliber, I can assure you."

Ashley batted her eyelashes—again. This was surely the performance of her life. "That just proves my point, Uncle. Jane's been away way too long to really know what it means to be from Bienville."

"Oh, I'm pretty sure I know what it means."

Wheeling away, Ashley focused her attention on Zara, who was still across the stage talking to her parents. "As for her, she's, she's . . ." Ashley trailed off, closing her mouth, opening it again, closing, opening, like a DVD player on its last legs.

Ohhhhh nooooooo. There it was. A prime example of how Bienville is, shall we say, majorly behind the times?

See, we all knew what Ashley was about to say—that Zara was African American. And while I wasn't a hundred percent up on my M&M history, at least not yet, I was pretty sure her being a Maid was a first for Bienville's most beloved yet conservative tradition.

The minions inhaled sharply.

Walter Murray Hill's right eye started twitching.

31

For Ashley had just broken a cardinal rule of Southern belle-dom:

8. DO NOT acknowledge uncomfortable subjects in public.

And while Ashley hadn't actually brought up a subject that was going to make some people feel awkward, she had been *about* to bring it up. Which was close enough.

And now that she had put it out there, she was in Southern-girl purgatory because she couldn't take it back.

Ashley backpedaled so hard she nearly crashed through the wall, especially since Zara, maybe sensing she was the subject of our discussion, now headed in our direction. "Well, well, now, I . . . ummmm . . ." Ashley stammered.

Walter cleared his throat nervously. "Now, girls, let's not turn this into something it's uh, not."

Ashley grew ten inches with blustery indignation. "Certainly not. This is far from something it's not. And I am far from a, a, a . . . some of my closest friends are black!"

Mallory frowned in confusion. "Really?"

This whole conversation was starting to make my blood boil. Moments like this made me not even want to admit I was from a small town in the Deep, Deep South.

Ashley glared at her. Then she fluttered a smile in Uncle Walter's direction. "Anyway, Uncle Walter, if y'all would be so kind as to let me finish what I was saying, I was merely going to point out that Zara is not from here, either."

"It's true. I'm not," Zara admitted, joining the group.

"See! What a terrible time you're going to have catching up on all our decades of rich history! I just feel for you!"

"My parents are from here, though. Jay and Felicia Alexander? So I've visited here every summer of my life."

I stopped in my tracks. "Wait, your last name is Alexander?"

Zara nodded, and Mallory went into pre-flip-out mode. "As in Alexander Communications? As in one of the biggest satellite cable corporations in the country?" Zara nodded again, and Mallory surged fully into flip-out mode. "Oh my God, Ashley, her daddy is my daddy's newest client! They just moved here! They are, like, the richest people ever to live in Bienville!"

Walter nodded proudly. "And they've just honored Bienville by moving their national headquarters here. Opening up a lot of jobs for us, okay!"

This was so not going Ashley's way and, well, she finally lost it. Gone was any attempt to play the good little Southern belle. "That's just great, Uncle Walter, but this is a travesty! This is not the Court I expected it to be, and if you do not see that Katherine and Courtney get put on immediately, I am afraid Mallory and I will have to resign." She nudged Mallory in the ribs.

Mallory blanched. "And give up the dress? Ashley!!!!! I've been waiting for this forever. . . ." Mallory trailed off as she felt the bloody daggers Ashley was aiming at her. "Okay, I suppose it's not what I signed up for, either, Mr. Walter."

Mr. Walter shook his head. "I'm sorry to hear that, girls. It's a real disappointment, what with your families' legacies with the Maids and all. Do me a favor and put it in writing, so we can go about selecting alternates as soon as possible." He gave a little bow and walked off.

Ashley nearly keeled over in shock. "But, but . . ."

Mallory, however, seemed to have finally found her own tongue. "No, no, we misspoke! We didn't mean it. We're not quitting!" She frantically called after Mr. Walter. "Anyway, you didn't say the name of the alternate! Maybe Courtney or Katherine made alternate!"

"Oh, you're right there, Mallory." Walter fished the results out of his jacket. "In all the excitement, I neglected to announce the alternate."

Ashley grabbed Katherine's and Courtney's hands. "Good call, Mal."

Mallory squeezed Katherine's and Courtney's other hands, forming one big circle of hope and expectation. "I'm sure one of y'all got it."

I have to admit, even I was curious to know who would be the sixth victim. Uh, Maid.

"And the alternate, who will fulfill all Magnolia Court duties in the event that a Maid cannot, is . . . Miss Caroline Jeannette Upton."

"Caroline Upton?"

"Caroline Plumpton?" Ashley blurted it out before she could stop herself. Rule number 8 was officially out the window.

Everyone turned to Caroline, so quiet in the wings that no one had paid her one bit of attention. Now she was the center of it, to her obvious horror. Hives were rapidly breaking out all over her chest and face. "No, no. Not me. I'm sure this is a mistake."

Walter smiled gently. "No, it says it right here, Caroline. Welcome to the Court."

"But I don't want . . . I mean, uh, it can go to one of the other girls. I am happy for someone else to do it."

I mock-dropped my jaw. "Are you kidding me? We get to roll around the country all decked out in our Scarlett O'Hara dresses telling people how wonderfully modern our little old town is. This is an honor!"

"It sooooooooo is!" Suddenly, out of nowhere, a fully recovered Brandi Lyn rocketed into our midst, enveloping Ashley and Mallory in a giant hug. "Hello, Magnolia Maid sisters! Oh my goodness, can y'all believe it? I'm going out of my mind with joy, aren't you? I am so sorry about fainting! I usually have great stage presence, everybody says so, but I was just so excited, it undid me. I won't let it happen again, though, don't worry. Isn't this exciting! We are going to have the greatest year ever, aren't we just?!"

Silence.

I surveyed the scene—Mallory distressed and fearful that her long-longed-for dress was going to get taken away, Caroline insulted to her face and terrified at being seen in public, Brandi Lyn and Zara insulted behind their backs.

35

And the grand cause of these problems, the very reason for their existence?

A very furious, very determined-to-have-her-own-way D-Girl by the name of Mary Ashley LaFleur.

Sweet Winds of Change! It was at that moment I understood why I had been selected to the Magnolia Court.

I had a higher purpose. A calling, if you will.

If I knew Ashley LaFleur, and I was pretty sure I did, she was not going to stop until she had complete control of the entire organization. And I may not have had anything in common with my new Magnolia Maid sister, but if I had to be part of this Court, then I was going to fight Ashley's power with every ounce of mine and then some. I felt compelled to create just a little truth, justice, and beauty for the four girls standing miserably before me. It was the right thing to do.

I beamed a smile brighter than Christmas at Brandi Lyn, threw my arms around her, and tossed my hat into the fires of Southern Belle Hell. "Why, yes, Brandi Lyn. This year's going to be simply divine."

Chapter Three

Fifteen floors above the city, in a building on the edge of the Bienville Bay, the highly exclusive Petroleum Club boasts an impressive 360-degree view all the way down to the Gulf of Mexico. Its membership consists of the executives who run the local oil industry. Grandmother was a lifelong member because of her father and her husband, my grandfather, both big oilmen back in the days before the oil spill ruined everything and people started cursing the very resource that had made them rich. The club's wine cellar rivals the best in New York City. Their steaks sizzle as the waiters bring them to the table. On any given weekend night, a jazzy band plays music that Old Bienvillites, both young and old, can boogie down to.

After the Magnolia Pageant, the Petroleum Club was packed and buzzing with talk about what had happened earlier that night at the Bienville Civic Center.

"Shock of the century!"

"Some real humdingers in the choices this year!"

"The Lennoxes are suing!"

"Oh yes, and so are the DeVilles!"

Grandmother, thrilled beyond belief that I had made the Court, got us a table with the best view in the house, plied me with a beautiful filet mignon, and let me have a couple of glasses of champagne as long as I didn't get too tipsy.

But all I could think was: this town is a ghost town.

Because the ghosts of Cecilia, of my grandfather Digger, even of my father, were hovering over our table all night.

With practically every bite of filet, someone stopped by to greet Grandmother and to tell me how proud Cecilia or Digger would have been of me, how sweet I was to try to help out Brandi Lyn Corey. Even some of Cosmo's old business associates, men I barely remembered from back in the day when Cosmo and Cecilia threw barbecues down at our house every weekend, came over to say hello, to ask after him and say it was good to see me back in town. "Tell old Cosmo that Jack Banning said hello, would you?" *Sure, Jack,* I thought. *I'll make that priority number one during my once-a-month conversation with my dad. Priority numero uno.*

As soon as Jack Banning excused himself, I swallowed another bite of meat and turned to Grandmother. "I don't know if I can take this."

"Take what?"

"Constantly being reminded that she's not here."

"Cecilia?"

I nodded. "It's all people can talk to me about. And every

time someone brings it up, I feel like I just want to scream. I just want to forget about it. I don't want to be reminded of it every single day."

Grandmother poured me another glass of champagne. "Honey, you can't ignore it. You can't act like it never happened."

"Yes I can."

"No. What you should do is bring her into your life more."

I snorted. "Grandmama, you've had too much champagne. Because, um, since she's dead, I'm pretty sure I can't bring her into my life more."

"Just because she's not here doesn't mean she's not here." She pointed at her heart. "I talk to both Cecilia and Digger every single day."

Now, y'all, my grandmother is a very serious, no-nonsense kind of lady. To hear her talking about chatting with her dead husband and daughter, well, it just didn't sound like the woman I had known and loved for seventeen years at all! "And they talk back . . . how exactly, Grandmama?"

"Honey, they don't talk back with voices. Well, sometimes they do, just not all the time. Signs. They send signs."

"You can't be serious. Oh my God, you are!"

"Yes, ma'am, as a heart attack. I ask your grandfather what he would do in certain situations all the time and he is always sending me signs."

"Give me an example."

"Well, I asked him what to do about the house on Magnolia

Street." She was talking about the stately home she'd been born and raised in. "I'd been thinking it might be time to sell it and move into something a little smaller."

"But that house has been in the family for over a hundred years!"

"Well, I know, honey, which is why I don't want to sell it, I really want to hold on to it for you, but it's been feeling a bit too big for me by myself lately."

"So what did Granddaddy say?"

"Nothing. He just showed me that it wasn't time to sell yet."

"Cut to the chase, Grandmama. You're killing me! How did he show you?"

"He sent you home to me."

Wow.

"And then when I got you here, I asked Cecilia if there was something special she wanted me to do for you. The very next day the call for Magnolia Maid tryouts was in the newspaper."

Okay, this was so out there, frankly, I didn't know what to say, what to think. All I knew was that suddenly I felt nervous, very nervous. "Do you really believe this, Grandmama?" I asked quietly.

"The Lord works in mysterious ways, and I do believe this is one of them. You know, you might benefit from trying to talk to your momma, too, young lady. This is such an important time in your life. I bet she's got a lot to tell you."

And now my instinct was to run. As far, as fast as I could.

Away from the good people of Bienville constantly reminding me of my dead mother. Away from my grandmother who was so ardently suggesting that I remove the bricks in my wall to let her in even more.

Luckily, at that moment, Grandmother's best friend since forever, Louisa Mandeville, came over and launched into a whole monologue about the things they used to do when they were Magnolia Maids.

I laughed at an anecdote or two, then politely excused myself to go powder my nose. Instead, I beelined to the viewing deck on the roof of the Petroleum Club and found sweet solitude. In the fresh air, far away from the constant attention, I felt like I could breathe again. My eyes meandered across the view, which certainly lived up to its exclusive reputation. Tonight, a full moon cast a glow over everything it touched. Ships and tankers were docked in the port. Oil rigs rose from the sea in the distance. The lights of Mobile shone far away on the horizon.

Farther south, the Bird River was a gleaming ribbon. My eyes traced it from the bay inland until they arrived at a bend. The bend where Cecilia, Cosmo, and I lived when I was a little girl. Living at the river was Cosmo's doing. Coming from a Greek shipping family, boats and ships, rivers and oceans, they were in his blood. He got antsy whenever he was away from them too long, so he convinced Cecilia to let him buy a piece of land down on Bird River and build them a house, what they call a Creole cottage. It was set on stilts to prevent flooding during bad storms and hurricanes, and to my little-girl self, it looked as majestic as a castle. Cecilia got her wide verandah and outdoor kitchen, Cosmo got his sprawling view of the river from almost every window and a trophy room for all his boating paraphernalia. Eventually, I came along and got my own bedroom and a sitting room filled with all the toys money could buy.

The boathouse contained three boats, all named for my mother in one way or another: *Ceci on the Sea* was the sailboat. *Go Ceci Go!* was a high-speed powerboat. And *The Majestic Miss C* was a fishing yacht for the days when Cosmo would motor deep out into the Gulf of Mexico and come back with an ice chest full of Spanish mackerel that he skinned and boned himself. He'd call Cecilia on the way home and say, "We've got fish for dinner!" and by the time he pulled up at the dock, she would have the house filled with laughter, champagne, and friends ready to eat the bounty of Cosmo's trip to sea.

When I try to remember my little-girl days, it's not full scenes that come to mind but swirls. Tiny flashes of sights and sounds. Cosmo's warm, tanned arms scooping me up off the dock and setting me down into the boat. Cecilia sunning herself on the bow as Cosmo threw fishing lines over the back. Me skipping on the sandy beach of an uninhabited island no bigger than a sandbar. Giggling at the feel of wind in my face when Cosmo opened the speedboat up to maximum velocity.

And then Cecilia fell.

That I remember clearly. It's permanently etched in my brain—not swirling at all. It happened on the dock in front of our house. She wasn't even doing anything weird. She was just walking and carrying me. I was about five, maybe too old to be carried, but exhausted from a long day on the river. One minute I was half asleep in her arms, the next I was flying through the air and into the water—a good thing, because I wasn't hurt at all. Just scared and spluttering, until Cosmo dove in and pulled me to the surface so that he could swim me back over to the ladder and hustle me up onto the pier. "What the hell, Cecilia? What happened?" She was still splayed out on the wooden slats, pulling herself together. Studying the pier around her where she had made the misstep. Looking for some cause for the sudden fall. "I don't know. I couldn't move my leg." Cosmo helped her to her feet, and they both chuckled and chalked it up to too many Heinekens underneath the afternoon's hot Alabama sun, and off we went back into the house.

Until she fell again.

And again.

Bit by bit, the "random incidents" could no longer be passed off as the result of too many cocktails or a snag in the carpet. Out of nowhere, Cecilia flew down an entire flight of stairs, landing hard on her butt and cracking her tailbone. After tripping into the stove and knocking over a simmering pot of gumbo, she ended up in the emergency room with third-degree burns all over her arm. An unexpected careen into the Cocoa Puffs cereal display at the Piggly Wiggly was not only publicly humiliating but required two stitches above her left eye. Falling became a regular part of Cecilia's day.

It was endangering her life.

Here's what I remember about first grade: Miss Mary Melinda teaching us to sing "Puff the Magic Dragon" and read and write our names. Running out the doors of St. Peter's School for Girls to see that it was Henry, not Cecilia, who was picking me up AGAIN at the end of the day to take me to Grandmother's house. Snacking on oatmeal cookies and milk in her breakfast room until little Luke Churchville came home from school. His family lived two doors down from Grandmother's and he became my constant playmate. We played in a tree house we built until Cecilia came to get me. I would ask where she was, and the answer was always quite believable. "Oh, she's over to New Orleans doing some Christmas shopping, Miss Jane," Henry would say. "She's playing tennis at the club with Lacey Wilkes," Grandmother would tell me.

Cecilia wasn't playing tennis or shopping in New Orleans. She was in doctors' offices and laboratories first here in Bienville, then later in Mobile and Houston when Bienville doctors couldn't come up with any answers. She was apparently quite determined to keep things normal for me; she and Cosmo never talked about her health problems in front of me. I knew something was going on, though. How could I not when I was the one who wiped gumbo off her arms while she cried in pain? When I was the one who sat with her at the bottom of the stairs and read her Madeleine stories until she convinced herself to stand up?

Here's what I remember about second grade: Cecilia and

Cosmo both coming to pick me up from school one day. What a delicious day that was! Cosmo never came to get me! He was always working in his office at the Maritime Building until at least five o'clock! They took me to their favorite restaurant, The Revelry, and they let me order chicken fingers and fried shrimp and a Shirley Temple with extra cherries and french fries and cheese poppers *and* Mississippi mud pie! I stuffed myself until I couldn't breathe, barely noticing the glances they kept exchanging. Cosmo repeatedly started sentences with "Janie, *agapemenee mu,*" but then Cecilia would shoot him a look and he'd close his mouth and stare out the window at Bienville Bay while she asked me a question about my day.

It wasn't until we got home that they told me. "Mommy is sick, *agapemenee mu,*" Cosmo said. And then came a big, long disease name that I couldn't wrap my seven-year-old mouth around, but that was okay, they told me. I could call it by its letters, ALS. "What kind of medicine do you take for it?" I asked. There was no medicine for it, they said, which very much perplexed me. "Every time I go to Dr. Taylor, she gives me medicine. Why don't they have any for you?" "They just don't, honey," Cecilia said, and a tear trickled down her cheek. "You have to be a big girl, Jane," Cosmo rasped. "You have to help your mother. She is going to need you a lot from now on."

Here's what I remember about third grade: Spending an afternoon at Alabama Medical Supply shopping for Cecilia's new motorized chair after her latest fall sent her to the hospital with a concussion and a dislocated shoulder. The doctors informed her it was better if she didn't walk anymore. Even a walker couldn't support her enough. "That's okay," Cecilia chirped. "I can't walk, but my hands are good as new! I can cook! I can bake chocolate brownies with my Janie. We'll be just fine!" I immediately dubbed the chair "Scooter-boy" and lurked about waiting for opportunities to steal it while Cecilia was in the bathroom or sitting in the wing chair on the sun porch reading. I rode Scooter-boy everywhere there was a smooth surface. Up and down the elevator Cosmo installed. Into the handicap van he bought. Down the ramp he built to the dock. "Your mother has more vehicles than I do now!" he joked. Then he lifted her into the boat and we zipped off into the blue.

Fourth grade: I learned to crack open eggs, knead bread, take casserole dishes out of the oven—the things that Cecilia could no longer do so well now that her hands were acting up on her. It was so much fun, helping her out every day after school. Sure, I wanted to be out playing with my friends, but I loved these afternoons in the kitchen talking and cooking with my mother. I relished the sense of victory that came when we brought a beautiful and delicious feast, the result of our chopping and mixing and measuring, out of the oven. But that all ended the day of the bread knife. It was a Thursday afternoon, and we had baked cranberry-pineapple bread for something—a Girl Scout badge, maybe? Cecilia was in the middle of telling me that my friend Teddy Mac was coming to spend Saturday with us so his mother could go shopping in Dallas when I noticed that she was having trouble cutting the bread. "Mom, what's wrong?" "No, nothing," she replied, struggling again to wrap her fingers around the knife. When it became obvious that her hand was not planning to cooperate anytime soon, I tried to console her. "It's all right, Mommy," I said. "I'll cut it."

She didn't say a word. She dropped the knife and quietly navigated Scooter-boy down the hall and into the elevator, where she sequestered herself. I had no idea what to do. She refused to come out no matter what I said. Cosmo wasn't home; in fact, he wasn't even in town. By then, his business was taking him more and more to Greece and London, so he was no help. And when she started crying, a deep, mournful keening, I really didn't know what to do. I went back to the kitchen and sliced the bread and attempted to coax her out with it, but all she did was take the elevator to the second floor to get away from me.

I called Grandmother.

"Cecilia! Open this door!" Grandmother had been in the middle of semifinals for the Bienville Ladies' Bridge Tournament, but she was at our house within twenty minutes of answering her cell.

"No!" called Cecilia, her voice muffled by the two sets of elevator doors.

"Cecilia Jane Fontaine Ventouras! You may be an adult, but the Lord God says honor your mother, and as your mother, I say open this door right now!"

The door creaked open to reveal Cecilia's face was swollen

and shiny with tears. There's nothing worse, when you're a kid, than seeing your parents cry. It makes you feel like the world's coming to an end. "Oh, Mommy!" I cried, pushing my way into the elevator and maneuvering myself into her lap so that I could hug her hard. As if my tight squeeze could make her tears, and this cruel disease, go away.

Over my head I heard Cecilia say, "I can't do this, Mother! I can't live this way."

Grandmother wrapped her arms around Cecilia and me and rocked us both as if we were little babies. "Darling, what's happening to you I would not wish on my worst enemy. But the Lord, he never gives us more than we can handle. You have to keep your spirits up. You have to live each day He gives you to the best of your ability."

"But this disease is eating away my abilities!" Cecilia cried. "I can't even cut bread anymore! Soon I'll be a lump of—"

"Hush, you hush now. I'm calling Henry, and it's all going to be fine, you hear me?" said Grandmother, and three days later, Henry and his wife, Charisse, moved into the guest quarters above our garage so that he could take care of the house and carpool me wherever I needed to go. Charisse handled the cooking and took care of Cecilia, which, as her disease ravaged the motor neurons connecting her brain to her muscles, meant things like pureeing her food into mush so that she could swallow it, putting her on the toilet, bathing, and dressing her. Cecilia never cried again, though. At least not that I ever saw or heard.

Even when people stopped coming to see us. Her friends. They didn't know how to talk to her because she couldn't talk anymore. My friends. They didn't know what to say to me. My father. He . . . frankly, I don't know what he thought. He just stopped coming. Everyone stopped coming.

Except Luke Churchville. But even he, in the end, was taken away from me.

Fifth grade: How packed the church was. How loudly we sang "Shall We Gather at the River?" How kind Reverend Burbank sounded, even if I wasn't listening to a word he said. Cosmo, finally returned, his face carved ice, squeezing my hand so hard I thought it would break. Me, Cosmo, Grandmother pouring what remained of our beloved Cecilia into the Gulf of Mexico. Gray ashes meeting deep blue sea. The current sweeping them off into the Gulf Stream, knowing that it flowed in the direction of the Bahamas, then North Carolina, before curving up toward Europe and the north Atlantic. *That's nice,* I thought. *Mom always said she loved London.*

Alone on the viewing deck of the Petroleum Club, I wondered if maybe Grandmother was right. That maybe Cecilia could guide me. Maybe she could hear me. Maybe she could help me. I glanced south, toward the gulf, vaguely in the direction of the place where we had poured her ashes in the water all those years ago. "Okay, Cecilia," I said out loud. "Can you hear me?" No answer. I forged ahead. "Let's just pretend this is going to work. Tell me, why do you want me to be on the Magnolia Court? What in the world am I supposed to do on it? What in the world am I going to do with these girls? Besides give Ashley a hard time, which will be fun, don't get me wrong. But this whole thing is sooooo not me, Cecilia, can't you tell? How in the world am I going to survive it? Cecilia? Cecilia? Mom?"

I studied the horizon. Stars twinkled, but not a one fell from the sky in symbolic response. Ships and boats plied the waters, but none used Morse code to signal an answer. The wind whistled, but I caught no secret messages.

I sighed. Bienville was a town full of ghosts.

And I was the most haunted ghost of all. "SOS, Cecilia," I said as I turned away from the night sky. "SOS."

Chapter Four

And so I settled into the slow lane called May in Bienville.
Because I had gotten kicked out of Stanton Hall so late in
my junior year, Grandmother determined there was no
need to enroll me in any one of Bienville's fine educational
establishments, public or private. The result was daily
lessons throughout the month of May at home with Mr.
Charles Dumas, tutor to Bienville's upper crust. Mr. Dumas
was tolerable, even if he was periodically besieged by sinus
flare-ups that made him snort like a horse. God bless him, he
had a tendency to drone on about the Hundred Years' War,
even when discussing Algebra II. How he was able to find a
connection between the Fibonacci sequence and the Battle
of Calais is beyond me. At least the medieval tapestries of
Joan of Arc were pretty.

In general, I had nothing much to do, and no one much
to do it with. I finished Mr. Dumas's assignments like a good
little girl. I fired up my Netflix queue with constant requests

for *Veronica Mars* and *Alias*. And I ran. Oh, how I ran. I know, it's an odd thing for a smoker. Maybe it's because I feel like I need to make up for the fact that I am destroying my little pink lungs with every puff. Also, I have a truckload of nervous energy. I'm not one of those people who is constantly on the move, but every once in a while a wave of anxiety crashes over me and I feel like I have to move or I will die. And since we wouldn't want that, I run.

Grandmother's house was in one of the oldest neighborhoods in Bienville, Magnolia Oaks, and as such, it was a stone's throw from downtown. Every day after the mid-afternoon rain shower, I stepped out the front door, turned right, and took off at a slow jog through the residential streets canopied with oaks and lined with grand old homes on giant plots of land. That time of day, the humidity is insane, so I often felt like I was breathing water vapor. But I kind of liked that I would get so sweaty so fast. At Commerce Street, I picked up speed, racing cars heading into the business district. At Government Boulevard, I turned right, ran past town hall, the city courthouse, and the chamber of commerce (where I sometimes waved at Mr. Walter). I'd hit the port and run along the docks, dodging forklifts and weaving my way through shipping containers. Then I'd loop back home, throw myself in the shower, and call it a day.

But I never, ever, ever turned left. Coming out of Grandmother's, I most consciously avoided turning left. In fact, since returning to Bienville, I had studiously avoided even glancing left out of the very far corner of my eye at the house that was two doors and three oak trees down from me.

At 511 Magnolia Street.

Home of the Churchvilles.

Last known residence of one Luke Churchville, my childhood best friend.

It's not my fault things ended the way they did. It's not his fault, either. All that blame, in my humble opinion, resides with Cosmo. Luke and I didn't do anything wrong. It was a huge misunderstanding, really. But when you've been so close for so long, and then suddenly it all explodes, there are a lot of loose ends and unknowns.

So I felt nervous. So nervous that I wasn't sure what I wanted. To see Luke or not to see Luke, that was the question. Hmmm. Better to keep that boy tightly sealed in his little box, all bricked up in the wall of tragic fame. If I didn't see him, I didn't have to deal, right? So I never turned left.

But, of course, the day came when curiosity got the best of me. Maybe it was my new Magnolia Maid status (not!) that gave me the gumption to mosey in the direction of 511 Magnolia. Or maybe it was the extra-strength espresso I had just gulped down.

Whatever it was, a few days after the pageant I decided to turn left. I chanted Bienville's motto ("Fill our city with sweet perfume, plant a magnolia and watch it bloom!") and inched my way over to the spacious home I had practically lived in during that terrible time after my mother's death. I wondered if the tire swing was still hanging from the giant

53

oak in the backyard. If Mrs. Churchville still maintained a greenhouse for her orchids. Was it still strictly off-limits to kids, something that Luke and I learned the hard way? What about the clubhouse we built together? Was that still there? We must have been about eight the year we pooled our allowance money together to buy plywood out at Lowe's and slap up a structure that came out as decrepit and treacherous as an ancient fishing shack. We didn't care, though. It was our second home until the Churchville family dog, Daisy, claimed it and infested the place with fleas so bad that Mrs. Churchville swore she'd make Luke and me take a flea bath if we ever crawled in there again.

"You looking for Mr. Luke, Miss Jane?" I jumped at the sound of Henry's voice. He had come outside to trim the azaleas back.

"Oh, hi, Henry." I acted as nonchalant as I could. "Yeah, I haven't seen the Churchvilles at all since I got back."

"That's 'cause they built themselves a big house out by the new golf club. Moved a coupla years ago."

Aha. Luke wasn't there. He wasn't residing in the house two doors and three oak trees away from me. I didn't have to worry about running into him at any old moment. Hearing that, every single cell in my body breathed a sigh of relief. Honestly, until that moment, I didn't realize just how tense I had been.

"Oh, that's nice. Who lives there now?"

"Dr. Paxton and his wife. They got three girls. Little things." As if to punctuate his statement, the front door of the house formerly known as Luke's swung open, and three feisty little sisters bounded out to a family-sized SUV shrieking over who got to put in the DVD.

"Good to know," I said, and took off running. Yes, it was very good to know that Luke Churchville wasn't living in the middle of my street anymore. I didn't have to run into him. And as long as I stayed away from the new golf club, the Churchville family church and, oh, just about every social event in this fishbowl of a town, I could keep it that way.

Chapter Five

"Now, Jane, I want you to be sweet." At breakfast a few days later, Grandmother was giving me advice on how to conduct myself at the very first meeting of the Official Magnolia Maid Court.

Ugh. Be sweet? *Be sweet?* Boy, is that straight out of the Southern belle handbook. It also happens to be Grandmother's catchphrase, something she says to her little dog, Chienette, when she's baring her teeth on the verge of chomping up the mailman. It's something that she's been saying to me since I was a little girl. "Be sweet, Jane, and share your Barbie playhouse." "Be a sweet girl and eat all your peas." I'm convinced my first words were "be sweet."

Truth is, there's nothing sweet about me. I hate being sweet. It's Southern belle code for "Don't make waves." "Don't ruffle feathers." "Keep your opinion to yourself because it might upset somebody else." A good Southern girl practices the three *D*s, according to Grandmother. Decorum.

Dignity. Denial. Bite your lip, nod your head. Accept the circumstances, for you cannot change them. Deny that they are even bothering you. Basically, it means let everyone walk all over you, then go complain about them behind their backs.

Besides, the last time I was "sweet," all it did was land me in a heap of trouble with Cosmo and get me banished from Bienville.

"Do you hear me, Jane? Promise me you won't do anything improper."

"I can't promise that, Grandmama, you know me."

"I do know you," Grandmother continued. "And I know that now that you're back, I don't want to lose you again. So will you please promise me you won't do anything unseemly and get yourself taken away from me again?"

As established, the last thing in the world I want to be is sweet. Especially with the Magnolia Maids. But it was Grandmother asking. "Okay. I'll try." And I meant it. I really did. I really thought, *I'll try to be sweet. To everyone.* If only Ashley weren't such a bitch. If only Mizz Upton weren't such a pain in the butt. If only . . . oh, a million and one if-onlys, so little time.

When Henry dropped me off at Mizz Upton's house (an appropriately dark and sinister brick Tudor over in the Dauphin District), I found Zara lingering out front. Opportunity number one to be sweet. "Hey, Zara! How in the world did a good Sidwell Friends girl end up in a place like this?"

Zara swiveled around and cracked a smile. "Sidwell? How did you know?"

"You moved here from DC, you're a girl of a certain class and stature. Sidwell. That's the school for you. Me, I went to Foxcroft."

"Out in Virginia? That's a great school."

"So I've heard. I wasn't there long enough to find out."

"You transferred?"

"Nah. Got kicked out."

Zara looked at me like I had just told her I was an alien or something. She clearly had no idea how to process this information. "Oh. I'm sorry."

"Don't be. If I hadn't gotten kicked out, I would never have ended up back in Bienville, all Magnolia-fied up, and that would have been a real tragedy, wouldn't it?"

Zara caught the twinkle in my eye and grinned again.

"So seriously, what's a nice girl like you doing in a place like this?"

Zara's grin turned polite and pasty. "Oh, you know, my parents thought it would be a great way for me to meet new people. Get to know the town."

"Couldn't you have taken a tour?" I rooted around in my bag for a cough drop to quench the intense desire for a cigarette that standing in front of Mizz Upton's house had given me.

"Would have been a lot easier." She laughed. "Oh no. We've been busted." Zara pointed at the bay window of

Mizz Upton's living room, where Brandi Lyn was waving at us with great zest. She disappeared from our view and appeared moments later throwing open the front door and pulling us inside.

"Hey, y'all! Guess what we're talking about?"

"I just couldn't tell you."

"Dandies! Who is yours going to be?"

I frowned. "Dandy? As in 'Yankee Doodle'? 'Stuck a feather in his cap—'"

"'And called it macaroni'?" Zara finished my sentence. We raised our fists in a jab, which brought us both to giggles.

Brandi Lyn joined in the giggling fun. "No, sillies!"

Zara and I climbed the steps as an icy voice called out from the living room. "She's talking about escorts." I recognized that voice. Ashley. She and Mallory were perched like princesses in a couple of wing chairs by the fireplace. They clearly had arrived early enough to assess the layout of the room and establish themselves in the power positions. "Magnolia Maids need age-appropriate male escorts for certain occasions, like charity events and Mardi Gras balls." Ashley tsked in Mallory's direction. "See? Didn't I tell you?"

Mallory shook her head in deep, agreeing concern. "They don't know anything."

Zara and I flopped down next to Brandi Lyn on a couch so big and puffy that it sucked you in to the point that you'd have to struggle to get out of it. These were the opposite of power seats. I smiled ever so *sweetly* in Ashley's direction. "Well, I guess we'll just have to learn, then, won't we?"

Brandi Lyn turned to me again. "So who is yours going to be?"

"I don't know. I just moved back here."

"And you, Zara?"

Zara shrugged. "I just moved here, too."

Ashley arched an eyebrow at Mallory. Mallory arched one back. "Total disaster," Ashley said.

Brandi Lyn smiled. "Oh, I'm sure it will be fine. Zara and Jane are so lovely. They'll find cute boys soon enough. Anyway, JoeJoe's gonna die when I ask him to be my dandy."

"Is that the guy who leapt off the balcony for you at the civic center?" I asked.

"Isn't that the most romantic thing in the world?" Brandi Lyn cooed. "He just adores the whole Civil War thing." She turned to Ashley. "Do you think he can wear his Confederate uniform to events?"

Ashley rolled her eyes. "No, Brandi Lyn. It's either morning suits or casual wear, depending on the occasion."

"And you, Ashley?" Engaging others in conversation, that's sweet. *Look how sweet I'm being,* I thought. "Who is your dandy?"

Ashley straightened up proudly. "My boyfriend, James Hardison the third."

"Ooh. A third. How exciting!" Did I deserve an award or what?

"Our fathers are partners in Hardison and LaFleur."

"What a match made in heaven."

"Isn't it? And I feel so sorry for y'all," said Ashley. "Not having a steady boyfriend you can depend on to be your dandy. Or even knowing any of our Bienville boys."

"Thanks, Ashley," I replied. "I'm sure we'll figure it out. Hey, Mallory, who's your dreamboat?"

Mallory blushed. "I haven't decided yet."

Ashley got a conniving look on her face. "Mallory has more of a free-form attitude toward boyfriends."

Mallory blushed even more. "Ashley! That makes me sound like a . . . *slut*."

"If the shoe fits."

"Y'all don't listen to her! I can't help it. I like boys. I just have a hard time making a decision."

"You mean you haven't met a boy you didn't like yet."

"That's okay, Mallory," I said. "What's wrong with being a slut?" Okay, I was trying to be sweet. . . . That one just didn't come out right. Thank God Mizz Upton and Walter Murray Hill chose that moment to come in from the kitchen.

"All right, y'all!" Mizz Upton called, a big smile on her face, her omnipresent blown-out bob bobbing every time she nodded. She motioned a maid—not the Magnolia kind— to set a heavily loaded tray onto the coffee table. "We have sweet tea, cream cheese and olive sandwiches, and lemon squares! Help yourselves. But not too much! You don't want to be bloated for your first dress measurements."

Walter Murray Hill chuckled. "Oh, I'm sure we won't have any bloating. This is the best-looking group of girls in town."

Mizz Upton dismissed the non-Magnolia maid and glanced around the room, finding something amiss. "Caroline! We're starting, Caroline!"

Moments later, Caroline trudged down the stairs from the second floor, book in hand. "Excuse me, Mother, but do I really need to attend? I already know all this stuff from the other years."

"Well, you need to bond with your sister Maids, don't you, honey?"

"I'm the alternate, Mother. I'm not that important."

Mizz Upton looked like her patience was being sorely tested. "Something might come up where you will be called upon to serve the Court and if that ever happens you need to be prepared to serve well, sweetie. So do sit down. Please." The last few words probably would sound polite on paper, but trust me, said out loud, they were nails hammered into a coffin.

I felt so bad for her, I said, "Yeah, come join us. Have a lemon square."

Caroline beelined to a seat across from the couch and did indeed grab a lemon square, until her mother slapped her hand away from them. "What did I tell you?" Caroline snatched back her hand, completely embarrassed. Yikes. That was awkward.

Walter Murray Hill cleared his throat. "Now, girls." He

shook his head. "No, I can't call you girls anymore. From here on out, you'll be known as Maids."

Oh boy.

"On behalf of the Bienville Chamber of Commerce, I welcome you to the sixtieth Magnolia Court. This is going to be our most exciting year yet, right, Martha Ellen?"

Mizz Upton, fake smile cemented in place, bobbed and nodded. "It already is, Walter! In my fifteen years as the Official Etiquette Mistress and Head Advisor of the Magnolia Maids, I have never seen such a, well, *diverse* Court."

Ashley raised her hand. "I saw in the paper that people have been calling the selection of the Court the shock of the century."

I rolled my eyes. "Obviously they don't read up on international affairs much." Uh-oh. Couldn't help that one. Just slipped out.

Mr. Walter held up a hand. "Now you girls don't worry about those letters to the editor, okay. We at the Magnolia Maid Organization will make every effort to protect and support y'all at every single event. And I'm sure the lawsuits from the Lennoxes and the DeVilles will be going away any day now."

"Lawsuits? Seriously?" I gasped.

Ashley jumped in. "Yes, Jane, people do take this seriously. Maybe not you, but other people."

Walter Murray Hill cleared his throat. "That's right. We do take this seriously, and we are not going to let a few contradictory voices interfere with official Magnolia Maid business. You ladies are going to have the time of your life representing our fair city to folks around the country!" He launched into a sales pitch that would have made a game-show host proud, with Mizz Upton backing him up with delicious little details. We'd be marching in the Macy's Thanksgiving Day Parade. That thrilled Brandi Lyn to no end because she'd always wanted to go to New York City. There would be a presidential inauguration next January, which cheered Zara up since she could see her friends in DC again. Ashley got excited about the Memphis in May festivities because she had family there. And we all agreed that our trip to Los Angeles for the Rose Bowl would be the perfect opportunity to scope out the yummy likes of Channing Tatum and Shia LaBeouf.

Mizz Upton bobbed her head again. "But our very first event, coming up in six short weeks, is right here at home. Your debut . . ."

". . . at the Annual Magnolia Festival at Boysenthorp Gardens!" As Walter Murray Hill completed her sentence with a bang, Ashley and Mallory worked themselves into a frenzy of delight.

"OMG, OMG, OMG!"

"Can you believe it? The best days of our lives are finally here!"

Mizz Upton held out a hand. "Now, Maids, there's good reason to be excited, but we have a whole lot of work to do. First, there is . . ."

Walter Murray Hill cut her off. "Before you get down to

business, Martha Ellen, I have to tell you, a special request came in the other day. I mean, you could have knocked me over with a feather." He paused dramatically, really working the "game-show host on the verge of announcing the big prize" angle. "Get your passports out, Maids! You're going to Spain!"

Every ounce of air in the room disappeared as we all gasped in unison. The Ashley/Mallory excitement buzz spread all over the room. Even I sat up. Spain? Sangria and bulls and cute Latin boys Spain? Not bad. It was Mallory, though, who got the first response out. "Abroad? No Magnolia Maid's ever gone abroad before!"

Mizz Upton's blonde bob nearly bobbed off her head in excitement. "Why, Walter Murray Hill, you rascal, you didn't breathe a word about this!"

"Just found out myself, Martha Ellen, isn't it something? We have been invited by our sister city, Ronda, to attend the annual bullfighting festival! I got a call direct from the mayor himself."

Mallory threw her arms around Ashley. "Oh my God, we're going abroad. We haven't even had out debut yet, and we're already making so much history!"

Brandi Lyn's hand crept up. "Um, Mr. Hill. I don't have a passport."

"Oh, I don't, either," replied Mallory.

"Me neither," said Ashley.

Caroline shook her head, too.

"I do," Zara said. "My family travels a lot."

"I've practically had one since I was born," I added.

Zara and I exchanged glances. None of these girls had passports? This is *exactly* what I meant about Bienville looking at the world from afar.

Brandi Lyn sighed. "Is this a problem that we all don't have them yet?"

Walter beamed. "No, it makes you one hundred percent Bienville born and bred, which is exactly why you're Bienville's best! We'll get it all taken care of later in the year. Well, you ladies have a lot to talk about, so I'm gonna let Martha Ellen get going with you. Before I leave, though, I just want you Maids to know I am here for you. Just give me a ring if you need anything, if you have any old question. I mean anything. Walter Murray Hill is here for you, okay."

He went around the room shaking hands with each of us, adding the extra squeeze with his left hand and looking us each in the eye before he made his exit and left us alone with Mizz Upton. And let me tell you, all of a sudden I had a newfound appreciation for his game-show-host self.

The moment that he was out the door, Mizz Upton's bob stopped bobbing and she turned into Cruella de Bienville. "Throughout the entire time I have known him, Walter Murray Hill has been quite the optimist. He always thinks our Maids are beautiful. He relentlessly trusts in their ability to rise to the occasion. He believes that each Maid can learn and uphold all the rules of the Magnolia Court. Usually, I take great comfort from his optimism. This time I believe him to be completely and utterly wrong." She turned what can only be described as a baleful eye around the room, one that turned benevolent only when it landed on Ashley and Mallory. "Due to the unauthorized and ill-advised selection process this year, I believe we are at the most detrimental starting point ever in the history of the Magnolia Court. Preparing you to present yourselves as proper antebellum ladies, with a complete cornucopia of Magnolia Maid and Bienville knowledge in six weeks' time, is possibly the most insurmountable task I have faced in my entire life." She launched into a litany of things we had to do, which included such delightful tasks as:

1. Working with the dressmaker to design our antebellum dress uniform and suffering through various fittings along the way.
2. Creating a fund-raising plan to raise the gazillion dollars necessary for us to travel far and wide.
3. Memorizing the Magnolia Maid Manifesto, handbook, and official poem, and being able to recite them upon command.
4. Procuring our dandies for events occurring later in the year.

Ugh. Listening to Mizz Upton's cantankerous voice was not my idea of a good time, so when she went off on a tangent about sisterhood and the importance of the Magnolia Maid poem, I receded into the depths of my own mind. Get a dandy? Really? I know I was acting all nonchalant about it earlier, but it was actually stressing me out. It used to be that the logical choice would have been Luke. But now? I got into an argument in my own head about whether I would ask him to be my dandy if I ever saw him again. Answer, after much internal debate: No. Mainly because I could never use the word *dandy* with a straight face. Ever. That led to my other internal argument about whether I actually wanted to see Luke Churchville again or not see Luke Churchville. See Luke, not see Luke. See Luke, not see . . .

It was a pretty all-encompassing debate, until I realized that Mizz Upton had exited the room, leaving us to our own devices. I whispered to Zara, "What's going on?"

"We're supposed to have a 'get to know each other chat' and elect a queen."

"A queen?" Huh? "What is this? The Feudal Ages?"

Caroline whispered to me, "You really should read the handbook, Jane. It's all in there."

Meanwhile, up in her power chair, Ashley whipped a clipboard out of her Lilly Pulitzer bag. "Maids, can I get your attention, please? I've taken the liberty of going ahead and developing some recommendations for how we should proceed." She handed out a packet of information to each of us. "I think our charity should be LeanTeen. It's a great new organization that promotes healthy lifestyle choices for inner-city youth. Exercising, eating fruits and vegetables, avoiding unnecessary weight gain. And for our fund-raisers, we can do a combo carwash and bake sale."

Mallory jumped in. "Oh, I love that idea! My cousin Lucinda and her Maids did one, and they raised tons of money. Tons."

Something about this sounded so very wrong to me. "Excuse me, Ashley, carwash and bake sale? How do you keep the baked goods from getting soaked?"

"Oh my!" Brandi Lyn cried. "I don't think soggy cupcakes will sell."

Ashley leveled us both with deadly stares. "Don't be ridiculous. Any idiot can aim a hose in the right direction."

True. But still. "I don't know, you guys."

Mallory giggled. "You *guys*? What are you, Jane, a Yankee?"

"Sorry. I seem to have misplaced my drawl. Let me try that again." I did a little shimmy, tossed my hair, and jumped back on the horse. "I don't know, *y'all*, I think we should do something different."

Ashley and Mallory frowned. "Why do something different?" asked Mallory.

"Mr. Walter said he wanted things to change, soooo, I don't know. Let's do something unique, maybe more related to current events."

Zara, good Sidwell Friends girl that she is, got an idea immediately. "Oh! What about the oil spill?"

"Exactly. I mean, here Bienville is, literally a sitting duck for all that oil spewing into the gulf. Isn't there something we can do for the community? You know, to help out people, the animals, the beaches, something? What about a beach cleanup? Save some birds?"

Mallory frowned. "I don't think anyone's ever done anything like that before."

Ashley grimaced. "It sounds dirty. I do not want to be parading around the beach getting bird gunk all over me. Ewww."

"It's oil, Ashley," I said. "It *is* dirty. And you could take the spill a little more seriously. Everyone in the region is affected by it. Everyone."

"I know my daddy's going to make a fortune off all those lawsuits he's filing!"

I gaped. Wow. "Okay, bully for you and your expanding shoe collection, but could you possibly consider those who are actually suffering? Say the folks who have lost their livelihood? The shrimpers, the people who run hotels by the beach? And oops, hate to tell you, but you may not be eating any oysters down at the Oyster House for a while because all the beds have been closed due to, yikes, being *toxic*."

Ashley shrugged. "All true. I'll give you that. But seriously, Jane. This idea is trashy. It does not fit in with the Magnolia Maid image. You know, clean, neat, presentable."

"Mr. Walter said the times and the Magnolia Maids, they are a-changing."

Ashley groaned. "Didn't you hear? Nobody around here likes change, Jane. Nobody. Caroline, tell her."

"Nobody likes change," Caroline parroted. "But I do think it's a nice idea."

"Thank you, Caroline." I smirked at Ashley. She sent Caroline a dark, dark look.

Brandi Lyn waved. "Excuse me, I'm so sorry, but aren't we supposed to be thinking about a fund-raiser? This sounds great for a charity event, but I don't understand how we make money off it?"

"I do." Everyone's attention turned to Zara, whose face was actually animated for the first time since we'd met. "I know exactly how to do it. A beach cleanup fund-raiser. We did one at this camp I go to in New England." Zara explained the concept: your organization chooses a beach to work on, divides it up into increments, say of ten or twenty feet, then solicits contributions for each segment of beach that is cleaned up. Donors pledge anywhere from one cent to a dollar per section. "I've done it twice and both times, it's turned out to be really fun. You're out in the sun all day, jump in the water whenever you get hot. And we had lots of people, even total strangers, join in and help us. It was cool."

I brought my hands together in a prayer position and quasi-bowed to Zara. "Genius, Zara. That's what I'm talking about. We clean the beach, raise some awareness about the environment, make some money, have some fun. It's a win-win-win-win situation."

To my delight, my Maid sisters/sister Maids started getting excited:

Mallory, quite surprisingly, kicked it off. "Y'all! This is so creative! No Magnolia Maid Court has ever done anything like this!"

"I know! Let's go door-to-door asking people for donations. Set up a booth at the mall!" cried Brandi Lyn.

71

"People all over the country are worried about this. We could set up at all the local tourist attractions so that out-of-towners can donate, too!" added Caroline.

"And don't forget corporate sponsors," Zara said. "My parents will definitely chip in."

Mallory gasped with delight. "Oh my gosh! This would be so perfect to get the dandies involved with, right, Ashley?"

Ashley, meanwhile, had been receding into the wings of her power chair, the expression on her face turning increasingly sour as our conversation escalated. "I don't know if my complexion can take a whole day in the sun like that."

"We'll take breaks in the shade," I countered.

That did NOT appease her. "And I have one question." She leveled a death stare at Zara, like a viper ready to strike. "Why don't you tell us all the truth? How much did your daddy pay to get you on the Court?"

Talk about a conversation killer. It was so awful. We all just sat there in stunned silence. No one knew where to look. My eyes searched out poor Zara, who was managing to look incredibly serene, but it was obvious that her comfort level had sunk from tolerable to nonexistent.

I fixed Ashley with a death stare of my own. "You know what, Ashley? Uncool. You're out of line."

"It's a legitimate question."

"It's totally rude and uncalled for and you know it." I turned to the circle of girls. "I move that we change the subject before things get any more inappropriate. What about this queen business? Anyone have any thoughts?"

Ashley nudged Mallory's leg with her foot.

"Ow! What? Oh! I nominate Ashley for queen."

Ashley acted ridiculously demure, especially given how rude she'd just been. "Oh, Mallory. Wow. I'm so honored."

"I can't think of anyone better to be a queen. Don't you agree, Caroline?" Mallory nudged Caroline with her foot.

Caroline glanced up from the lemon square she had snagged in all the awkward silence and nodded. "Yeah. I mean, you're a great student council president. You'd be wonderful on this, I'm sure."

My jaw hit the ground. Really? Caroline was supporting Ashley for queen? Had she not heard Ashley totally insult her on pageant night?

"Great. We have one candidate," I said. "And since this is a democracy, you need an opponent. I nominate Brandi Lyn."

Brandi Lyn paled. "Really? Me? Oh my goodness!"

"Don't you go fainting again, Brandi Lyn. It's obvious. You're thrilled about being a Magnolia Maid, and you're nice to everyone. You should totally do it."

Zara raised her hand. "I second it."

And with that, swear to God, steam erupted from Ashley's ears as she realized she had lost every iota of control she ever thought she would have over her Magnolia Court. "Excuse me! Her boyfriend works at EZ Lube!"

"Yes, he makes real good money there," chimed in Brandi Lyn, all enthusiastic.

"I don't give a damn if he makes a million dollars a minute. He's a redneck. And so are you. And I will not let you be head of my Court!"

With that Ashley finally jumped up and down on my last nerve. "See! This is exactly why you should not be queen. It is NOT your Court! It's ours! You're pissed that your little BFFs didn't make it, and now you're out to make all of us miserable! We'd have to be stupid to put our fate in your hands."

"You'd be stupid not to!" Furious, Ashley shot up and got in my face. "My father is willing to donate ten thousand dollars if I get elected queen!"

I stood my ground. "And how is that any different from you accusing Zara of having her daddy buy her way on to the Court? Could you be more of a hypocrite?"

We were ready to take it outside—if you can imagine a world where Southern belles are willing to take it outside—when suddenly a sharp clap smacked us back to reality.

Mizz Upton, a look of appalled anger on her face, stood in the doorway.

"What?" I quipped. "Is it lunchtime?"

Mizz Upton's voice shook with fury, but she spoke so calmly and quietly, I almost had to lean forward to hear her. "A Magnolia Maid never raises her voice."

Ashley smoothed her hair, put that prissy look back on her face, and took a seat. "I am so sorry, Mizz Upton. It's just that Jane, well, her attitude is so aggressive and unfriendly. It's got me a little concerned that she may not be a team player."

"I'm sure it does." Mizz Upton glared at me. "Jane, could you please conduct yourself in a manner becoming a Magnolia Maid?"

I snorted. "That's a question you should ask Ashley. She's the one trying to play dictator!"

"I am sure Ashley's just trying to guide the discussion."

"If by guide you mean completely and totally dominate."

Before Mizz Upton could respond, however, there was a knock at the front door. She moved toward the foyer. "Maids, we simply do not have time for this fracas. We will address it later. Dinah Mae Marshall is here."

"Oh my!" Now Mallory looked like she was going to faint. "Somebody pinch me! It's time for the *dresses!*"

Chapter Six

From the first moment that Dinah Mae Marshall, official seamstress to the Magnolia Court, opened her mouth, I knew I was going to love her. "Lord God, child," she said to Mallory. "Get your arms off me. I'm no hug baby for you to love on." All four feet ten inches and eighty pounds of Dinah Mae Marshall struggled to push a fawning Mallory away from her. She looked to be about two hundred and thirty-seven years old, which meant she had been making antebellum dresses since the days of Scarlett O'Hara. Just kidding.

But Miss Dinah Mae's reputation so long preceded her that Mallory swooned at the mere mention of her name. She had run right over and threw her arms around Dinah Mae and cried, "Oh, Miss Dinah Mae, I've been waiting to meet you my whole life! I have! Ever since the very first time Ashley and I played Magnolia Maid dress-up when we were five. Oh my gosh, it is such a pleasure to meet you. My cousin Lucinda, she was a Maid a few years ago, she simply adores you." She squeezed Miss Dinah Mae twice more before Mizz Upton was able to separate them.

We Maids lined up in the dining room so that Miss Dinah Mae could inspect us. And inspect she did, like a drill sergeant studying her new recruits. Silent. Stern. Harumphing to herself. Finally, she turned to Mizz Upton and said, "Well, Miss Martha Ellen, this has got to be the sorriest bunch a belles I ever did see. Where'd you get these gals from?"

News flash! Mizz Upton seemed almost *intimidated* by this tiny force of a woman. I wouldn't have thought it possible if I hadn't seen it myself. "I-I'm so sorry, Miss Dinah Mae," Mizz Upton stammered. "It wasn't my choice this year. The Jaycees, they took it out of my hands."

"You think you gonna get them all whipped up into shape in time for the Boysenthorp?"

"I guess we don't have a choice, now do we, Miss Dinah?"

"We sure don't." Miss Dinah stopped at Brandi Lyn, who greeted her with her friendliest smile, until Dinah Mae sniffed and said, "Hmmph! Girl, you got some bosoms we got to hide or those boys, good God a-mighty."

Brandi Lyn turned beet red. "I'm sorry, Miss Dinah. I've got a minimizer I can wear."

"What you sorry for? The good Lord gave you that, didn't he? Miss Dinah'll take care of it." She moved on to Zara and paused. Straightened up. "Child, there are two days I thought I'd never see come in my lifetime. This is one of 'em."

Mizz Upton nodded enthusiastically. "We're diversifying this year, Miss Dinah. Getting into the twenty-first century!"

Miss Dinah paid her no mind. She was too busy studying Zara. It was a funny sight, like a toddler standing next to a basketball player. Miss Dinah shook her head. "Girl, you ate those Wheaties all up, didn't you? You gonna wear Miss Dinah out, making a skirt long enough to cover those legs." She moved on, but not before whispering proudly to Zara, "You represent good, now, you hear me?"

Zara nodded. Vigorously. "Yes, ma'am."

She looked each one of us up and down and immediately identified which body part was going to make her "work." Mallory's neck was long, "just like her mother's," so Miss Dinah would have to be careful she didn't come out looking like a giraffe. Caroline "had meat on her" (a pronouncement that made Mizz Upton cringe in horror), but that was okay, Miss Dinah had a special nip pleat that would help out with that. Ashley—this is hilarious—had legs shorter than her torso, which was going to mess up the bodice/skirt ratio.

Ashley's face bloomed scarlet. "My legs aren't short! What are you talking about?"

"Don't you argue with Miss Dinah. I made over three hundred of these dresses before you was born. I know from these dresses."

"But . . ." Miss Dinah Mae had already moved on to me, and I was having a hard time dealing with the fact that she was staring me in the eyes like she could see into my soul.

"Something's going on with you, child. You the queen?"

"No, ma'am. We don't have one."

Miss Dinah glanced over at Mizz Upton. "That true?"

Mizz Upton, looking like she was going to poop a bag of peanuts, nodded. "The girls haven't elected a queen yet, Miss Dinah."

I laughed.

Miss Dinah glared at me. "You think that's funny? Miss Dinah don't think that's funny." She kept staring, and y'all, I don't know if you've ever had a woman six inches shorter than you stare you down until you felt like you were five inches tall, but seriously, that is exactly what she did. I shrank.

"You the spitting image of your mama."

There it was, the first mention of Cecilia all day. I took a deep breath and braced myself for the onslaught of sadness. Odd. It didn't come. I just nodded and gave a little smile. "Yes, ma'am. That's what people say."

"She was a sweet girl. Didn't have no attitude like you."

Awww, man! How did she know I had attitude? I'd been trying to be sweet all day! Sort of. "I suspect not, ma'am."

"Show me your arms."

"Ma'am?"

"Lift up those sleeves and show me them arms." I did and she grabbed both arms, turning each one over and inspecting them. "Turn around and lift up your hair."

I did so. "What's going on?"

"Hush your mouth." I felt her yank the neck of my T-shirt down so that she could see my back. She was searching here and searching there and suddenly it dawned on me what she was looking for. Suddenly, she emitted a sound of annoyance and slapped me on the shoulder. "Lord, girl, the stupidness in the world today! What in the good name o' the Spirit am I supposed to do with *that*?"

One time when I was in the tenth grade, I was allowed to go to a coed school, and there was a really cute boy there, Hank Mayers. We dated for a bit and had a good time, and on this field trip our class took to Atlanta we took our relationship to the next level. No, not *that* level. We snuck out in the middle of the night and went down to Little Five Points and bought beer with fake IDs and drank it on the corner. Then we went and got tattoos together.

I woke up with a hangover and the image of Cartman from *South Park* inked on my shoulder, just under where my bra strap goes. Hank woke up with a heart and JANE FOREVER on his arm. Sadly, we didn't last another twenty-four hours. The next day we were both kicked out of school for sneaking out in the middle of the night, and I haven't seen or heard from him since.

Only later did it dawn on me that Luke Churchville was ace at imitating Cartman, and had even made the character part of his e-mail address: cartmanluke@hotmail.com.

Gosh, I hope Hank lasered my name off and got another girl's put on.

Needless to say, the Cartman on my shoulder did not go over

well. Miss Dinah Mae fussed about how in the world she was going to sew the off-the-shoulder neckline high enough to cover the tattoo. Mizz Upton turned a peculiar shade of green when she saw it, then tersely eeped, "Let's have a chat later, Jane, why don't we?"

Then Miss Dinah Mae took everybody's measurements and informed us we'd be selecting our embellishments (Magnolia-speak for ruffles and ribbons) and be assigned our dress colors the following week—whoop-de-doo-doo! Then she'd get busy making our gowns, for which we would be required to do at least two fittings, probably more, given that we all had these body abnormalities, and a final dress check. Quel joy.

To my surprise, Brandi Lyn stayed after orientation to "chat" with Mizz Upton as well. What had she done wrong? She was so Magnolia-happy, how could she possibly be thrown in with the likes of me? Mizz Upton called Brandi Lyn and me over to sit with her in the living room. She put on what I'm sure she thought was her most sympathetic face. "Now, girls. I have been thinking, and while it greatly pains me to say this, I believe y'all might want to reconsider your commitment to the Magnolia Maids."

Brandi Lyn furrowed her brow. "I feel very committed to the Magnolia Maids. One hundred and ten percent."

"She wants us to quit, Brandi Lyn." I aimed my most unsympathetic gaze in Mizz Upton's direction. "And Mizz Upton does not hate saying it. Not one bit."

Blinking rapidly, Mizz Upton tried to paint a portrait

of politeness on her face. Not that it worked. "Now this is exactly what I see as your personal challenge, Jane. Magnolia Maids are the epitome of Southern grace and femininity. And your behavior and attitude so far, well, we would be kind to say that it merely *lacks* those qualities."

"But Mizz Upton, I've been nothing but sweet today, right, Brandi Lyn?"

"Um, sure. And you were so nice to me the other night when I was fainting and all. It was sweet of you to try to catch me!"

Mizz Upton raised an eyebrow. "What was that little altercation with Ashley then?"

"Oh, she was so offensive, Mizz Upton! She asked Zara if she bought her way on to the Court. Then she insulted Brandi Lyn and her boyfriend. I had to say something!"

"This is one of the things that concern me, Jane: you're unpredictable. You say what you think."

My brow turned into one giant furrow. "Excuse me, ma'am, but isn't that a good thing? Shouldn't we young ladies be encouraged to say what we think?"

"Well, no, Jane, that's just it. You're no longer a young lady, you're a Magnolia Maid." She threw her hands into the air. "See, this is where it's become obvious that leaving Bienville has had a most negative impact on you. Those outside influences, they have diminished your respectability in ways that I just can't combat. Your clothes, your tattoo, the fact that you've been expelled from so many fine institutions—honestly, I will never understand how in the world that got past the judges! It is so clear that you are unpredictable and uncontrollable and absolutely not fit to be a Magnolia Maid!" She calmed herself down for a millisecond. "I saw you trying to behave today, I did, but it's a case of too little, too late. I simply cannot send you out into the world not knowing what's going to come out of your mouth at any given moment or what kind of inappropriate situation you're going to get yourself into. It would reflect badly on me and the entire Magnolia Maid Organization."

She sighed deeply, leaned forward, grasped my hand, and painted another portrait of faux sympathy on her face. "It's not your fault, though, dear. If your mother were alive, if you had been raised properly, I'm sure you would be a young woman of much higher caliber. Everybody's saying so." She gave my hand a pat.

A "you don't belong here" pat.

A "nobody wants you" pat.

A "you poor thing" pat.

I just stared at her hand in shock. And when she removed it, I continued to stare at the skin she had touched, a mass of emotions and thoughts scurrying through my head. I'm not good enough. Leaving Bienville has ruined me for all eternity. I'm not high caliber, and everybody knows it. *Everybody knows it? Everybody was saying it?* Of course they were! Behind my back! It suddenly dawned on me—every encounter I'd had since I got back, every time that someone said how wonderful my mother was or asked me how I was doing, they were just looking for something to gossip about! Of course they were all judging me. They were watching and waiting for me to mess up in public so that it would give them something to talk about. *I was part of the show.* Mizz Upton was just the first one to let me know.

Meanwhile, Brandi Lyn blinked tears from her eyes. "But Mizz Upton, ma'am, what about me? Why should I reconsider my commitment?"

"For one thing, your personal style is just a wee bit bolder than what we consider appropriately feminine." Mizz Upton took both of Brandi Lyn's hands in hers and continued. "And being a Magnolia Maid is also a very expensive proposition, dear. I am concerned that you might not be able to afford the investment we expect of our girls."

"But I've already thought about that! I'm planning to take on extra shifts at the Krawfish Shack, and my boyfriend, JoeJoe, said he'd help me, and Momma and Daddy, they're gonna chip in!"

"And that is so generous of them! But Brandi Lyn, I feel so guilty about the toll that seven-thousand-dollar dress is going to take on your family."

Brandi Lyn whitened. "Seven . . . Seven thousand dollars?" Funny how the cost of the dresses wasn't mentioned—not even ONCE—during the entire course of orientation and competition.

"Oh dear, didn't you know? I would think that anyone who tried out would know. Isn't that just common knowledge?" Mizz Upton quickly repressed a flash of a grin and placed a "well-meaning" hand on Brandi Lyn's shoulder. "Wouldn't you just feel terrible if they lost their house or a car over this? I just don't think it's the right choice for your people."

Now I'm sure Mizz Upton thought she would just deliver her pronouncements and that would be the end of Brandi Lyn and me giving her a giant Magnolia headache. What she could not have expected, though, was that Brandi Lyn Corey would be so devastated by the news that she would immediately erupt into a volcano of hysterical lava, spewing tears and hiccups all over the place.

"Nnnnnnnot be a Maid? Not be a Maid?! But I, I've worked so hard! I already sacrificed! It's . . . It's a key part of my five-year plan! I can make this work! I know I can!" Brandi Lyn wailed even louder.

"Don't make this more difficult than it has to be, honey," Mizz Upton said. "It's good form to resign when asked to. Just go ahead and write your resignation letters before we get too much further into the training. You can send them care of Mr. Hill at the chamber of commerce." She got to her feet and dismissed us with a sliver of a smile and a truckload of condescension.

We didn't move. Brandi Lyn continued to bawl, and I, well, I was frozen solid with a dark, angry hurt that had invaded every cell of my being. Fine, they didn't want me? I wasn't good enough for Bienville? Great. I would go home right that very minute and craft that letter like nobody's biz-nass.

But there was something about people wanting me to fail that bothered me. If Brandi Lyn and I resigned, they would win. Mizz Upton would win. Ashley could claim victory. It would serve as proof that we weren't good enough, and I was NOT ready to accept that judgment yet, no matter how rebellious I was. No way was I going to let Mizz Upton and Ashley beat us out so early in the game. No way.

Instead, I was going to invoke another version of the Southern belle. They wanted a Magnolia Maid? Fine. They'd get one.

A *steel* one.

"Mizz Upton, I do so hate to say this," I said, dripping my sweetest drawl onto every word. "But Brandi Lyn and I regret that we are unable to resign at this time." I stood up and pulled Brandi Lyn to her feet.

"Excuse me?" Mizz Upton looked horrified.

"We do?" Brandi Lyn gaped at me.

"We do. Brandi Lyn, she's trying to scare us. She can't make us quit."

"This is no scare tactic! I am doing what is best for the organization."

"Well, I have a hunch that the Jaycees and Mr. Walter Murray Hill would have quite a different opinion. They elected us to the Court, what, three nights ago? I don't think that they would be so happy to hear that you are strong-arming poor innocent girls into believing they aren't, in your personal opinion, good enough, when the judges clearly decided we are."

"Don't you dare talk back to me, Jane Fontaine!"

"Fontaine *Ventouras*. I'm sure you recall that my mother—gasp!—married a non-Bienvillite, Cosmo Ventouras? And with all due respect, I'm not talking back, Mizz Upton. I'm just saying that we'll leave when the Jaycees themselves invite us to leave. Until then, we'll be showing up for any and all rehearsals and other events that you have planned for us. Come on, Brandi Lyn." I put my arm around her and led her out of the house, but not before Mizz Upton got her last word in.

"Fine. But I am filing probation reports first thing tomorrow. And if you don't follow every single rule, meet every single expectation to a tee, I will have you out of here before the first magnolia blooms at Boysenthorp Gardens, so help me, God!"

"You're so brave. Oh my stars, Jane, you were so brave back there." Brandi Lyn and I were still in the middle of our grand exit, me walking a mile a minute in my John Fluevogs, Brandi Lyn teetering along as fast as she could in her Payless specials. "I never could have said what you did. I wanted to, but I couldn't do it."

"Yeah, well, this is my specialty: bringing authority figures to their knees." I sparked up my first cigarette since the day's activities began. "Jesus, what a bitch! You didn't deserve that, Brandi Lyn."

"Well, thank you. You're so sweet. But please don't take the Lord's name in vain."

"Don't take the Lord's name in vain? Are you for real?"

"The Ten Commandments are." We were in Bienville, Alabama, for God's, uh, *goodness'* sake. Of course she was for real.

"Okay, okay, you're right. I'm sorry."

As we brought our speedy grand exit to a halt, Brandi Lyn put a hand on my arm. "Jane, that's terrible what Mizz Upton said back there. About your mother. I'm so sorry. I didn't realize until today that she had passed."

"Thanks, Brandi Lyn."

"It must be hard."

Brandi Lyn's bright blue eyes grayed over with compassion. It wasn't the "lost little lamb" look that I had just learned was one hundred percent fake. It was so real, that expression in her eyes. And I didn't feel obligated to respond, to pretend, to decree, "I'm fine, everything's okay." Brandi Lyn never knew my mother. She just knew *me*. She cared about *me*.

All of a sudden I felt the warmth of her hand melting the icy fury that had been flowing through my system. A river of rushing rapids piled up behind my eyes, and two slow, quiet streams escaped down my face.

Quick, Jane, I thought. *Change the subject before you flood the entire neighborhood!* Yes, yes, that was a very good idea indeed. But first I took Brandi Lyn's hand in mine and squeezed it—tight—and nodded. She squeezed back and pulled me into a hug that seemed to last forever.

Not so good for flood control. Not at all.

88

I took a deep breath or twenty-five thousand, then slowly extricated myself from Brandi Lyn's embrace. I took a shaky drag off my cigarette. "So, um, tell me, what in the world is a five-year plan?"

Breathy with excitement, Brandi Lyn informed me that a five-year plan was this really amazing thing where you thought about what your goals in life were and how you were going to achieve them with a series of well-thought-out deadlines and mini-goals! She had perfectly mapped out her life for the next five years:

1. Get selected for the Magnolia Maids. Gain valuable travel and cultural experience.
2. Earn full scholarship to the University of Alabama's journalism school just like Selma Andrews had. (I knew who Selma Andrews was, right? The news anchor for CNN? She was Brandi Lyn's hero. Well, Selma had gotten her start at Bama on a full scholarship before going to journalism school at Columbia, and BL wanted to follow in her footsteps.)
3. Build résumé with sorority and club membership, at least five a year. Take key leadership position in at least two extracurricular activities per year.
4. Make honor roll each semester. Graduate summa cum laude. (To which I responded, "Wow. You're smart!" and Brandi Lyn humbly replied, "I'm blessed.")
5. Intern each summer at a radio or television station in order to build exposure and contacts.

6. Get first reporting job at a local news station in a small, probably Southern market.

Brandi Lyn stopped there because she had reached the five-year limit. "I'll have to assess my progress about halfway through, of course," she said.

The thought of so much industry and planning gave me a headache. I lit yet another cigarette. "You've thought that far ahead?"

"You have to set goals, Jane, if you're going to achieve anything in life."

"Me, I can't think beyond, like, ten minutes from now."

"Let me help you with that! I just love brainstorming and planning and figuring out ways to achieve goals!"

"Uh, sure. I'll let you know when I feel like getting my life on track." I puffed again on my cigarette. "But how 'bout you and me work on a five-week plan instead?"

"That's a good start! What do you want to do?"

"Declare war on Mizz Upton."

"War!"

"Not shoot-a-gun, fire-a-cannon kind of war."

Brandi Lyn was baffled. "Then . . . ?"

"A war to be the most perfect Magnolia Maids ever!"

Brandi Lyn sighed with relief. "Well, that's obvious. Of course we want to be the best Magnolia Maids we can be, right?"

"You do. But I've only just now decided to."

"So why's it got to be a war?"

"Brandi Lyn, Mizz Upton's going to be after us now. You heard her say it, right? She's declared war on us. If we're going to make it through, we're going to have to be not just good Magnolia Maids but perfect Magnolia Maids. Fight fire with fire. And to do that, you and I, we're going to have to change. We need a makeover."

"I don't mind change! Change is good. And I *love* makeovers!"

I laughed. "Someone in B'ville who believes in change? Thank Go—goodness."

"Thank you, Jane." Brandi Lyn waved at someone over my shoulder.

I turned to see JoeJoe pull up in his perfectly maintained monster of a Ford truck.

"This makeover idea sounds great! Now I've got to get home and work on my finances. Honestly, I thought the dresses cost about seven hundred dollars, not seven thousand! My goodness! I've got some thinking to do!"

She hopped up into JoeJoe's truck and greeted him with a big kiss. She was about to shut the door, when suddenly I got an idea. "Hey, Brandi Lyn! Will you come to the Episcopal Church with me on Sunday?"

She gasped in delight. "Oh, Jane, you have a church home? I'm so happy for you! I'd love to!"

I watched the truck kick up dust as it sped off. *Now that's a sweet girl,* I thought.

Chapter Seven

I flopped down, exhausted, at the dinner table and laid there like a gravy-soaked biscuit. "I need some money."

Grandmother raised an eyebrow. "More than your allowance?"

"Whatever it costs to get a tattoo lasered off."

Grandmother raised the other eyebrow. "You have a tattoo?"

"On my shoulder, right exactly where the back of my dress has to come down, and Miss Dinah Mae is having a conniption fit over it."

"I don't recall signing any sort of permission form saying that you could get a tattoo."

"You don't need one when you have a fake ID."

"Remind me to search your room for it tomorrow."

I laughed and dove into the roast beef and mashed potatoes that Charisse had whipped up for us. So much better than boarding school barf-a-roni.

"Other than that, how was your first day?"

Hmm. How was my day? What should I actually tell her? Under normal circumstances, I would go ahead and confess all. Tell her exactly what had happened, that I was in serious Magnolia Maid danger and that Mizz Upton had declared war on me and Brandi Lyn and that I had declared it right back. After all, Grandmother knew every bad thing I had ever done to get kicked out of boarding school. None of this would be news to her. It would seem like just another notch in the old bad-girl bedpost.

But she was so thrilled that I had been selected for the Court, so delighted that I was following in the footsteps of a long list of Fontaine women. No doubt she would be deeply upset if I told her what had happened. She would be on the phone with Mizz Upton, Mr. Walter, the chamber of commerce, the higher echelons of Bienville government, anyone affiliated with the M&M Organization in about two seconds flat demanding to know why I had been treated this way. Did I want to stir up that kind of trouble? Jane B.M.M.—before Magnolia Maids—would have leapt at the opportunity to up the drama quotient. But Jane A.M.M.? I couldn't do it.

"My day was . . . well, I decided to take your advice and act sweet. And I made a new friend. Two, actually. And we learned all this cool stuff about the dresses, and the city, and . . ."

Grandmother cleared her throat and uttered a most suspicious "Hmmph."

I giggled. "Now Grandmama, what you just did there? Not exactly what I would call a ladylike utterance."

She shook her head. "What goes on in your own home doesn't always have to be ladylike. And when one is shocked by the behavior of another, a 'hmmph' can be a most appropriate expression."

"Well, what's so surprising?"

"You truly managed to avoid making waves today?"

"Maybe I've decided to turn over a new boat." Her eyebrow raised even higher. "No, seriously I have, Grandmama!"

Her eyebrow lowered but the suspicion still played around her lips. "What a lovely turn of events this is, then."

I continued eating and trying to act like I was the sweetest girl in the world, but her gaze lingered on me until I couldn't take it anymore. "Okay, okay! It was not that fun! But it's true I tried to be sweet, and I did make some friends, kind of. But Mizz Upton can't stand me, and do you have any idea how much work we have to do?"

Grandmama slapped the table with a giggle. "There's my girl! Oh, you had me scared there for a minute!"

"I have to learn all this history, and we have to plan these lame events, and the dresses! Do you have any idea how much they cost?"

"Don't you worry about the money, darling."

"That's great for me, but Brandi Lyn, she's freaking. And the girls! There are some serious snobs up in that joint! One in particular."

I waited for a reprise of Grandmother's "be sweet"

lecture, but to my surprise, she chuckled. "That's exactly how Cecilia felt."

"*My* mother? Really?" My jaw dropped mid-chew, and a piece of roast beef fell out. Talk about manners unbecoming a Magnolia Maid.

"Oh yes. Well, she didn't word it in quite the unladylike way you did."

"Sorry."

"But she considered some of the girls quite snobby. She would come home with the most horrendous stories of bitchery."

"Wow. I thought Cecilia was all light and perfection."

"We always think that about our parents. It's never true. Cecilia behaved herself most of the time, but she nearly gave me a heart attack or two. And she could be quite critical of the organization."

"Then what in the world did she see in it all?"

Grandmother got a mischievous look in her eye. "After supper, let's go up to the attic, why don't we, and I'll show you."

Mother's Magnolia Maid dress was pink. Close to twenty-five years old, it looked as if it had been worn yesterday. Grandmother had stored it on a mannequin made to size and hidden it away in the cedar closet so that pesky moths and color-stealing sunlight couldn't get to it. Tiny white rosettes trailed around the arms and the bodice, meeting in the V of the sweetheart neckline Miss Dinah Mae had talked up that

95

afternoon. The thing was voluminous—there was enough fabric there to clothe a dozen orphans! Seriously, the skirt trained out *six feet* behind the dress! It must have billowed beautifully as Mother floated through Boysenthorp Gardens on a sunny June day, twirling her parasol and winking at cute boys.

Suddenly, it dawned on me. "Oh my God. She was the queen, wasn't she?" I pointed at the long train and the rosettes. We had learned that afternoon that the queen's dress could be any of the Court's favored pukey pastel colors, but what distinguished her from the other Maids was the addition of the white rosettes, uh, "magnolia-ettes," the excessively long train, all-white accessories, and a tiara worn at indoor appearances.

Grandmother nodded and pulled the dress off the stand. "Try it on."

All I could do was stare and think: that was my mother's? That thing? It was just so weird to think of her in that dress. To think that she had had a body that fit into it. I know that doesn't make any sense. Of course she had a body. Of course she had clothes. Duh. But there was something so . . . mystical about the fact that this had been her dress. And that today I had spent all day getting measured for my own. Somehow it made me feel *connected* to her.

I slipped out of my tank top and jeans and into the bazillion layers that made up the skirt. When I got the last one on, I could barely move. "Grandmama! This thing weighs a ton!"

"It's all that taffeta."

"No wonder those antebellum belles were always fainting and fanning themselves."

Grandmama buttoned me into the bodice. She led me over to an antique mirror in the corner and we studied the reflection. The dress was just a little bit big for me, especially in the chest, but it was weird. I looked so different. I barely even looked like myself. "This is so crazy! It looks like I stepped out of another era!"

Grandmama nodded. "Cecilia always said she felt like she was wearing history. How she loved to put on that dress and go to her appearances! That girl could talk on and on about the South and Bienville's place in Gulf Coast history. You know, she met your father in this dress."

"She did?! How come I never knew that?"

She shrugged, puzzled. "I guess with everything that happened, it's just a story we forgot to tell you."

I leaned into the sound of Grandmother's voice as she recounted how it had happened. Bienville was hosting a shipping convention that year, and hundreds of ships had come in from around the world. The Maids were playing hostess down at the wharves, when the man who is my father arrived from Greece with his father. The Ventouras family was huge in the international shipping industry. They had tankers and barges all over the planet, and they had come to Bienville in search of the next big oceangoing vessel. The minute he met my mother, though, my twenty-one-year-old father lost all interest in ship buying and fell madly in love.

97

"Your mother, she had lots of boys calling around the house all the time, but she loved this Cosmo from the moment they met. He came over to the house every afternoon for a week to court her. I was entirely against it, of course."

"Really? Why?"

"They were so young and he was going home to Greece in a few days and I just didn't want her to get her heart broken. Of course, the fact that he wasn't American, and even worse, not Southern, quite upset your grandfather."

"Aw, that's so sweet, Grandmama. Looking out for your daughter."

Grandmother laughed. "She didn't listen to a word I said. Every night she snuck out the window and met him down at the Dew Drop Inn."

My jaw dropped again. "Okay, now you're saying she was a rebel? Like me?"

"Well, she was in love, honey! They carried on the entire time he was in town. After he left, they became pen pals."

"What's that?"

"Back in the days before e-mail and FaceSpace and all that, people used to write letters by hand and send them in the mail."

"Oh, yeah, those things you put stamps on. I've heard about those."

Grandmother studied me in the dress and sighed. "Most days I think you don't look a bit like her, but now . . ." A tear formed in the corner of her eye. "Just think. If Cecilia hadn't worn this dress, she never would have met your father and they never would have married, and you never would have ended up here with me today. My darling girl."

Shoot, I even wiped away a tear at that.

We both studied me and the dress in the mirror. "Would you like to wear it? As your Magnolia Maid dress?" she finally asked.

I stood there, dumbfounded for a moment, then quickly shimmied the bodice off my shoulder. "No, ma'am. No, thank you. Too many ghosts."

Oh, Sweet Jesus and Junipers! I just realized: the first time I see Luke Churchville, I MIGHT BE WEARING A MAGNOLIA MAID DRESS.

HORRORS!!!!!!

Chapter Eight

Speaking of sweet Jesus, what I did NOT tell Brandi Lyn when I issued the invitation to church on Sunday was that I kinda sorta had an ulterior motive. Guess whose family goes to the Episcopal Church?

You got it.

I was dying to know: did Luke Churchville know I was back in town? Yes, of course, he had to. I'm sure the gossip mill had jettisoned that into his in-box the minute I crossed the Dauphin County line.

The real question was: how did he feel about my return?

Was he thinking about me?

If so, was it in a good way? Perhaps he has been imagining a scene such as this: I am looking supercute in my favorite lucky 7 jeans, and I am in a restaurant, maybe The Revelry downtown, with friends (to be determined), and it's super-crowded, so we have to wait in the bar for a table even though we can't legally drink. I am pushing through the crowd to the bathroom, when I feel eyes on me. I know it's him. I turn slowwwwwwly to see that he is as handsome, as adorable as ever, only taller and with broader shoulders. Luckily, my lipstick is perfect, and I, too, am as adorable as ever. Powerful magnets of destiny draw us together.

"I missed you," he says.

"I missed you back," I reply.

We live happily ever after.

Awwww.

Or was he thinking of me in a bad way? Something along the lines of . . . it's the hottest, most humid day in Bienville history. There is no water left in the bay because it has all been sucked into the air. If you live in Minnesota or California or someplace that has no such thing as humidity and you have no idea what I am talking about, go get in a steam room at the gym and sit there. All day long. And try to go about your daily business.

No one can breathe, and anybody who curled their hair today lost it the minute they stepped out the door, even though it's only six feet from the air-conditioned house to the air-conditioned car.

For some reason, I have chosen this very day to go jogging, and not only that, but I have chosen to go at high noon. My body is drenched in forty-seven layers of sweat. Seriously, I feel it running down between my boobs, down my back, down my legs.

Suddenly, I hear someone call out my name. I turn and see a car—I'm thinking a Jeep Cherokee, black. In the passenger side, someone waving at me. I can't tell at first who it is . . . wait, it's Luke Churchville! Despite the fact that I feel like overwatered shower scum, I smile and wave. Delighted to see him.

His response? He throws a wad of chewed gum at me. It lands on my cheek, slides off. The Cherokee races off, peals of cruel laughter trailing behind it.

There is nothing good about that fantasy reunion. Nothing.

So it was with some trepidation that I eluded Grandmother's attempts to drag me to First Presbyterian so that I could instead cart Brandi Lyn off to First Episcopal, but I just had to do it. I swiped the keys to the Caddie and drove out to Government Boulevard, a.k.a. God and Gun Road because along it lies church next to gun shop next to church next to gun shop as far as the eye can see. At Faith Joy's Live Bait and Bible shop (the sign reads, GIVE A MAN A FISH AND HE'LL EAT FOR A DAY. TEACH A MAN TO FISH AND HE'LL EAT FOR A LIFETIME.), I took a right into Mac's Woods, where Brandi Lyn lived.

I immediately thanked God that Ashley wasn't with me. If she had been, she surely would have figured out a way to make Brandi Lyn's place of residence a cause for double secret probation. Let's just say that the style of Mac's Woods didn't exactly mesh with that of the historical district of Old Bienville. For one, big pickup trucks that slurp way too much gas were parked in driveway after driveway. Other than that, though, the recycling/reusing/repurposing habits around here were a testament to reducing the carbon footprint. Almost every front yard was filled with broken-down pickups, boats, trailers, and truck cabs to be fixed someday, one day. Then there was the yard art: old clawfoot bathtubs and wheelbarrows that served as planters, rotting tractor tires that had been converted into sandboxes for the kids. Ancient La-Z-Boys and prehistoric sofas, rather than expensive Lowe's lawn furniture, adorned the front porches, providing comfy seating for passing the happy hours away.

Brandi Lyn's house was no different. Three pickup trucks stood at attention in the front yard, one of them JoeJoe's monster truck. When I drove closer, I noticed that JoeJoe was messing around under the hood. "Gun it!" he yelled, and a guy in the driver's seat mashed the gas pedal, causing the truck to let out a mighty burp followed by a nasty screech. JoeJoe yelled for his helper to shut it down.

"Hey, JoeJoe," I called as I made my way by them.

"Hey, Jane, how ya doing?" He introduced me to the guy in the front seat and another one under the hood—Sammy David and Eddie Dean Corey, Brandi Lyn's older identical twin brothers. We shook hands, or we would have, except there was so much grease on all of them, I just ended up doing a little wave. "Nice to meet y'all."

"Go on up to the house," said JoeJoe. "Brandi Lyn's waiting on you."

"Up to the house" a man in a wifebeater stained with chewing tobacco pushed the screen door open for me, his eyes never leaving the early morning NASCAR commentary playing on a TV from the last millennium.

"Sammy Dean Corey, get a shirt on! Letting that girl in like that on a Sunday morning!" Brandi Lyn's momma called out from the breakfast room, where she was ironing a dress to wear to her Sunday morning service. "I swear, am I the only one with any class around here? Sammy Dean, you hear me?!" Mr. Corey grunted and tore his eyes off the TV to head out of the room.

"Hey, Jane, hey!" Brandi Lyn ran down from upstairs, her hair in curlers and her body encased in a bathrobe. She gave me a quick hug.

"Brandi Lyn, why aren't you ready? We're going to be late!"

"My curling iron broke! It took me forever to find my hot rollers. They're just about cool, though. Have a seat and I'll be ready in two shakes of a billy goat leg." She skedaddled out of there so fast, she nearly ran into her father, who returned with a plaid shirt that he rebelliously left completely unbuttoned. He parked himself back in his La-Z-Boy, not acknowledging my existence until the NASCAR show went to commercial. "You part of this Magnolia crap Brandi Lyn's all up in arms about?" he asked.

I giggled. "Yes, sir."

Mrs. Corey looked up from her ironing. "Sammy Dean, don't call it crap, honey."

"It's all right, Mrs. Corey. I kind of think it's crap, too."

Mr. Corey hooted with laughter, while Mrs. Corey frowned at him. "Sammy Dean, we agreed, what Baby wants, Baby gets."

"I didn't agree to no seven thousand dollars when I signed that permission slip, though, now did I, Cora? No siree. Seven thousand dollars for a dress. Goddamn Queen of England don't dress that good."

"Daddy!!!!!" Brandi Lyn yelled from her bedroom.

"Sorry, Baby." Mr. Corey threw a quarter into a giant pickle jar overflowing with quarters. "Brandi Lyn don't like me cussing."

Mrs. Corey shook her head. "I done tole you, Sammy Dean, the dress ain't gonna cost seven thousand dollars because Baby's gonna make it herself. It's just a thousand for the fabric."

"Oh, what a great idea," I jumped in, trying to calm them down. "Really? Brandi Lyn's gonna make the dress herself?"

"Well, sure. Baby makes most her clothes."

"Wow. She must be a really good seamstress. Those dresses are so complicated."

"Oh, child, yes. That girl can do anything, right, Sammy Dean?"

"Girl's got more talent than any of those screamers on *American Idol*."

"I'm sure she does," I replied.

Moments later, as I drove us out of the neighborhood,

Brandi Lyn pulled down the sun visor and started teasing her hair with a pick and a rain shower of Aqua Net.

"Okay, you know what?" I asked. "This is going to have to be part of the change."

"I know. I got to get me a new curling iron and fast."

"No, I mean your hair is just a wee bit too . . . big."

"Big!" Brandi halted mid-tease, she was so horrified. "Hair can't be too big!"

"Look, Brandi Lyn, I know people love their big hair down here in the South, but what you're doing? It's the Mount Everest of hair."

She looked so defeated. "Really?"

"I'm afraid really."

Brandi Lyn reluctantly returned the Aqua Net to her purse.

By the time we pulled into the parking lot of First Episcopal, it was already more than half full. Shoot. I had hoped to get there early so that I could stake out the best position for observation. Oh, well. As we joined the people filing through the front door, Brandi Lyn asked me how long my family had been attending First Episcopal.

"We don't. We go to First Presbyterian."

She looked confused. "Then why didn't we go there?"

"Because Ashley and Mallory and Mizz Upton and all of those folks attend here, so I figured that it would look good if we made an appearance."

"Oh, Jane, you're so smart!"

I led Brandi Lyn up the stairs to the balcony, checking

everywhere I went for the likes of Luke. Historically, his family sat downstairs in the second row, right under the nose of the priest. With a name like Churchville, you've got to be a staunch Episcopalian, right? When Grandmother allowed me to attend with Luke, however, his mom would let us sit up in the balcony, the known hideout for all lapsed Episcopalians, squirmy kids, and bored teenagers. We'd perch in the very last row, giggling and drawing pictures all over the fellowship log. I figured there was a fifty-fifty chance that he would be up in the balcony now.

Brandi Lyn and I took seats in the front row of the balcony. We could see everything from there: the altar and podium, the organist playing the prelude, members of the congregation milling around on the floor below. I waved at Mizz Upton and Caroline, who waved back. Mizz Upton tersely nodded her head. The only thing we couldn't see from where we sat were the pews underneath the balcony. But I figured if Luke Churchville was here, I'd most likely be able to spot him easily.

And then what?

Well, I didn't have the least little idea of that. I didn't have a five-year plan for this endeavor, let alone a five-minute plan. I was just curious, okay?

Meanwhile, Brandi Lyn and I performed fashion espionage, examining the sea of heads and coifs down below us for hair, makeup, and clothing tips. Brandi Lyn sighed and shook her head.

"But Jane, they all look so boring, don't you think?"

"Hey, I'm the one with the tattoo and the butt-hugging jeans. To me, everybody looks about as interesting as a five-year-old wearing Garanimals. I'm just saying that if we want to kick it Magnolia style, this is probably what Mizz Upton is expecting."

Brandi Lyn pondered that, which is when I noticed that—gasp!—the Churchvilles had arrived! They were down below, with Mr. Churchville leading his pack, followed by Mrs. Churchville, Lindsey (who was no longer a pesky little nine-year-old, but an achingly awkward pubescent teen), and little Betsy (who had grown into an adorable ten-year-old). I scanned the aisles behind them, but no Luke. Hmm. Where in the world could he be?

Unfortunately, I had no more time to look. The organist launched into the processional, and the priest marched down the center aisle followed by the associate priest, the altar boys, and the choir. Brandi Lyn and I leapt to our feet along with the rest of the congregation. Together we limped through the very mysterious thing called the Episcopal Church service. I had forgotten how confusing they always were to me. The Episcopalians don't print a bulletin the way we do at the Presbyterian Church, so it's hard to know what is happening and when it's happening and when to stand and when to sit. The most confusing thing of all is when to kneel. Presbyterians don't kneel at all, and apparently they don't at Brandi Lyn's church, either, because we were both left sitting in the pew when everyone moved to the kneelers in front of them. We quickly rectified the situation, slipping onto our knees and bowing our heads. To my surprise, Brandi Lyn actually prayed along with the priest, throwing in her own amens after just about every sentence he uttered. I jabbed her in the ribs and shushed her.

"What?" she mouthed.

"Don't say 'amen' unless the minister tells you to, or at the end of the prayer," I whispered back. I glanced around to see if anybody had heard her . . . and almost choked on my own breath.

He was here. Not ten feet away in a row two back from us, on the opposite aisle. He must have slipped in during the opening hymn. I could easily have thrown a prayer book at him. Easily.

And y'all, all I can say is that time, good genes, and the soccer team or swim team or whatever it was had been more than generous to Mr. Luke C. He was more magnificent than even the most magnificent fantasy I had invented in my head. All blond curls, cupid-esque ringlets (where had those come from?), broad shoulders, lean muscled arms encased in a vineyard vines oxford.

And I finally had the answer to the question that had plagued me since the moment I returned: how would I feel when I saw Luke Churchville again?

Like I wanted to run all the way to China. That's how. What had I done? Sneaking into his church on his turf was the *worst idea ever*! I was such an idiot! Had he seen me? Please, God, no. Maybe, if I just sat real, real still, then he wouldn't see me during the rest of the service. Brandi Lyn and I would wait until everyone had left at the end, then we'd sneak out and I'd be safe, completely and totally safe. Yeah, that was a good plan. . . .

A plan that was completely and totally ruined five minutes later when the choir stood to sing a breathtaking rendition of "In Christ There Is No East or West." Brandi Lyn became so overcome by the beauty of it all that she stood up and pulled out a lighter—a lighter! She flicked it on, raised it into the air, and waved it back and forth like people did at U2 concerts in the 90s, like you see in old video footage on YouTube. Kids stopped squirming and teenagers stopped writing notes to each other as every eye in the balcony swiveled in our direction . . . including LUKE CHURCHVILLE'S! The corners of his lips curled up as he watched her sway in time with the music, then his gaze traveled in my direction.

I jerked my head forward fast in hopes that he hadn't recognized me. I clutched at Brandi Lyn's hand, desperately trying to make that lighter disappear. But instead I knocked it out of her hand and sent it plummeting into the congregation below!

Crap! I closed my eyes. Brandi Lyn's widened. Then we heard an angry yelp from below. That was it. I grabbed Brandi Lyn's hand. "We're outta here," I whisper-screamed, and dragged her up the aisle. We bolted past the slew of staring faces, including Luke's, and clambered down the stairs and out the front door.

Brandi Lyn gawked at me in a breathless frenzy. "Jane,

what in the world?! No one's even been saved yet!"

"That's just it, Brandi Lyn. People don't get saved in this church. Episcopalians are really . . . sedate with their services."

"Well, in my church, we like to make a joyful noise unto the Lord."

"Okay, that's totally cool and I would love to see that sometime, but let's get out of here before . . ."

Before, say, an angry voice whispers, "Excuse me. You forgot something."

Oh, shoot. I prepared myself to face some mean, old church lady, furious that we had broken the well-established rules of conduct.

I whirled around, already offering up apologies, "I'm sorry, ma'am, we just . . ." But instead of a rabid matriarch, there stood a willowy prepster of a boy, our age, in a pink jacket and a screaming-pink flamingo tie. He had one eyebrow raised, the lighter dangling from his fingers, and to my surprise, a big welcoming grin on his face. "I see you still know how to create a stir, don't you, be-yotch?"

"Teddy? Teddy Mac Trenton!" I burst out laughing and swept the richest boy in Bienville into my arms and hugged him hard.

Chapter Nine

There is a lot of *old* money in Old Bienville and there's a lot of *big* money in Old Bienville. But no one has bigger or older money than the family of Teddy Mac Trenton. His mother was a Hawkes, Lacey Wilkes Hawkes, to be precise, and she came from a long line of Bienvillites, people she easily described as rumrunners and pirates who raped and pillaged their way into a fortune before civilizing themselves and settling down into the legal business of importing and exporting. Lacey Wilkes, for that was her full given name, was loaded. So loaded that she completely flouted local convention while at the same time serving as Bienville society's unofficial tastemaker. She'd been through a string of husbands, at least five, to my recollection. She always professed absolute and eternal adoration for each one, at least until they started stealing money from her or cheating on her or visiting prostitutes that ended up singing like canaries to the local press. Teddy Mac was the result of marriage number two, to a real estate developer from Memphis who had returned home after the divorce due to irreconcilable differences. Lacey Wilkes always survived her heartache and devastation, primarily due to her extensive indulgence in retail therapy, her everlasting belief in love, and her devotion to young Teddy Mac, who she called her "Teddy Toy" and declared the only man worth trusting. In return, Teddy Mac adored his mother and served as her little houseboy. He fetched her cocktails, lit her cigarettes for her back when she smoked, and performed tap dances for her guests upon request.

Lacey Wilkes was frequent fodder for the Old Bienville gossip mill. Everyone loved talking about the husbands who came from all over the place, about how poor Teddy Mac had to deal with that series of stepfathers, how Lacey Wilkes took off for weeks on end to Dallas or Paris or New York to indulge in the retail therapy that was the only thing that could get her over her latest breakup. I can't tell you how often I overheard the women of Old Bienville state that Lacey Wilkes was "ostentatious as a Texan" or "had the morals of a Yankee." But Lacey Wilkes didn't care what the ladies said, and they certainly kept their mouths shut whenever she donated a wing to the Bienville Infirmary or wrote a check to somebody's pet charity. No, everybody in town knew what side the bread was buttered on: Lacey Wilkes's.

Teddy Mac and I had always gone to different schools, but our mothers were friends, so every once in a while I would end up at Hawkleigh for an afternoon playdate. Yes, the Hawkes's family estate was so grand it had a name. Picture a Southern plantation house, a two-storied Greek Revival palace with wide verandahs upstairs and down, fronted by an alley of majestic oaks. You could almost see Miss Scarlett and her sisters on the front steps. The lawn was beautifully landscaped, and I loved to play hide-and-seek amongst the azaleas. But Teddy Mac always dragged me up to Lacey Wilkes's closet which, unlike Mrs. Churchville's orchid house, was wide open to kids. We played dress-up while our mothers sipped bourbon-spiked lemonade and gossiped on the verandah downstairs.

"Jane, Jane, Jane, kudos on the most dramatic Magnolia Maid Pageant ever!" Thirty minutes later we had repaired to the Dixie Cup Diner out on Grand Boulevard for giant breakfasts of sausage, biscuits, and milk gravy.

"Oh, you were at the Magnolia Maid Pageant?" Brandi Lyn had what can only be described as a mystified expression on her face. She had worn it ever since we ran into him.

Teddy Mac clutched Brandi Lyn's arm. "Wouldn't miss it for the world! Of course, it's usually a done deal which girls are gonna get selected. The same old boring same olds, but this year, I tell you! Mother and I nearly fainted ourselves, we were so surprised! Look, I got the best picture of you catching Brandi Lyn on my iPhone!" He brandished an action photo of Brandi Lyn, legs sprawling, me all mouth wide open as I struggled to keep her from falling.

Brandi Lyn went red as the checkered tablecloth.

"Charming, Teddy Mac. Charming," I said.

"Anyway"—he dug into another sausage biscuit—"I hear Ashley LaFleur is fit to be tied."

"Hell, yeah. She's conniving all sorts of ways to toss us out of there and sneak Katherine and Courtney on."

"They are such sheep. Don't have an original idea in their heads. Just follow her around doing whatever she tells them. Being all judgmental." He turned to Brandi Lyn and fluffed at her big hair. "You, girlfriend, I love this look you have going on. Amy Winehouse, with a dash of Dixie, wouldn't you say?"

"Well, thank you, but . . ." Brandi Lyn looked pained. We exchanged glances.

"Uh-oh. Did I just step in conversational do-do?"

"Teddy Mac, we have a problem." I explained our entire situation about being on Magnolia Maid probation and about how we needed to shape up if we were going to get off it and fit in according to Martha Ellen Upton's specifications.

Teddy Mac howled with laughter. "Oh my lands, I know just what you girls need! Southern belle drag!"

"No, not *drag*." Brandi Lyn raised her eyebrows in horror. "It's not an act. We need to *be* fine ladies of the South."

"Oh, honey, everything's an act. All the world's a stage, don't you know?" His arms swished out so far that he nearly hit Brandi Lyn in the face. She jumped back fast, spilling coffee all over the place. "And I am just the one to help you with this."

Teddy Mac called for the check and skedaddled off to the

little boys' room, giving Brandi Lyn the chance to turn to me with great concern as she wiped up her coffee. "Jane, your friend, is he, um, well . . ."

"What, Brandi Lyn?"

She squeezed her eyes shut tight. "Do you think he's homosexual?"

"Well, I haven't seen him in six years and we haven't exactly been Facebooking, but I would hazard a guess and say the answer's hell yes with sugar on top. Want to ask him?"

"No, no, no! Jane, that would be so rude!" Brandi Lyn sighed. "It's just I've never met a homosexual before."

"Seriously. Never?"

"Lord's truth. Have you?"

"Yes. I mean, definitely in boarding school there were a couple of people who were out of the closet and a few who, well, we had our suspicions."

"Really?! Well, how should I act? I'm just not sure what to do."

"You do what you normally do. Be yourself. Be Brandi Lyn."

And Teddy Mac was back. "Okay, dumpling babies, let's get to work."

I raised an eyebrow at Brandi Lyn. "Are you in, Brandi Lyn?"

She pasted a nervous smile on her face. "I'm ever so excited."

When we were little, Teddy Mac and I played dress-up in his mother's walk-in closet, which at that point was the size of a small bedroom. But the space that Teddy Mac led us into, after a tour of Hawkleigh that left Brandi Lyn wide-eyed in shock (she kept saying, "You live here? This isn't a museum?"), was not a closet. It was big as a house. "Mama had a whole new wing built onto the back of the house about three years ago," Teddy Mac explained. "We just didn't have enough room for what we need."

"Damn, Teddy Mac, Carrie Bradshaw would give up half her Manolos for this thing." I paced the east wall, studying the collection of evening gowns and fur coats.

"My whole house could fit in here!" exclaimed Brandi Lyn.

"Isn't it obscene? We just love it!"

At that moment, a voice trilled up from downstairs. "Teddy? Teddy Toy?"

"Up in the wardrobe, Mother!"

Lacey Wilkes Hawkes swooped in on a cloud of angel-blonde hair and White Shoulders perfume. Seriously, she looked otherworldly. Well-preserved. "Now, Teddy Toy, you disappeared from church and I do not appreciate that. Do you know I looked for you a whole ten minutes! And then I had to leave. You know these shoes were killing me."

"Beauty equals pain, Mother. You knew the new Louboutins weren't broken in yet."

"But they're so pretty. Evil, pretty things." Lacey Wilkes sank into a wing chair to take off the evil things. That's when she noticed me and started screaming like a banshee.

"Mother, what in the world?" Teddy Mac rushed to her side.

"Cecilia?"

"No, Mother, Miss Cecilia died years ago. This is her daughter, Jane."

"Oh, of course. So tragic, Cecilia leaving this earth so young. But she was still beautiful, at least she had that." Lacey Wilkes composed herself as I walked over to put out my hand. "Hi, Mrs. . . ." I trailed off.

She jumped up and hugged me. "Oh, honey. I'm back to Hawkes. What with all the getting married and getting unmarried, I could never remember how to sign a check, what a disaster. So I just went back to my maiden name. Much easier that way. Teddy Toy, fetch Mother some champagne. My nerves, I'm so unsettled since Skip and I hit the rocks."

Teddy made his way over to a closet within the bazillion-square-foot closet, revealing a fully stocked bar, including a mini-fridge filled with every alcoholic beverage known to man (or woman, in this case). He poured his sweet mother a glass of bubbly.

She swigged it down fast. "I swear I thought I had laid eyes upon Cecilia's ghost. Such a tragedy, her declining the way she did. I did love her so. Anyway, Teddy Toy and I were just delighted that you were selected to the Magnolia Court. And who is this?" She beamed at Brandi Lyn, who stammered out her name. "Land sakes! The girl who fainted!"

"Yes, ma'am, I'm afraid so."

"Darlin', don't be afraid. You got everybody talking."

"I know. I looked such the fool."

"Honey, please. The year Cecilia and I were Magnolia Maids, I fainted a good dozen times, I'm sure. But that was the anorexia. I've recovered, as you can tell." She gestured at her by no means fat, but by no means anorexic, figure. "I couldn't take any more stitches in my head. I even broke my nose once! But that turned out fine. Got a brand-new one in Houston and my first husband to boot! Teddy Toy, what was his name?"

"Dennis."

"Oh yes. Gosh, he was adorable." She giggled. "If a bit of a man-whore. Anyway, it's so delightful to see you girls in my closet." Lacey Wilkes's expression suddenly turned to horror.

"What's wrong? Are you feeling faint again?" Brandi Lyn looked terrified.

"No. I am the rudest thing in the world, and that is not okay! Forgetting to offer you a drink. Y'all want champagne? A little mimosa? We have orange juice up here, don't we, Teddy?"

Brandi Lyn gaped at her response and I had to laugh out loud. My mother had always called Lacey Wilkes a tornado of whimsy in heels, and she certainly was that. She was what is called Down South "a character." It was hard to keep up with her tangents and the hands constantly clutching at her throat or at someone else's arm to make a point. I had to take a mimosa just to chill out from watching her in action.

Brandi Lyn declined on account of she doesn't drink, but she would take a Coke, diet of course. Then Teddy Mac got down to the business of explaining what we were doing up there in Lacey Wilkes's wardrobe.

Lacey Wilkes howled at the idea of turning us into proper young ladies. "Although, darlings, I'll tell you, not a soul in Bienville thinks I'm proper. I'm just too rich for them to pick at. But I am not surprised to hear Martha Ellen Upton is gunning for you, Jane. Not one bit."

"I take it you've heard about my boarding school experiences."

"Oh no, not that. It's that she hated your mother. Simply could not stand her."

My eyes widened. "What?! Someone actually hated Cecilia?"

"Why, yes, honey, she beat Martha Ellen out for queen."

I laughed. "Well, that explains a lot."

"Martha Ellen got it in her head that because her daddy was in the chamber that she was a shoo-in for queen. But that girl was just as sour then as she is now, and not one Maid voted for her. Not one. It was Cecilia, and it was U-nanimous, you can be sure about that."

Brandi Lyn and I exchanged glances. "Gosh, Jane, it's good you declared war on her then," she said.

Lacey Wilkes nodded. Suddenly, she was all business. "Now. Let's start in the summer dress department, shall we?"

"Exactly what I was thinking!" Teddy Mac urged us over

to an entire wall demarcated with a sign reading, SUMMER. "Now, Brandi Lyn, your outfit looks fit for a young Shania Twain."

"Really?" Brandi Lyn beamed. "I made it myself."

"Did not!"

"I did, I did!"

"Girl, oh my God, Mother, do you see this?"

"You should be designing for those country music stars. Shania, and who's the other one I like, TT?"

"Carrie Underwood."

"Oh yes, she's a cutie. She'd look adorable in something like that. Tell me you're going into fashion design."

Brandi Lyn looked down demurely. "Y'all are so sweet. Really. I'm planning to be a newscaster, though, but wouldn't it be fun to design on the side?"

"I couldn't agree more," replied Teddy Mac. "What I'm thinking, though, is that your look is a little too star, not enough lady."

"Not enough lady?"

"It's the difference between a Marilyn and a Jackie. Marilyn's all boob-y and sex, sex, sex, but Jackie's all sedate and proper. We just need to Jackie you down a bit. Bienville is not *The Hills*, you know. Those Hollywood vixens wouldn't know sedate if it hit them in the face."

Disappointment flittered across Brandi Lyn's face. "Jane kind of told me the same thing, but I like the way I dress."

"Well, of course you do, because you look like a star! But those Magnolia Maids are about being ladies. Just think of it as your new act. What do you think of this?" He held up a colorful shift.

"Oh!" she exclaimed in delight. "Why, it's magical. This herringbone stitch is so intricate!"

"Doesn't it just bring out the color of the fabric? I was nervous about it, but it worked out so much better than I could have imagined."

"Than you could have imagined?" I asked. "Teddy Mac Trenton, did you make this dress?"

Lacey Wilkes glanced up from pouring herself another glass of champagne. "Honey, he did more than half the things in here. That's why we needed the closet expansion, to keep up with his creations. Isn't my Teddy just brilliant?"

Teddy waved a hand at her. "Mother exaggerates. I do the designs, but we have a girl who cuts the patterns and sews the outfits."

Lacey Wilkes plastered Teddy Mac's head with kisses. "Aren't I the luckiest mother in the world, to have my own dress designer for a son?"

Even I was impressed. "Damn, Teddy Mac, you've come a long way from playing harem princess."

"Honey, that was the start of it all!"

She and Teddy Mac chattered on about whipstitches and hemlines and bodice choices and all sorts of things that I didn't really know—or care to know—what they were. Brandi Lyn whipped off her country star gear, down to her undies (to my surprise, but she seemed to have forgotten that Teddy Mac was male), and let him go to work.

With all this Teddy Mac–Brandi Lyn BFFing going on, I had tons of time to obsess over my ludicrous Luke Churchville sighting. Had he actually seen me? Did he have any idea I was there on a scouting mission? If he had seen me, what was it like after all these years? Was I more cute or less cute than he would have imagined? Did he even think of me at all? Now what was I going to do the next time I saw him? Maybe it wasn't too late to go back to boarding school.

Brandi Lyn ended up with ten dresses, a few skirts, some simple sleeveless tops, and a half dozen pairs of shoes. She and Lacey Wilkes wore the same size shoe, although all the clothing would have to be altered a bit. Luckily, Lacey Wilkes also shared Brandi Lyn's big chest, but she had a bigger middle, too, despite years of Jenny Craig, liposuction, and biannual spa treatments at Canyon Ranch up in Massachusetts. Teddy Mac took Brandi Lyn's measurements and promised to send everything out to Laverne, the seamstress, for alterations and to make an appointment with his mother's hairstylist to update her 'do. Brandi Lyn protested, claiming their overwhelming charity was just too much, but Lacey Wilkes batted her words away like a pesky housefly.

"No, no, no. I will not tolerate this talk. It is my pleasure to support your cause and, by the way, I can always have Teddy Toy whip me up something new when I need it. So you just hush and go look beautiful and be sure to drive that Martha Ellen Upton crazy with your propriety." The last words came out as a slur. Lacey Wilkes had downed most of the bottle of champagne and she was now wobbling more than ever. "Teddy Toy, Mother's feeling a little tired now, so I'm going to take me a nappy-poo. But, honey, you are going to have a time getting this one out of the black." She wagged a finger at me and teetered out of the closet and down the hall to her bedroom.

I braced myself. "I know. I have a feeling this is going to be painful."

"You just need a little color and sparkle, dumpling," Teddy Mac said.

"Oh hell no." I backed away in horror. "No color. No sparkle. No cute."

"Oh, Jane," Brandi Lyn chortled. "Let Teddy do his magic. I think you'd look gorgeous in deep pink."

"Nooooooo! I don't care if it's deep as the ocean. No pink of any kind! Help!!!!!" But she and Teddy Mac attacked me with a couple of Lacey Wilkes's sundresses and before I knew it I was in front of the three-way mirror gazing at myself wearing a red-and-white polka-dot sundress with a snazzy kick pleat in the back.

Brandi Lyn exclaimed, "Jane! You're from another era!"

"Well?" Teddy Mac waited breathlessly.

"It's . . . cool. Kind of retro. Sassy."

"That's your look, then. Forties vamp. Sassy and original, but ladylike all the same. Let me see what else I can pull out for you." He paused. "But, Jane. This is going to cost you."

"Oh yeah, fine. I'll write you a check."

"That's not what I mean. There's something else I'd like." A sly grin crossed his face.

"Ohhhhh-kay . . . ," I drew out.

"Once your Magnolia Maid dress is done, will you let me try it on?" Okay, that is so not what I was expecting. My jaw hit the ground and Brandi Lyn gasped. "Pretty please? Sugar on top? Just one time?" Brandi Lyn and I burst into laughter.

Teddy Mac huffed away. "Forget it."

"No, Teddy Mac, it's fine. Really. I was just taken by surprise. You seemed so serious, I was worried there for a second. Honestly, you can try on my dress whenever you want. But on one condition . . ."

Teddy Mac arched an eyebrow at me. "What?"

"You agree to be my dandy."

Both Teddy Mac and Brandi Lyn screeched with delight.

My guess is that was a yes.

Chapter Ten

"Just what do you think you're doing?" Ashley hissed at me under her breath a few days later.

"Learning the flight formation," I replied. "What are you doing?" The flight formation, for those of you who are not ducks, geese, or other migratory birds, is the official walking pattern of the Bienville Magnolia Maids. The queen plays the role of the lead bird, and she is flanked by two Maids walking exactly four feet to the side of her and four feet behind her (four feet being the minimum amount of space to accommodate the span of the hoopskirted antebellum dresses). Behind those two Maids trail two more. According to the *Magnolia Court Handbook*, when performed correctly, the Maids will appear as a graceful, sinuous unit, like ducks in flight, hence the term "flight formation."

But when you've had a vote for queen that morning that ended in a deadlock—half the votes for Brandi Lyn and the other half for Ashley—it's a little harder to appear as any sort of unit. Mizz Upton was at a loss as to how to effectively teach the fine art of gliding like little Maids all in a row. In fact, she barely even struggled to hide how pissed she was. Instead, she furrowed her brow and dropped little snark bombs like, "Well, I guess we'll just have to make do." "This won't be perfect, but try, Maids, please." "We have no idea where you'll each be positioned when you do this in the real world, but use your imagination."

So there we were, out on her gigantic back lawn, each taking turns in the "queen" position, all of us except Caroline, who, as alternate, would not be required to do the flight formation except in the case of a Magnol-emergency. She got to sit in the corner to "watch and learn," but I saw her sneaking peaks into a paperback romance, lucky dog. The rest of us lined up on marks Mizz Upton had placed in the ground, then stood quietly by as she used a yardstick to make sure we were in the exact four-by-four position. She counted, "One-two-three," and we took off again, right foot first. . . .

But Mallory started a beat late and Zara ran right into her. Brandi Lyn set out on her left foot and ended up "throwing off the look." Ashley veered instead of walking a straight line and bumped me in the butt. Most ironically, I was in the queen position at that moment, ha-ha-ha. Some variation of this mess had been happening all morning. Finally Mizz Upton called a potty break.

"I'm not talking about the flight formation and you know it!" Ashley continued. "You're all *decent* today."

"Thanks, Ash, I just love my new makeover," I simpered.

"This isn't a makeover! You're being nice. You haven't said one sarcastic thing all day. You're wearing a, a *sundress*."

"You know, it just suddenly came to me . . . I can wear black and still look feminine!" I fluffed out the skirt of my dress. "The daisies really pop on the black background, don't you think?"

"No, well, yes, but . . ." Poor thing, she was flustered. "You're even doing the flight formation right, for God's sake!"

"Please don't take the Lord's name in vain," Brandi Lyn singsonged from her perch on a swing hanging from the giant oak that shaded the Upton's entire backyard. Ashley rolled her eyes in exasperation.

I took Ashley's hands in mind. "I've come to see the error of my ways, Ashley. It was like a flash of lightning, I had a vision, and suddenly this deep appreciation for all things Magnolia Maid-y washed over me like the gentle waves of Bienville Bay."

"You expect me to believe that?" Ashley gestured toward Brandi Lyn. "And what's up with her? She looks all decent, too. Oh my God! Y'all are on probation, aren't you?!"

Brandi Lyn sighed. "Please, Ashley, I know it's hard, but please don't use the Lord's name in vain. Please. God does not want to hear that."

Ashley ignored her, keeping her eyes focused on me. "That's why Mizz Upton made you stay after last week! She put you two on probation and you're trying to get off it by behaving for a change!" She looked downright gleeful, the little detective.

I held my tongue—yes, I know, not the usual thing that I do—but I couldn't quite figure out what she was on about. If I admitted it, what would she do with the information? What could she possibly do? If I denied it, would it end up biting me in the back at some future, unforeseen point? From the gleam of certainty dancing in her beady little eyes, I just knew she was up to something. I just didn't know what.

Which is why I dragged Brandi Lyn downtown to the chamber of commerce to meet with Walter Murray Hill the minute Mizz Upton called lunch break.

"Well, girls, what a delight!" He ushered us to sit down in two wing chairs flanking his desk. "Jane, I heard about y'all's idea for the beach fund-raiser. Excellent idea, just excellent. Exactly the kind of thing we're looking for!"

"Thank you, sir. It was a team effort. Well, mostly."

"Go, team!" He took a seat in his power chair. "Tell me. It's not very often that I get a personal visit from one of our beautiful Maids, let alone two. What can I do for you?"

"Well, Mr. Hill . . . ," I began.

"Please, call me Mr. Walter."

"Mr. Walter. I don't know if you're aware of this, but Brandi Lyn and I have been put on probation."

The grin slipped right off Mr. Walter's face. He leaned back in his chair. "No, Jane, I don't believe I was made aware of this."

"I'm sure it must have slipped Mizz Upton's mind."

"I'm sure it did. And I appreciate you keeping me posted on this situation. Now what are you on probation for, exactly?"

"Sir, unfortunately, I have in the past, exhibited a bad attitude that gets my mouth in trouble every once in a while."

"And a tattoo," Brandi Lyn chimed in. "Mizz Upton wasn't happy about that, either."

"A *tattoo*?" Walter Murray Hill's lips formed the word with an odd mixture of titillation and disgust.

"Yes, sir," I confirmed. "The tattoo was probably the straw that broke the camel's back."

"Yes, yes, I can see that it could be."

"But don't worry. Miss Dinah Mae Marshall is figuring out how to cover it up. My shoulder ruffles are going to be a bit wider than average."

"All right, all right." Mr. Walter turned to Brandi Lyn. "What about you, young lady? What are you on probation for?"

She shrugged. "I'm not real sure, Mr. Walter, sir."

"What do you mean you're not real sure?"

"Seriously, Brandi Lyn didn't do anything wrong," I said. "Except sport quote bold fashion unquote."

"What's wrong with bold fashion?"

Brandi Lyn beamed. "Oh, Mr. Walter, I feel the same way! But I think Mrs. Upton is upset because I refused to quit. Well, Jane refused for me. Thank you, Jane."

"You're welcome, Brandi Lyn."

Poor Mr. Walter, confusion ran rampant over his face. "You were asked to quit?"

"Yes, sir. Mizz Upton was real concerned about my being able to afford the dress and all the outfits."

"You look perfectly fine to me."

"Thank you! Miss Lacey Wilkes Hawkes helped me out with some clothes. Wasn't that sweet of her?" Brandi Lyn modeled her cute little blouse for Mr. Walter as he digested the very timely dropping of the Hawkes name into conversation.

"Lacey Wilkes, huh?" He nodded, impressed. "She's a good girl. Always been a big supporter of the Maids, okay."

"Mr. Walter," I said. "We just wanted to let you know that we are taking our probation very seriously and that we are doing the best job we possibly can."

Brandi Lyn nodded. "That's right. Jane and I have made a pact to be the best Magnolia Maids we can possibly be."

"We just have one tiny little question. Mizz Upton told us we were on probation, but she didn't tell us how to get off. And we can't find that information anywhere in the handbook. Do you know the answer?"

"You mean to tell me you don't know?" Mr. Walter's face turned a rather unattractive shade of middle-aged-man red as his hand reached for the phone.

By the end of day, Mizz Upton sat both me and Brandi Lyn down and stated that there had been "a wee bit of an oversight." Was it my imagination or was there a wee hint of a glare in my direction? "It has been called to my attention that it must have slipped my mind to have you sign this." She presented us with official notices of probation. They basically said that if we obtained any more demerits we would be subject to immediate expulsion from the Magnolia Maids. Under Reason for Probation, she had handwritten in perfect cursive "argumentative," "unladylike attitude," and "unbecoming personal presentation" for me and "inappropriate attire" for Brandi Lyn. She informed us that the probation period was officially one month.

"From today?" I asked.

"From the day that I put you on probation, of course."

"Great." I scratched out the date on the document and dated it a week ago, to the very day that she had put us on probation. This time, there wasn't a hint. Mizz Upton *definitely* glared at me. I shot her a sugary sweet smile right back. "We want to be accurate, don't we?"

I have to say, in the weeks that followed, the trips to Mizz Upton's for further Magnolia Maid instruction were actually quite entertaining. This being B'ville, of course, all the other girls found out we were on probation, so Ashley made it her daily goal to get me and Brandi Lyn to slip up in hopes that we would be booted off the Court. "Brandi Lyn," she simpered one day. "Your hair is soooo different."

Brandi Lyn flushed with pleasure. "I have a new stylist. Don't you love it?"

"Weh-elllll . . ."

"You don't like it, do you?"

"No, it's not that. It's just that I miss your big hair! It suited you so well!"

"Jane says this fits better with the Magnolia Maid philosophy."

"Oh, honey, don't go changing because of the Magnolia Maid philosophy! You have to be yourself. And this bob, well, it just isn't the Brandi Lyn we've all come to know and love."

"That's not what Mizz Upton told me."

"She's just old-fashioned, right, Mallory?"

Mallory nodded vigorously. "And I luvvvved your short skirts! They showed off your legs so nicely!"

"You should wear them more!"

Brandi Lyn furrowed her brow. "That's so sweet of y'all, really, but Teddy Mac Trenton and I have come up with this whole new look and I just love it! It's classy, don't you think?"

Curses. Foiled again.

With me, Ashley presented an array of needling remarks. "You know, Jane, I read the other day in the *Bienville Gazette* that girls with behavioral problems are just screaming for proper love and attention."

"Jane, did you hear? Your chances are so high of getting Hepatitis C if you've had a tattoo. I read it in *Vogue*. I hope you didn't get yours at some unclean place. . . ."

"So, Jane, what are you going to do about getting into college, what with your awful school record? You must be terrified!"

When none of those got a rise out of me, Ashley turned to being faux polite/true mean to the others. She asked Zara if she could trace her family tree all the way back to Africa. She told Caroline that she couldn't "help but notice that you're stress eating again. As your friend, I just have to tell you, you're fat and you really need to do something about it or you're never going to get a boyfriend."

This stuff really pissed me off, I mean really, but I bit my tongue as I had promised to and fought Ashley's fire with a new brand of my own—the *Magnolia Court Handbook*, of all things! Who would have guessed that reading it from cover to cover three times would turn out to be the best weapon ever? It provided me with such grenades as "Oh, dear Ashley, a Maid never raises uncomfortable subjects in public, *Magnolia Court Handbook*, chapter six, page twelve." "A Maid never calls attention to another's physical condition, including pregnancy, unless it is mentioned by the other first or if assistance is necessary, chapter seven, page twenty-four." This really made old Trashley see red. Who would have believed how much fun you could have with rules? So refreshing!

Time to interrupt our programming for some smokin'-hot news items:

LUKE CHURCHVILLE TOTALLY DRIVE-BY STALKED ME!

I am so serious. It happened a few days after the Episcopal Church incident. There I was on the roof outside my bedroom window lighting up a ciggie. (I had determined upon moving back to Grandmother's house that this was the least likely place to be caught smoking. After all, she wasn't going to haul her sixty-five-year-old self out there looking for me.) Anyway, it was around ten o'clock at night, when I suddenly spied a car turning onto my street a few blocks away. I didn't give it much thought UNTIL IT SLOWED DOWN as it approached my house. I'm talking, to a crawl. What in the world? It was some kind of older diesel sedan, oddly familiar, with headlights bulging like the eyes of a frog. I could see the outline of a face turned to look at my house. Whoever it was had angled their head in such a way that he/she/it could glance upstairs in the direction of my bedroom window. Seconds later, the car moved through the beams of a streetlight and that's when I saw—fanfare, please—the face of Luke Churchville! Turned up. *Looking at me.* Our eyes locked, and one Mississippi, two Mississippi, three . . .

His face jerked forward. The car, his dad's old convertible Mercedes, I think, sped up, and the moment was over. But the damage was done.

A grin spread across my face. Ear to frickin' ear. He was looking for me. Luke Churchville was drive-by-stalker looking for me. Nice.

News flash number two: MR. WALTER APPROVED THE BEACH CLEANUP FUND-RAISER! Mizz Upton was clearly not thrilled to relay that news to us, but we girls were psyched. With the exception of you know who! So now, in addition to rehearsals and dress fittings, we were out on a regular basis soliciting donations for the event, which we had decided to do the first Saturday in June.

News flash number three: MALLORY AND BRANDI LYN COMPLETELY BONDED! The other day Brandi Lyn ran late into rehearsal wearing her waitress uniform from Karl's Kajun Krawfish Shack, apologizing up a storm. "Oh, Mizz Upton, I am so sorry! We got slammed down at the Shack! All these English guys are in town from the oil company that caused the spill."

Mallory went berserk. "Oh my gosh, you work at the Krawfish Shack? I love the Krawfish Shack!"

"Ugh. Why?" Ashley grimaced. "It stinks in there."

"That's just because you don't like fish, Ashley. But the Kajun cheese fries are the best on the gulf, I swear."

"I know!" enthused Brandi Lyn. "Do you ever get them with bacon?"

"I love them with bacon!" That, right there, sparked the Brandi Lyn/Mallory love connection, but it was the arrival of Miss Dinah Mae with the fabric for our dresses that set it aflame. We had been asked to rank the hideous pastel colors in order of preference for our dresses. Each girl had to be in a different color and that color was finally determined by Mizz Upton and a team of experts. But we got to weigh in. As we all shared our top picks, Brandi Lyn and Mallory discovered that they had chosen the same three colors and ranked them in the same exact order, wasn't that amazing!? When Mizz Upton announced that Brandi Lyn got lavender and Mallory got spring green—their first and second choices—they worked themselves into a frenzy of compliments about how beautiful each would look.

As for the rest of us, Caroline was left with pukey peach, poor thing, not a good color on anyone, but she was the alternate, so she had to take what she could get. Zara was happy to learn that her dress would be yellow because it looked good with her complexion. Ashley and I were the disappointed ones: Mizz Upton put me in pink and Ashley in blue. Huh? Pink was nowhere near my list, and blue was Ashley's third choice! I offered to trade with her, but Mizz Upton wouldn't hear of it. Apparently, she and the committee strongly felt that pink went with my Greek Southern skin and that blue would compliment Ashley's eyes.

Sweet Thorns in a Thornbush! Me in pink? Ugh.

News flash number four: I was STILL OFFICIALLY LUKE CHURCHVILLE-OBSESSED. Great Gorgeousness on a Gin Blossom, I cannot tell a lie. He had grown himself up into a hottie pa-tottie, and sighting him at church had been enough to stir any straight girl's senses, but the fact that he had done a drive-by look-see of my house meant he now had taken up permanent residence in my head. Everywhere I went, I pictured the two of us together. On my morning jog down Bird River Parkway, I would see us cruising in his dad's old convertible, singing retro eighties tunes at the top of our lungs. When I passed the Picklefish Pizza and Sandwich Company, I pictured us munching muffulettas on the roof and making fun of the Friday night revelers as they stumbled out of the bars and clubs that line Le Moyne

Street. Sprinting through Bienville Square, I imagined us dashing, hand in hand, through the fountain, trying to make it through before another stream of water spouted up.

Ewww. Could I get any more Harlequin romance all up inside my head?

Alas, I couldn't help it. Everywhere was Luke Churchville; Luke Churchville was everywhere.

The thing is, we were best friends at one time. Shouldn't we see each other again? More than once, I pulled out my phone and scrolled down to his number. Yes, I had his home number in my phone. Stalkery, I know, but hey, what if he decided to call me one day? I'd need to know it was him before I picked up the phone, just to have my game face on, right? But then I'd scold myself, "Jump into reality, Jane! You haven't talked to him in five years! You can't just call out of the blue." There were just too many unknowns. I had no idea what he was like now. He could be a total jerk for all I knew.

I suspected Ashley and Mallory would know his 411.

Not that I would ever, EVER deign to ask them.

But then news flash number five: I *did*. Sort of. "Hey there, do you have a sec?" No, that wasn't me on the verge of asking Ashley or Mallory about Luke Churchville. It was *Mallory* asking if *she* could talk to *me*. Hmmmmmm. Breaking ranks with Ashley to converse *avec moi*? Intriguing. That merits a news flash, so I'll make it number six.

"Sure." We were midway through our Magnolia training torture, a mere three weeks away from our grand debut at Boysenthorp Gardens, and we were gathered in the multipurpose room of the chamber of commerce for the first fitting of our dresses. Miss Dinah Mae had called and said she was going to be late with them, so we were just twiddling our thumbs until she arrived. I followed Mallory down to the ladies' room. "What's going on?" I asked.

Mallory's shoulders heaved in a sigh. "Well, it's just that . . . Jane, you know we do have our problems and all."

"And all."

"But you are a really honest person, always saying what you're thinking, right?"

"Pretty much so."

"Telling the truth all the time?"

"Enough to get me in trouble on a fairly regular basis. What is it?"

Mallory sighed again. "I can't really say."

"Nice chat, Mal. Let's do it again sometime." I moved to go, until she latched on to my arm.

"No, Jane, wait, please!" Worry seeped from her words, so I waited. "What if you knew something that would upset someone really badly, really hurt them, and other people knew it, too, but you swore to the person doing the something that you wouldn't tell anyone, and you didn't want to hurt that someone person by telling them but you think maybe they should know?"

Did anyone catch that? "Try again, Mallory, with a little less confusion, a little more information."

"Oh, I can't! I was sworn to secrecy. I can't break that promise!"

"Okay, empty the contents of your makeup bag." Blank look, but Mallory did it, and out came at least five hundred dollars in beauty products. "Okay, pick a product."

She picked a Smashbox lipstick in a berry color called Sublime. I held it up. "This is you. Pick another product." She handed me a compact of M.A.C. Studio Fix. "Okay, give this one a role in our drama."

"The someone who would be upset really badly," Mallory said.

"And wasn't there a person you swore you wouldn't tell?"

"She can be the miniature bottle of Chanel Number Five. Actually, ooh. Can I be the Chanel Number Five?"

"Whatever. Okay, so that means that the lipstick is who?"

"The person I told I wouldn't tell."

"Great. Now, act it out with the makeup."

"Okay. So Smashbox lipstick, that's the person who swore me to secrecy."

"I get it."

"Well, Smashbox is cheating with Studio Fix's boyfriend." She picked up a bottle of OPI nail polish. "This is Studio Fix's boyfriend."

"Oh no!"

"Yes! It's terrible!"

I picked up the Chanel N°5. "And you, Chanel, you are the only one who knows?"

Mallory bit her lip. "No. That's the problem, Jane. It's getting around, and Studio Fix is going to find out, I just know it, and I am terrified—simply could not be more terrified!—as to what's going to happen when she does."

I paused. "What does Ashley think about all this?" Mallory was silent. "Ohhhhhh. She's one of the parties, isn't she?"

"I am totally and completely sworn to secrecy."

"Okay. Here's what I would do if I were Chanel Number Five. I would think about who was more important to me, Smashbox or Studio Fix. And then I would decide based on that whether or not to tell Studio Fix."

"But then Smashbox will hate me!"

"It's a tough world, Mallory. It's either lipstick or foundation."

Looking sad, Mallory stuffed her makeup back in her bag and moved to leave. "You're right. Thanks, Jane."

I thought, *Well, here's my chance. It's now or never.* "Wait, Mallory, I have a question for you. Do you know this guy, his name is ummmm, Luke Churchville?"

"Luscious Luke! He's friends with my brother. He's just the cutest thing since Bradley Cooper!" Her eyes widened with excitement. "Oh my God, do you have a crush on him?"

I acted as cool as I possibly could. "No, no, nothing like that. We just used to be . . . neighbors. And his family doesn't seem to live on my street anymore."

"Oh no, they moved out by the golf club. So, what? Do you want to try to see him?"

And here we were back to the same question that kept

eating at me: did I or did I not want to see him? Suddenly, I felt incredibly nervous.

Mallory could tell. "Oh, you know what, I think his family's on a trip to Hilton Head right now. I don't think he's even here."

"Oh. Okay."

"But if you want I can totally tell my brother. We could meet them over at Picklefish or something one night."

No! I screamed in my head. *No way, no how, not in this lifetime!*

What I actually said was, "No, that's okay. I'll run into him sooner or later." The last thing in the world I wanted was some orchestrated reunion. Where we'd be in the spotlight and everyone would be all excited and watching, all, "Look at the cuties, they haven't seen each other in ages, do you think they'll fall in love again?"

Last thing in the world.

And now, for news flash number seven: MY FATHER IS COMING TO TOWN!!! I came home from brunch with Teddy Mac one day to find Grandmother out on the back porch, staring into her glass of sweet tea and swirling the ice around like a teacup on that Disney World ride. Swirl, swirl, swizzle, swirl. "Jane, darling, I need to talk to you."

"Ooh. Sounds ominous."

"Your father called this afternoon."

"There we go. *Is* ominous." I acted all calm and cool as I sank into the seat beside her. "Does he want me to call him back?" These little phone calls from my father happened about once a month. He'd call in from London or Athens or wherever it was he happened to be, and demand to know how the hell I was. Such lovely conversations they were. In between caring, concerned questions like, "You're not embarrassing me, are you, Jane?" "What's this about straight Cs, Jane?" "You're a Ventouras. Aren't you smarter than that?" He'd bark out orders to his secretary or put me on hold to pick up another call. Eventually, he'd come back on the line and tell me to "Straighten up, make the family proud, be good." The only nice thing about these calls was getting to hear my father's voice. He has such a beautiful voice, as deep and sun-kissed as the Aegean Sea that surrounded his beloved Greek Isles. It was layered with the British accent he acquired from growing up in London after my grandfather moved his shipping conglomerate there, and if he weren't always berating me for something or other, I could have listened to that voice all the livelong day.

"So what did old Cosmo have to say for himself?" I took a swig of sweet tea.

"He's coming to the Magnolia Court Debut."

I spit my mouthful of tea all over the verandah. Mizz Upton surely would have kicked me off the Court if she'd witnessed this violation of all things ladylike. "Here? At Boysenthorp Gardens? Are you kidding me?"

"He wants to see how you're getting along now that you're back at home."

"Well, I'm fine, thank you. Didn't you tell him that?"

"Of course I did. Truth be told, I suspect he wants to check up on me as well."

"Well, you're doing great!" I groaned out loud. "What's his problem? I haven't seen him in ages and now he decides to pop over for a visit? What for? I haven't gotten kicked out of anything lately!"

"No. In fact, you've been better than I ever could have expected."

"Please, Grandmama, call and tell him not to come. I don't want to see him right now. Please. Please, please."

"Well, I'm not going to do that." She looked down into her tea glass again. "I invited him."

My jaw hit the ground. "*You* invited *him*? Why would you do that?"

She sighed. "As you know, I do not entirely approve of the choices your father has made in raising you since your mother passed way."

"No kidding." Grandmother shot me an expectant look. "No kidding, *ma'am*."

"It is one of the great sorrows of my life that your mother did not live long enough to raise you into a young woman." Her voice caught in her throat at the mention of Cecilia. "I realize your father may not be the most present and accessible of parents, but he is your father, the only father you have, and you need to appreciate him more."

All I could do was stare at her. "Unbelievable. Seriously. I see the man, maybe, I don't know, twice a year, he has zero involvement in my life on a daily basis, and you're telling me that *I* am supposed to appreciate *him*?"

"You live in the lap of luxury, Jane. He pays for your schooling, your clothing, your allowance," she replied. "Your life could be so much worse. You should be thankful for what you have instead of resentful of what you don't."

How could she say this? There's no way she could mean it. Not with our history. But she had that whole stern-look/furrowed-brow thing going on which meant she wasn't just serious. She was dead serious.

"Really, Grandmama? Is that what you're selling? That I should be happy because he throws a few bones in my direction every once in a while? Uh-uh. Sorry, I'm not buying." I stood up from the table. "And excuse my profanity, but if he's going to be the world's crappiest father, then no one should expect me to be anything but the world's crappiest daughter." I grabbed my purse. "I'm going for a drive."

As I stomped off, Grandmother yelled after me. "Family is family, Jane. You may not respect that right now, but you will one day!"

"Why? Why, why, why, why, why?" I punctuated each "why" with a punch of the steering wheel. The speedometer was hovering around eighty and the steel girders of the Bienville Bay Bridge were flying by. There's something about hitting and stomping and pushing things that feels oh so satisfying when what you'd really like to do is put somebody's eyes out.

"Get out of the way, blue hairs!" I punched the horn and slammed on the brakes to avoid a couple of sweet little old ladies out for their afternoon drive. "If you can't keep up, get out of the way! Or I'm calling the nursing home!" Seriously, the centenarian in front of me was clutching the steering wheel like a lifeline. Not exactly the model of a responsible driver.

Neither is a pissed-off seventeen-year-old flooring it up to ninety.

I used to call the man who is my father "Daddy." It's a term of such affection, one that implies cozying up in front of a fireplace to read a storybook, tugging on a shirt hem to beg for a lollipop, or the keys to the minivan so you can run to the mall and spend his money, depending on your age. "Dad" has a more serious ring to it, no longer little girly, a bit more mature, very much "I'm too grown up to call my daddy 'Daddy.'" "Papa," well, that was tailor-made for an old man, and "Father" has a formal ring to it, like you live in a castle with servants and minions. I've never known what to call my father because, well, he was never around, not after my mother died. Except for fleeting visits and monthly phone calls, I never knew where he was or what he was doing.

So "Daddy," as I called him back then, was never around, but then Grandmother strong-armed him into coming to Bienville to see me one Thanksgiving. Sound familiar? It's just like what she was doing with this Magnolia Maid Debut. That time, she had this big plan that Daddy and I would go off to Disney World for a little family fun. How excited was my twelve-year-old heart? RIDICULOUSLY. I had been telling everyone at school about it for days and days and weeks and weeks. Made everyone pea green with envy. Made myself pea green with excitement.

Thanksgiving came and Daddy did, too, with gifts of a sari from India that no self-respecting Bienville girl would ever wear—too weird!—and an overstuffed doll from England that would have been just right for a five-year-old. So what if they weren't a pair of Lucky jeans, who cared? Daddy was home!

But he wasn't. Not really. He was always on a call to Greece or e-mailing Liberia or conversing with his secretary in London. Grandmother had to steal his cell phone to get him to come to the Thanksgiving feast she and Charisse had prepared. Daddy politely complied, telling jokes, solicitously paying attention to Aunt Edna's Alzheimer's-induced tales from the war. Which war? I'm not real sure. But as soon as the dinner was over, he got up from the table and went back to calling Liberia because, hey, they don't celebrate Thanksgiving there. Might as well have been another workday.

Oh, well, I told myself. We're going to Disney World tomorrow. How many cell phone calls could he make from Space Mountain?

The answer: you wouldn't know unless you actually made it to Space Mountain.

We never did.

By supper time, not that anyone wanted to eat, considering we had crammed ourselves full of enough stuffing and cranberries and turkey to digest until Tuesday, Daddy had come up to my room and broken the news to me that, unfortunately, he wasn't going to be able to make it to Disney World. Some disaster had occurred with the Liberians and ship-docking rights, and he was going to have to fly in with a team of executives and fix it, stat! He was leaving on the next flight out of New Orleans.

Now what does a girl do under these circumstances?

Be sweet. That's right.

And I was. I told him that I understood, that business was very important, him being the head of an international shipping company and all, and I agreed with his placation that we would do it "some other time," which we both knew was a figment of our imaginations, but hey, might as well play along with it.

I expressed not one whit, one cent, one ounce, one teaspoon, of the disappointment that was pulling my stomach out through my eyeballs and shoving it back up my nose. I politely excused myself, then tore down to Grandmother's "summerhouse," flopped on a chaise longue, and sobbed my heart out.

I have no idea how long I was there before Luke came looking for me after he got back from dinner at his grandparents' house.

"Janie, what's wrong?" He panicked when he saw me comatose on the chaise. "Are you sick?"

"We're not going to Disney World."

"What, are you grounded or something?"

"Dad has to go to Liberia."

"Aw, that sucks. Really? I'm sorry."

"Yeah. It sucks." I stared off into space.

Luke tried to bring me back. "Yeah, it really sucks because you were going to go on 'Pirates of the Caribbean' and tell me how it's changed since the movie. Now how are we going to find out? Am I going to have to go myself?" He was being supersweet and joking and trying to cheer me up, but I wasn't having it.

He tried again. "Come on, Jane. Want a hug?" Now, this wasn't that crazy of a question. We had hugged on occasion, and right at that moment, I did want a hug. Nodding, I sat up and put my arms around Luke and he enveloped me in his. We hugged. But very quickly it became apparent that this wasn't our normal sort of hug, or merely a hug of comfort. Something was different, something was changing. Before either of us even had a chance to think about what was happening, our faces turned, our lips met, and the hug transformed into a kiss. A gentle, nudging first kiss. And it was sweet. So sweet.

Until Daddy walked in.

"Jane?" We barely heard him calling from the yard. "Where are you, honey, I have to leave in a . . . ?" He crossed the threshold just in time to see me and Luke scrambling to opposite sides of the summerhouse.

"Hi, Mr. . . ."

"Daddy! We were just . . ."

But Cosmo held up his hand for silence. Then he hit

the roof. Blasted through it. Entered the *stratosphere* with his rage. He blew up, called the Churchvilles, screamed at Grandmother that she was completely unfit to raise me, that she had turned me into a wild, undisciplined hussy, that I was too young to even know about boys! The Churchvilles were surprised to hear what happened, but not upset, and Luke being a boy and all, they certainly didn't flip out. Mr. Churchville just gave him a lecture about responsibility and called it a day. Me, I was forbidden to speak to Luke ever again and banished to the first of my boarding schools.

Gosh, Daddy Papa Cosmo Father Dearest, thirteen schools and counting later, I guess I showed you just how undisciplined and wild a child can be.

I slowed down when the bridge reached landfall again and assessed the situation. Where in the world was I? I pulled out my iPhone and used the GPS feature to determine that I was in Fairhope. Did I know anybody in Fairhope? No. Maybe I should keep driving, continue east on I-10 to I-95, then drive all the way down to the tip of Florida. Set up shop in some cool art deco pad in Miami Beach and entertain Europeans with my wit and intellect.

Or I could call someone and complain. But who? Who did I know? Who exactly were my friends? Did I have any? I careened through my contact list:

Brandi Lyn—she'd be genuinely sympathetic and concerned, but then she'd get all "The Sun Will Come Out Tomorrow" on me and I'd have to strangle her.

Caroline—if I could rip her nose out of whatever romance novel she had it plastered in, she would be quietly kind. But the cloud of sadness and desperation hovering over her was too much to bear on a day like this. And the thought of running into Mizz Upton made me want to puke.

Ashley—the mere fact that she was in my iPhone was a laugh! Mizz Upton had insisted that we all have each other's contact info so that we could be in constant Magnolia communication once the season got underway. Ashley helping me out with anything was as likely as a snowstorm in July, unless of course, she could figure out some way to use it against me.

Mallory—not quite as annoying as Ashley, but close enough. Besides, I had come to understand that she was as likely to play the optimism card as Brandi Lyn. "Jane, aren't you excited that your father wants to be a part of your life? I don't understand why you're so upset!"

Teddy Mac Trenton—the oh-so-fabulous Teddy Mac. He would get it. But with Teddy Mac came Lacey Wilkes, and I just couldn't take an afternoon of the whimsical tornado.

Zara—Aha. Zara! Gracious, sweet-as-pie, perfect mixture of humor and gravitas. And as out of her element and lonely as I was here in Bienville. I hit SEND, it rang, she picked up. "Hello, Zara? What's shakin', Magnolia sister?"

Chapter Eleven

I will say this: Jay and Felicia Alexander, the king and queen of satellite communications, do not skimp. There was no corner cut, no luxury not appointed to the nouveau French chateau they constructed on an entire acre of prime property in the Country Club District. It was evident even in the fancy cars lining the driveway that semicircled through their front yard: a Ferrari, a Mercedes SUV, Zara's little Porsche roadster, a few Cadillacs, a Lexus or three.

A housekeeper answered the door and ushered me through the foyer into a living room so expansive and freshly decorated it could have been the lobby of a five-star hotel. "Miss Zara, you've got company," the housekeeper announced into an intercom.

"Who's that?" a voice boomed out from deep inside the grand hall, where I spotted a dining table packed with dressed-down business execs. That explained the huge number of fancy cars out front. They barely glanced up from their work as a tall, imposing, linebacker of a man got up from the head of the table and approached me.

"You must be the famous Jay Alexander," I said.

"I don't know about the famous part, but I am Jay Alexander." He shook my hand but regarded me suspiciously. "And who are you?"

"Jane Fontaine Ventouras, pleased to meet you, sir."

"And you know Zara how?" Okay. A little imposing, this guy.

"Uh, through the Magnolia Maids. We're on the Court together."

"Humph." What did that mean? "Hmmph"? Luckily, Zara arrived at that moment. "You got a friend here, Z," he said.

"I see, Daddy. Hey, Jane."

"Hey, Zara."

"Is Daddy giving you a hard time?"

"No, I checked all my weapons at the door. We're good now."

Zara's mom, Felicia, glided over. "We're so happy to meet you, Jane. Z's told us a lot about you." I could see where Zara got her height, grace, and beauty from. Mrs. Alexander looked picture perfect, totally dressed to the nines even on a Saturday at home. She turned to her husband. "Cosmo Ventouras is Jane's father, Jay."

"Cosmo Ventouras? No kidding!" Oh, now a smile breaks through the sullen suspicion on Mr. Alexander's face? Mentioning *Cosmo* gets me out of suspicion jail? Apparently. "We put the satellites on a good half dozen of his ships. We just set a meeting with him in a couple of weeks, Felicia, did you know that?"

"Great! Terrific. You think he'd be interested in the new XZ-17 technology, Jay?"

As Jay answered Felicia's question, I raged inside my head. So that was the reason old Cosmo was willing to travel a bazillion miles to Bienville from wherever he was. Not to play cheerleader to my fabulous debut at the Magnolia Maids, but because he had a high-powered meeting with the biggest entrepreneur in the state. Of course. "Great, terrific" was right.

Meanwhile, Mrs. Alexander was beaming at me. "We're glad you're here, Jane. We're so happy to see Zara making friends. It's not the easiest thing in the world to move in your junior year."

Mr. Alexander threw his arm around Zara and pulled her to his side. "But what's the family motto, Z?"

"'Flexibility is the key to success.'" Zara stated this by rote, as if she'd been forced to memorize it in kindergarten alongside the ABCs.

"That's right," Mr. Alexander said. "Alexander Communications is built on that motto." His cell phone rang, and he answered with a bark of his name. "Alexander! Give it to me, Vito, how are those numbers?"

"That's our cue," Mrs. Alexander said as she and her husband headed back to the dining table packed with employees. "Zara, give Jane the grand tour, why don't you?"

The grand tour was in a word, grand. Lacey Wilkes Hawkes may have had the biggest closet in town, but I'm pretty sure that the Alexanders were the only people who had a *gift-wrapping room*. The place was filled with all sorts of rooms that usually only exist on English estates: a billiards room, a two-story library, a music room with an organ, a piano, a harp. Not to mention a most serious home theater.

I poured myself into the most comfortable lounge chair ever made by man. "Okay, I am never going to the movies at the mall again. That screen is bigger than the state of Texas!"

"Yeah, Daddy likes to watch his sports big. It makes him feel like he's on the field again."

"He was a football player?"

"Yeah, in college and then he went pro for a while, then he and Momma went to business school." She motioned to a side door. "Let's go out that way and I'll show you the lagoon."

Lagoon?

The lagoon, for those of you who don't live on say, some tropical island covered with them, was a dark-bottomed swimming pool meandering like a stream through an extravaganza of tropical plants and palm trees. A cliff rose up on one side, with a waterfall cascading down into the pool itself, sending gentle waves in the direction of the faux shore. It was fake as the day is long, but Lordy, it was beautiful.

"Sweet Tropic of Thunder, Zara, did we just teleport to Hawaii or what?"

"I know. Isn't it crazy? The landscaping was inspired by a picture I took in Kauai a few years ago."

"It's gorgeous." I noticed a set of stairs carved into the faux cliff that led up the side of the waterfall. "What's up there?"

"A hot tub."

"A hot tub? Okay, that's it. I'm moving in."

As we headed toward the four-car garage, Zara sighed. "I don't know. I think it's a bit much. Part of their master plan to . . ." She stopped mid-sentence and frowned.

"Master plan to . . . ?" I asked.

"Nothing."

"Oh, come on. Tell! Tell all to your sweet, little Magnolia sister!"

Laughing, Zara confessed that deep down inside she felt that building this giant house was phase one of an elaborate "move back to Bienville in style and prove to everybody that the local kids did good" plan.

"What were the other phases?" I asked.

"Two, donate an entire wing to the Bienville Infirmary and slap all the grandparents' names up on it."

"That was nice of them."

"Three, construct a humongous office complex to house the shiny, new headquarters of Alexander Communications."

"Which created like, hundreds of new jobs in our crappy economy in the process."

"Four, get me on the Magnolia Maids. Make a big splash and integrate it for the first time."

"I see what you mean. Everybody knows who y'all are now."

"I love Momma and Daddy, I really do, but sometimes, it

just all seems so fake. Like they have to show off all the time. 'Look at us. Look how good we've done.'" She led me up the garage stairs to what appeared to be a large junk room and we made ourselves comfortable on a couple of beanbags.

"Oh, please. You want to talk fakery? Let me tell you." I gave her the extended remix version of how I had gotten into a fight with Grandmother about Cosmo coming to town for our debut at Boysenthorp Gardens and how I was going to be expected to play the perfect daughter to his perfect father. "So I'm thinking, this is all bull, and he knows it and Grandmother knows it and I know it. And that he's just coming to check up on me to make sure I don't besmirch the Ventouras name in public. But then I get over here and your dad says that about having a meeting with my dad, and now it's so obvious, Cosmo's not coming for me. It's business. Ugh! It's just too much fake for a girl to take!" Now truly annoyed, I leapt up from my beanbag and paced the junk room.

Zara mulled this new information over for a moment. "Makes me wonder."

"Wonder what?"

"What's worse, a father who's never around or a father who is up in your business 24/7."

"Is that what your dad's like?" I asked.

Zara blanched. "Did he jump up from the table and run right over the minute you walked in the door?" I nodded. "Stare you down like you were a criminal?"

"Oh yeah. I felt like I had just been busted for shop-lifting."

"That's my daddy. Always has to know who is messing with his baby. It's embarrassing. Momma and Daddy are dying for me to make friends, but I don't even want to bring people over."

"Eww. That *is* obnoxious. Hey, what's this?" My pacing came to a screeching halt as I nearly ran smack into a black-and-white photo hanging in the air. Actually, there were dozens of photos hanging at about eye level, all clipped to a clothesline leading to what would have been a closet door, except a red neon sign above it read, IN SESSION. "Zara, is that a darkroom? Like for *film*?"

She nodded. "Yeah, it's my consolation prize. Momma and Daddy said if I'd move down here quietly, they'd build me a darkroom and studio." She gestured toward the other end of the space formerly known to me as the junk room. I noticed for the first time that the walls curved where they met the floor instead of joining at a ninety-degree angle, just like in the backdrops you see models posing in front of during photo shoots.

But what really intrigued me was a set of candid photos of three girls. "These photos are amazing!" I said, and Zara explained that they were of her best friends, Caitlin, Sabina, and Beatrice. She had taken them her last big day in DC, one of those paint-the-town-red kind of days, where they had perused modern art at the Smithsonian, devoured Ethiopian food in Adams Morgan, danced at an all-ages show in Dupont Circle. "It was the best way to spend the last day," Zara said wistfully.

I moved along the clothesline to a very different series of photos, this one of a very good-looking guy, older than us—I don't know, like twenty or so? The first picture was a candid of him studying a contact sheet through a viewfinder. Unaware of the camera, he was completely dedicated to the task at hand. He was unselfconscious, focused. The next photograph, however—*hello!* Clearly it been taken a moment later. The guy must have realized his picture was being taken, so he glanced up directly into the camera. But he didn't seem irritated by the distraction. Oh no, not at all. In fact, he looked so delighted that every inch of his face was smiling, from the curve of his lips to the crinkles around his eyes. I swear, even his eyebrows looked happy. "Who is this hottie?" I asked.

Zara froze. "A friend."

"A friend. What kind of friennnnnd?" I drew the word out playfully. "You took that picture, didn't you? The way he's looking into the camera, it's like fifty degrees warmer than 'friendly'!" Zara rose from her beanbag chair, suddenly becoming awfully interested in one of the paint-the-town-red pics. She was so not answering the question. "Oh, come on, Zara, you're killing me! This guy obviously adores you. Who is he?"

She shook her head. "I'd rather not talk about DC. If you don't mind."

I was on the verge of pressing for more dirt, but there was so much sadness in her eyes, I decided to go easy. "All right. Fine. Let's talk about something else then."

"Let's go back to your dad."

"My dad? Not exactly where I thought the conversation would head, but okay." I plopped back down on my beanbag. "Talk."

"Well, I'm just wondering if you're looking at this thing with your dad and your grandmother all wrong."

I raised an eyebrow. "How so?"

"It sounds like your grandmother really wants you to have a relationship him. Like she's really going out of her way to make that happen."

"Yeah, that's Grandmother. Family is really important to her." *So much so that she talks to her dead husband and daughter and encourages me to do the same.*

"So when's the last time you saw Cosmo?"

"Right after I got kicked out of the Banning School. He flew over and read me the riot act and got me situated at Foxcroft. That was last summer."

"A year ago? And you were all in rebel Jane mode then?"

"Definitely."

"But look at you now. You're all cleaned up, toeing the line. You're like a different woman."

Hmmm. This was true. Being back in Bienville was turning out to be the equivalent of getting a lobotomy. "So what are you thinking?"

"I just think it's an opportunity for you to show that you're doing great. That you're not this rebellious kid he's used to. That you're a lovely young woman of . . ." Zara giggled. "Magnolia caliber."

I snorted. "That sounds like a bullet I should be putting in my head right about now!"

"You and me both!" We laughed. "Seriously, Jane, think about it. Letting your dad see you now could really be good for you."

I stuck my tongue out at her and rolled my eyes, like the mature young woman I clearly had turned into. But on the way home, Zara's words ran rampant through my head. Maybe she was right. Maybe I could develop an adult relationship with Cosmo. Whoa! News flash in my head! I had never considered the possibility that our relationship could evolve. What was it that Jay Alexander said? That flexibility was the key to success? Hmm. If I were flexible, and didn't fight Cosmo's return, if instead I prepared for it . . . suddenly this fantasy of how cool life could be invaded my thoughts. I would be going to college next year (if anyone would have me), and college has breaks, and everyone wants to go to smokin'-hot places on breaks. . . . Cosmo was always gallivanting around to smokin'-hot islands, beaches, international ports on business. So maybe if I showed him I was responsible and mature, I could spend my college years gallivanting around with him. Getting to know him, dining at beautiful restaurants, sailing around Mediterranean islands on his sleek boats, gambling at fabulous casinos.

Wait a second! This was sounding a lot like one of Brandi Lyn's five-year plans. And, dear me, it was sweeter than a headache-inducing artificial sweetener. Not to mention awfully ambitious given the dark period of sadness and separation that we'd lived in since Cecilia's very first fall. And in the back of my mind wiggled a nagging thought: was I setting myself up for Thanksgiving at Disney World, part deux?

And yet . . .

Grandmother was waiting for me when I got home, elegantly poised at the dining table, projecting a visage of contained anger. I plopped down and waited for the lecture, and she delivered. Oh yes, Grandmother delivered. If I was going to reside in her house I was going to treat her and her home with respect. Observe a curfew. Refrain from using profanity. Help out with chores when asked to. I was not to walk out ever again while she was in the middle of conversation with me. I was not to go anywhere with my cell phone turned off except church and Magnolia Maid events. (It's true that she had tried to call me several times that afternoon, but I had set the phone on silent.) When she finished, I said, "Yes, ma'am, I'm sorry. I shouldn't have run out on you like that. I won't do it again."

My words washed over her, and she relaxed back into the dining table wing chair. "Thank you. You know, I worry about you, Jane."

"I know, and I appreciate it. I know you just want me and Cosmo to get together. To be a family." I leaned down to kiss her cheek. "It'll be good to see him. It will. Who knows? It might even be fun."

Chapter Twelve

"I can't. I'm sorry, Jane, but I really do have to vote for Ashley," Caroline said as she plunged a stake into the sparkling sands of Bienville State Beach. It was the first Saturday of June, the day of the big Magnolia Maid Beach Cleanup, and we were measuring sections of shorefront so that we could keep track of how much we cleaned, then collect our donations accordingly. Zara and Brandi Lyn were working at the other end of the beach.

"Give me one good reason why," I replied. Zara and I had decided that since there was no way in hell Mallory would ever break ranks with Ashley to tilt the queen vote over to Brandi Lyn, the only way to burst the deadlock was to get to Caroline.

As she searched for a reason, I handed her one end of the tape measure and paced with the other end along the white gulf sand. It was so glistening and gorgeous even at seven o'clock in the morning. Hard to believe that within a few days it would probably be besmirched by oil residue. When I reached twenty feet, Caroline joined me and plunged another stake in the sand.

"I know Ashley is a bit . . ."

"Malicious? Toxic? Spiteful?"

"Strong-willed."

"Nice euphemism, Caroline, for a girl who wreaks a hell of a lot of evil."

"She's not evil, Jane."

"Let's be real. Ashley only has the interests of Ashley in mind. She doesn't care about any of us or what we think. No way is she about being part of a team. But Brandi Lyn, that girl is one hundred percent genuine, and you know it."

"But Mother would curl up and die if she made queen."

"I know! Wouldn't that just rock?"

Caroline blanched. "Jane, please. You don't have to live with her. I'm already in so much trouble. Mother's mad that I only made alternate and that . . ." She clammed up as her face turned red and tears welled up in her eyes.

"About what?" I reached out and touched her arm. "Caroline, what's wrong? Are you okay?" She nodded vigorously, but the raindrops pouring from her eyes said otherwise. Her chest heaved with quiet sobs until a big one escaped her lungs. "Do you want to talk about it?"

She nodded. I coaxed her to a seat on the sand, and out poured what Mizz Upton was really furious about—she had put Caroline on Jenny Craig a few months ago and so far Caroline had failed to lose an ounce. In fact, she had managed to *gain* six pounds. "What is wrong with me?" bemoaned Caroline. "I eat the food they give me, and I try to exercise, I really do, but I can't help it! It's like there's a monster inside of me and it takes over. If I see cookies I have to eat a dozen. If there's Ben and Jerry's in the house, I have to eat the whole pint. I can't stop it. Mother is right. I'm a big, fat slob and that's all I'm ever going to beeeeeeeeee!" Caroline sobbed.

"Caroline, please. Don't talk about yourself that way. You're not a slob. You always look perfectly neat and presentable."

"But I *am* fat and you know it!"

Sweet Bars of Hershey! Here I was, trapped in a lose-lose situation, no matter what I said. I gave it my best. "I'm sure people might say you could stand to lose a few a pounds, but so could lots of folks."

"No one in my family. Not my mother. And have you seen my sister? She's a beanpole!"

"She's twelve!"

"And skinny and everybody loves her for it."

"Well, that's a stupid reason to love somebody." Seriously, do a few more or less pounds make someone more or less lovable? Here in the South, it seems like almost everybody gets fat sooner or later. What's the point in judging others for it?

"Jane, I'm so scared. What if something happens to one of the other Maids and I have to make an appearance? I'll look like a big peach whale. People will laugh at me!"

"No they won't." Except they probably would, darn it. "Caroline, if you really feel this way, don't you think having Ashley as queen would be the worst choice possible? There's not a bone of sensitivity in her body."

"Don't you think I know that? Don't you think I heard her call me Caroline Plumpton the night of the pageant?"

"Actually, I was kind of hoping you hadn't."

"Well, I did. I know that everybody calls me that. And I know that Ashley doesn't like me and also thinks I am a fat slob, and I can't stand her, either, but I just can't vote against her right now. I have to walk into my mother's house every day, and I can't have one more reason for her to look at me like I'm shower scum. I can't do it, Jane. I'm sorry."

I groaned. "Okay. I get it. We'll figure something else out." Like what? Hiring an assassin to off old Ashley?

We continued our measuring, and by the time we arrived at beach cleanup headquarters—a tent Mr. Walter had set up over a handful of picnic tables—Ashley and Mallory were lollygagging around on a bench in a big display of displeasure.

"Nice showing up on time, Ashley," I said as I tapped the nonexistent watch on my wrist. "Punctuality is such a good trait for a Magnolia Maid to develop. I believe that's listed in chapter five."

"Sorry, this isn't exactly my neck of the woods, Jane." Oops, there it was. Dig number one of the day. We chose this particular beach because it's situated at the point where the bay flows into the Gulf of Mexico, so it would most likely be the first place where oil would hit our community. As luck would have it, Bienville State Beach was pretty far out in the county, meaning in a poor section. It was far from the places where Old Bienvillites maintained their summer cottages. Ashley's little remark meant that this place was beneath her, in her esteemed opinion. And so were the people who used this beach. After all, only people who didn't have their own beachfront property had to use state beaches.

Ashley surveyed the shoreline. "And you really think we can clean this whole beach in six hours? It's pretty big."

"I do, if every member of the organization gets off her Magnolia booty and does her fair share of the work." I arched an eyebrow in her lollygagging direction.

Oddly enough, it didn't spark a snappy comeback. In fact, Ashley's face lit up like the sky over Bienville Bay on the Fourth of July. "Our dandies are here! Our dandies are here!" she squealed. She and Mallory sped over to a Land Cruiser that was careening into the beach parking lot as if a bunch of firecrackers had just been lit under it. Out poured some of Old Bienville's finest young scions: Ashley's boyfriend, James Hardison III; Mallory's pick of the week, Andrew Lancer; and this guy named Jules Dupree, who I vaguely recalled was Caroline's cousin. Talk about blasts from the past. God, I think I danced with all three of them at cotillion back when we were all a foot shorter and a ton gawkier. If I remembered correctly, James was a quiet sort while Andrew was the alpha male. A loud, obnoxious kid always looking for some sort of trouble. Not unlike me, ha-ha-ha. Jules, I don't know. Seemed like just another rich prepster with a lot of money and no real need to do anything to earn it.

We were all in the middle of hellos and introductions when I heard a second vehicle pull up beside the SUV. Oh no. Suddenly, every cell in my body switched to vibrate. I recognized the sound of that diesel engine! It was a Mercedes sedan, circa 1970-something. I remembered the sound of that door slamming. I'd heard it a million times coming from 511 Magnolia Street when I first moved to Grandmother's. *He* was here. I knew it. I sensed it moments before his Nike Zooms and his broad shoulders came around the back of the SUV. Before his golden locks popped into view. Before his now deepened man's voice called out, "Hey, everybody!"

Luke Churchville.

All I could think was, *Thank God I'm not wearing a Magnolia Maid dress.*

We used to play this game, Luke and I, when we were kids, in his attic at night where one of us would be It, and the other person would go stand and hide somewhere in the dark space. Except you wouldn't hide, you'd just go to a part of the room and stand really, really still while It stumbled through the dark trying to locate Not-it from the sound of Not-its breath. We got the idea from watching Jodie Foster in *Silence of the Lambs* during that super-creepy scene where she's trapped in the basement of the evil serial killer and he's stalking her while wearing the night-vision goggles, reaching out to touch her hair and she doesn't even know it. Ewwww. We did the same thing, only we didn't have any night-vision goggles. We just had breath and sound and feel. Still. It was good and creepy.

But now that Luke and I were actually breathing the same air—now that he wasn't safely sheltered by the roof of his car as it drove by my house, or ensconced harmlessly three church pews away, I wondered if I remained motionless— really, really still—maybe he wouldn't notice me and I wouldn't have to deal. I could just sneak over to my car and hurry home to safety.

But then Mallory bounded over and shrieked, "Jaaaaane! Oh my God! Look who's heeeeee-re!"

Great! Blow my cover, Mal, why don't you?! Here I was trying to make myself invisible, and she dashes over to me, giddily playing matchmaker and RUINING MY LIFE! She dragged me the remaining six feet over to Luke. "Luke! You remember Jane! Y'all were neighbors! Luke's going to be Zara's dandy, isn't that great!? Oh! Let me introduce you! Luke, Zara, Zara, Luke."

Luke and Zara politely shook hands.

"Nice to meet you," said Luke.

"It's nice of you to come out," responded Zara.

Mallory turned back to me. "Since Zara doesn't know anyone in town, I suggested we recruit him, aren't you thrilled?" Mallory beamed with pride at the result of her little scheme. "But Luke and Jane, y'all haven't seen each other in ages! You've got catching up to do! Talk! Talk!" she ordered. Then she ran off, dragging Zara with her, leaving Luke and me completely and utterly alone.

Now, as we all know, I usually have something to say about anything and everything, under any circumstances. But in this case, I was at a loss. A complete and total loss.

Luke wasn't. He twisted the cap off a bottle of water and downed a swig. "Oh yeah. Heard you were in town."

Hmmm. This was so not turning out to be my fantasy first encounter. "Yep! Here I am."

"Cool," he said. Not cool. *Ice cold*. That's how he was playing it.

I cloaked myself in nonchalance. "I heard y'all are living out by the golf club these days."

"For about four years now." Luke gulped down the rest of his water and looked beyond me. "Hey, Lancer! What are you doing with that shovel, man? This isn't a sand castle–building contest!" And he was out of there.

Alrighty then.

Luckily, a sudden flurry of activity masked Luke's tremendous diss and gave me a chance to try to regather my wits. Officers Meeks and Detroit from the Alabama Bay Watch showed up in a sleek, white truck, ready to dispense the rules of the game. Then JoeJoe's monster truck got a lot of attention when it rolled into the lot. Brandi Lyn rushed over to him and immediately and enthusiastically introduced him to the whole crowd. They were polite, don't get me wrong, but after a few exchanges of "Hey, so you work at EZ Lube" and "I sure do," the conversation shriveled into a painful silence and the Old Bienvillites went back to their exclusive conversations about so-and-so's upcoming kegger.

Teddy Mac made his grand entrance, fashionably late in a totally beat-up old Saab and wearing a formerly bright green polo shirt and khakis that had seen better days, oh, about five years ago. What I love about the truly rich is that they don't give a toot about showing their money. They don't need to. Teddy worked the crowd with handshakes and hellos, then slinked up to me and glared. "When I agreed to be your dandy, Jane, this was not exactly what I signed up for. Tell me there's some glamour in my future, please? Pretty please?"

"Don't worry, darling, I'm sure there's a ball or two in your future."

"I'm *certain* there's a ball or two in my future!" he whispered in my ear, making me laugh out loud. Thank God for Teddy Mac. He was like my own personal Advil, taking the pain out of the giant headache this day was turning out to be.

Mr. Walter called us together, and Officer Meeks, the delegate from the Alabama Bay Watch, began his speech. "Okay, folks, let's gather round! We're gonna get started here! As y'all know, oil has not hit our part of the coastal region yet, but it can and probably will within the next few days. So, in anticipation of that future cleanup, we're starting with a pre-cleanup."

Ashley batted her eyelashes at James. "I still think it would be a lot easier if we just hired a maid."

James shrugged. "I thought all y'all were the maids. The Magnolia Maids."

"Ah-ha-ha."

"It's a lot easier to remove tar balls and tar patties later if the shore is cleared of debris first," Officer Meeks continued.

Andrew Lancer snickered. "He said 'tar balls.'"

OMG, what dandy academy did these yahoos graduate from? These guys were sooooo seventh grade. At least Teddy Mac whispered his ridiculous remarks in my ear.

Mallory giggled and play-slapped her boy-toy on the arm. "Lancer!"

"He said 'patties,' too," Andrew replied, which made Mallory giggle even more. So it was definitely going to be that kind of day.

Officer Meeks continued over the ruckus. "What I want y'all to do is to take these bags and collect anything that is not natural to the beach environment. Cups, plates, beer cans, bottles, toys, beach gear. You'll be surprised what washes up onshore."

Ashley raised her hand. "Excuse me, this sounds a little dirty. And unsafe."

"Yes, it does. Thank you for making that point," he responded. "Definitely this is dirty work, I can't help that. But we want everyone to take safety precautions. I want gloves and sunhats on everyone." He opened up a cardboard box full of wide-brimmed hats, the kind with the sunflap on the back—quel fashion choice!—and industrial work gloves. "Also, people. Believe it or not, one of the biggest safety risks today will be our hot Alabama sun. It will get you faster than a mosquito in August. Put on sunscreen. We'll take breaks every thirty minutes, and I want everyone drinking a lot of water."

As we all clamored for gloves and hats, Officer Detroit continued. "Now, folks, this is very important. If you see anything that happens to look like oil, DO NOT touch it. If you find anything that has a sheen to it, or anything that looks like this . . ." He held up a photo of a ball of black, sticky-looking stuff. "It's a hazardous substance. If you are even the least bit suspicious, call me or Officer Meeks here on over and we'll take care of it. And if you find any wildlife, birds or turtles covered in oil, same thing."

Mr. Walter turned to me. "Jane, how are y'all going to do this?"

I stepped forward. "So, as everyone knows, we have gotten donations for every twenty feet of beach that we clean up. If you look out in the sand, some of us got here early—thank you, Caroline, Zara, and Brandi Lyn—and put up posts that mark every twenty-foot segment. So I'm thinking every Maid should take a segment with her dandy and get cleaning. Then move on to the next available one when you are done."

Teddy Mac raised his hand. "Where should we start?"

"Uhhh . . . on the gulf side? Since that will likely be hit first? Is that okay with you, Officer Meeks?"

"Makes sense. You can work your way into the bay."

But Andrew Lancer had another idea. "Or we could have more fun with it." He spread his arms wide and gestured at the far ends of the beach. "Why not have half the group start on one end and the other half start on the other, and we race to the middle?"

"Ooh, that sounds fun!" Mallory chirped.

Officer Meeks frowned. "I don't know about racing. Could increase the chance of heatstroke and injury."

"I concur," chimed in Mr. Walter. "We don't want any injuries, okay."

Luke kicked at the sand, avoiding looking in my direction. "It sure would make the time go faster."

Everyone looked so bummed. And he was right. Why not try to have some fun while doing this truth-be-told odious task? "I agree," I said. "What if we set some ground rules? No running. Everyone has to take scheduled breaks?" I beseeched Mr. Walter with a glance.

Mr. Walter looked at Officer Meeks. "This certainly is an enthusiastic crowd. What do you think, Dale?"

Officer Meeks gave in. "All right. No running, no sprinting, no jumping. Mandatory ten-minute breaks every half hour. Deal?"

"Deal!" we all screamed.

I turned to the crowd. "We need team captains!"

Andrew Lancer raised his hand. "Me versus Luke."

"I'm on Lancer's team!" shouted Ashley.

"Me too," screamed Mallory.

"No, no, no." I put one hand on my hip. "Nice try, Lancer, but last I checked, you aren't a Magnolia Maid. Girls? It's got to be two of us."

Lancer stepped back. "Just trying to help."

Ashley raised her hand high. "Me!"

"And you, Jane," said Brandi Lyn, "since you organized the whole thing."

"Okay, I'll accept that challenge."

Ashley scanned the crowd. "I get Mallory."

"Brandi Lyn!" I motioned for Brandi Lyn and JoeJoe to join me and Teddy Mac.

"Caroline." Oh, well that was good. Not being picked last had to be good for Caroline's self-esteem. But that meant that Zara was on my side. Which I would normally be over the moon about, but it also meant that Luke was on my side, which meant . . . uh-oh.

While Lancer, Ashley, James, and crew were high-fiving and congratulating themselves on how awesome their team was, my team had just landed in Awkward-ville. We were all just staring at each other like, gee what do we do now? What with Zara knowing no one, JoeJoe not being part of the crowd, me and Luke avoiding each other like the plague . . . what a perfect day it was going to be.

Lancer held up his hand to get everyone's attention as he outlined the stakes of the race. "First team to the middle marker gets . . . What do they get?"

"Pizza bought by the other team at Picklefish," Luke interjected.

"You're on!"

Then we all took off running despite Officer Meeks's warning.

When my team arrived at the end of the beach along the gulf, we all slowed down and surveyed the scene. It was nasty. Trash everywhere. "This must have been brought up by the storm the other night?" guessed Brandi Lyn.

"Might as well get started," I said. "Come on, everybody. To your stations."

Each pair took a segment of beach and we were off. Once we got down to business, I had to admit that I wasn't really into it. Picking up trash is mindless but really not that much fun. Plus, I was so weirded out by Luke being there (not to mention his lackluster hello) that I couldn't even focus. Darn it, couldn't Mallory have given me a little heads-up? This whole thing was so wrong. Luke was making polite chitchat with Zara, but I could tell he was studiously avoiding me. You would have thought I killed his favorite dog. Where was that sweet boy I used to know on Magnolia Street?

A few days after Cecilia died, Cosmo sat me down at the house on Bird River and broke my heart. "Jane. My darling. You know I need to travel a lot on business."

"Yes, Daddy."

"I can't leave you here by yourself. So your grandmother and I have talked and you are going to go live with her now."

"At the house on Magnolia Street?"

"At the house on Magnolia Street."

I just sat there a moment. He was leaving? Without me? "But Daddy, I want to go with you."

"I want you with me, too, *agapemenee mu*, but I'm on business all the time. I live in hotels and airplanes. Those are terrible places for a little girl."

"Why can't you do your business here? Can't people come meet you here?"

"Honey, we're so far away. Bienville is at the end of the world as far as these people are concerned. And our company is growing, Jane. It's very exciting. I need to be on the move."

I threw my arms around him and hugged him tight. "I won't be a bother. You can have your meetings and I'll sit in the corner and do my homework!"

"And where will you go to school? There's no school on the airplane."

"We'll find a tutor. Please, Daddy." I sniffled.

He sighed. "We'll have visits. You'll come visit me in Greece, see your grandparents. Or in London. We'll get you a passport and you can fly all by yourself like a grown-up young lady. That would be very exciting, right?"

I nodded, but really the answer was a big fat no. Owning a passport and traveling on an airplane by myself didn't sound nearly as good as having my daddy with me. But what choice did I have?

"Just promise me I won't lose you, too, Daddy, please."

Funny thing is, when I think about the expression on his face now, I swear it was like his heart was breaking, too.

He swept me into his arms. "I promise, *agapemenee mu*. I promise."

He sold the house, moved me to 505 Magnolia Street, left town. Grandmother fixed up one of the formal bedrooms for me on the second floor, making it kid-friendly with flowing curtains and cheery yellow walls and a four-poster bed with a canopy fit for a princess. In the sitting room, we set up a play area complete with a bright-colored rug, shelves filled with board games and books and puzzles. I did a lot of puzzles.

We built a life together, Grandmother and I. My whole routine changed. Walking to school with Grandmother in the morning instead of being driven from the river house by Henry. Getting picked up again in the afternoon by Grandmother, who claimed she just loved all the exercise she was getting now that I lived with her. Going home to play with Luke rather than reading to Cecilia. That's something I had done a lot at the end, when she couldn't turn pages or talk anymore. *A Wrinkle in Time*, all the Harry Potters and Lemony Snickets, *The Boxcar Children*, we loved those. Funny to look at it now, all those are stories about orphans of some sort, which is essentially what I became. I wonder how Cecilia felt, hearing me read those books and knowing that she soon would be leaving me motherless?

Early mornings with Grandmother, late afternoons with Luke. Those were my favorite times of day. School, however, sucked.

After Cecilia died, no one would talk to me. All the girls in my grade just ignored me, including Alexandra Maxim and Maria McBride, the ones I had been closest to. They didn't pick me for their kickball team. They didn't invite me to join them in the cafeteria, only made small attempts at polite conversation. It was like I suddenly had some contagious disease that they would all catch if they were nice to me. Grandmother tried to explain that it wasn't my fault. They felt uncomfortable about my mother passing away and they didn't know what to say to me, didn't know how to handle me. "Give it some time. They'll get over it," she said.

In the meantime, it was a pretty lonely experience. I couldn't wait to get home to Luke. Each day after snack, I would sit reading in the window seat of the music room, one eye trained on his driveway, expectantly waiting for Mrs. Churchville's SUV to pull in, home from picking up Luke at the private boys' school across town. He would burst out of the car and over to my house always ready with a plan. "Let's build a tree house!" "Wanna go over to Le Moyne Park and play catch?!" "Hey, Jane! My dad just got me Grand Theft Auto! You ready to lose, sucker?" Each afternoon, Luke swept into my lonely existence like a tidal wave of fun. We raced, ran, chased, played through every corner of every yard in our block on Magnolia Street. We were best friends. He didn't treat me like I was a pariah. He was always there. Always. Afternoons with Luke made me feel like a normal human being. Every once in a while, if suddenly I looked a little sad, he would say, "What's wrong, Jane? Everything okay, Janie? Want a Coke? Want a hug?" and he'd give me a

Coke or a hug or a noogie and say, "All right, ditch the tears, Janie. Time to ride bikes!"

Luke Churchville was unbelievably sweet to me when nobody else was.

I couldn't imagine where that Luke had gone.

By eleven in the morning, we had made some progress with our trash duty, but it was slow going because the beach was so wide. And we were starting to realize that Officer Meeks had been right about the dangers of cleanup duty—it was hot, sweaty, grueling work. The humidity had kicked in big-time, so during the next mandated break, my team and I waded—shorts and T-shirts and all—into the shallow waters of the gulf. We all figured that since the oil had not hit shore yet, we might as well enjoy the water while we still had the chance!

"Hate to say it, but this cleanup kinda sucks," someone said.

"Yeah," someone else replied.

"Are we ever going to finish?"

"I think the longer we work, the longer the beach gets."

Then silence. That was the way it had been most of the morning. Each pair did some chatting on their own, but there had not been much interaction. We were a bit of a mismatched group. Or you could just say we didn't know one another.

JoeJoe broke the tension, pointing to the next section we

needed to clean. "Beer cans, beer cans everywhere and not a drop to drink."

Luke grinned. "Nice one."

Dear Lord. That grin. Did it have to be so adorable?

Teddy Mac gestured at the other end of the beach, where Team Ashley was taking their break. "Hey, why are they having more fun than we are?"

It was true—Ashley's team seemed to be having the time of their lives. Even from a distance, it was obvious that she had lost her bad attitude, what with the boys being there and all. Although to be honest it looked like she was getting her boyfriend, James, to do most of the work for her. "Oh, James, could you pick up this bucket and move it for me? It's too heavy." "Eww! That is so disgusting! James, will you come get this?" James played the chivalrous gentleman at every juncture and did Ashley's bidding without an iota of complaint. *He must really love her,* I thought. Meanwhile, on more than one occasion I saw Lancer swing Mallory up on his shoulders, he-man style, then run into the water with her. At that moment, Caroline and her cousin Jules competed to see who could run farthest into the bay before they fell into the water.

"Ahh, the in-crowd," I said. "Always knows how to turn any situation into a party."

"So, Jane, if they're Team In-Crowd, what are we?" Zara asked. "Don't we need a team name?"

"How about the Outcasts?"

"The Unwanted."

"The Throwaways."

"The Redheaded Stepchildren," JoeJoe added. And with that we all laughed.

"Clearly, we have a winner," I announced. "We are the official Redheaded Stepchildren, even though not a one of us has red hair."

That turned the tables on the day in a big way. Suddenly, everything became a game for Team Redheaded Stepchildren. When JoeJoe found a lone Air Nike, Luke took a picture with his iPhone and put it up on his Facebook page asking if anyone had seen the other one. We entertained ourselves by posting more pictures of gross and lost things on our Facebook accounts. A disgusting bag of King Chicken leftovers now covered in maggots. Ewww. A deflated basketball. Some poor baby's dirty cloth diaper. Ewww, ewww, ewww. Our howls of laughter drew the attention of Lancer. He barreled on over. "What's going on? Too much laughing, not enough working."

Zara showed him a picture she was putting up on Facebook for her friends back in DC to see. It was of a handmade dollhouse she and Luke found settled amongst the beach grass. Colorfully painted like a Victorian house on the outside and covered with tattered wallpaper on the inside, it was completely devoid of furniture and dolls. Kind of sad, really.

To my surprise, Lancer was actually affected. "Some poor little girl is missing her house, isn't she?" He yelled over to his crowd, "Guys, let's get some chatter going!"

Within about twenty minutes, everyone was posting. Mallory had set up a Twitter account called "Magnolia-riffic" and started tweeting about how much we had already cleaned and how much more we had to go. We were all getting comments and feedback and postings—a lot of support—which gave me an idea.

"Hey, everybody," I called out. "Gather round! Let's make our posts work for us. Write something like 'there's still time to help.' That people can come on down and donate or put on some gloves and get to work."

Ashley's eyes lit up. "More hands on deck? Love it!"

I gasped. "Ashley, did you just agree with me?"

"Yes, but word to the wise. Don't get used to it."

Everyone got busy on their smart phones and within half an hour, no lie, we had a CROWD! Brandi Lyn and JoeJoe's friends lived nearby and used the beach all the time, so they were the first to show up. Then more friends and friends of friends drove down from town, and suddenly there were tons of people out grabbing gloves and bags and joining in. *The power of social networking,* I thought. *We might be able to finish this endless project after all.* A few folks asked if they could give us some more money, so JoeJoe cleaned out a plastic toy bucket somebody had salvaged and Brandi Lyn made a sign that read, DONATIONS HERE. It started filling up with dollar bills and change, and Zara's friends up north started pledging to send some cash our way. I was a wee bit surprised to see Katherine and Courtney show up, even if they had dropped their lawsuits against the Magnolia Maid Organization, but they kind of just ignored Team Redheaded Stepchildren—typical!—and joined Team In-Crowd for the pickup. Our fund-raiser was turning into a big ole B'ville social event, so obviously they needed to make an appearance.

Total news flash! And this time I mean that literally! The local news actually came to interview us. Midway through the day, the Local News 7 van pulled into the parking lot, and reporter Maven Rice started interviewing various bystanders. Lots of folks talked about what a great thing we were doing for the city. Then Mr. Walter dragged Ashley and me toward Maven. "It is your duty as team captains to give her the story, okay."

Maven stuck the microphone in my face. "Ms. Fontaine Ventouras, how did you come up with the idea of a beach cleanup as a fund-raiser?"

For the second time that day I blanked. What was happening to me? "Well . . . ," I floundered. "We really, thought, we wanted to help our community and . . . um, this seemed like a good idea. . . ."

Ashley, however, transformed herself into a passionate public relations expert. "Well, Maven, I think the question is, how could we *not* do this type of fund-raiser? As Magnolia Maids, we are Bienville, and Bienville is its natural resources. Our resources are threatened so we have to defend them." My jaw dropped. Go, Ashley! "And we are so grateful to everyone who has turned out today and supported our cause. You all have been wonderful." She waved to all our fans off camera, eliciting a giant cheer. Damn, she was good when she wasn't being all angry and vindictive.

Maven nodded. "On another note, I understand that you girls have yet to elect a queen?"

Ashley and I exchanged glances. "That's true," I said.

"That's very unusual for this stage of the Magnolia Maids process, is it not? Tell me, what is the holdup?"

Ashley and I didn't even look at each other this time. What in the world were we going to say? "Well . . . ," she started.

Miraculously, I found my sea legs and finished her sentence. "There's no holdup here, Maven. What's happening is that this year's Court is a very diverse Court. Unlike previous years. We are from different parts of town, different schools. Two of us have just recently moved back to the area. So we are taking our time to get to know each other before we select a queen."

Wow. That fine excuse burst out of my mouth like a cannonball at the circus. I hesitated to even look in Ashley's direction in the event she was balking at my answer. To my immense surprise, she was nodding right along with everything I said, even adding to it. "We just want to make the right decision," she said. "We need the best leader possible to guide us through all the appearances and events in the year to come."

Maven beamed at us. "Well, so far, it looks like you're doing a great job as a team. Good luck, Maids." She looked back into the camera. "I'm Maven Rice for Local News 7. Back to you, Chuck."

As soon as the reporters left, Mr. Walter came over and swept both me and Ashley into a giant hug. "Good job, Maids. Couldn't have asked for more, okay. Keep up the mighty fine work."

After he walked away, I turned to Ashley. "Don't take this wrong, Ashley, but you were great."

"Don't take this wrong, Jane, but so were you." We grinned at each other for a split second. "But we're still going to kick your butts." She ran back to her team and rallied them to get cleaning again.

I headed back to mine and we pushed through the last hundred yards toward the finish line. Surprisingly, I was starting to feel pretty good about the day, considering.

Until Teddy Mac hissed at me in the way that only Teddy Mac can. "What is going on here?"

"What do you mean?"

"You and Luke Churchville. Have not said word one to each other since he arrived. Did you think I wouldn't notice?"

"It's nothing."

"In some alternate universe, maybe. If I recall correctly, you and he were BFFs once upon a time. True dat or true dat?"

"True dat. But I don't think he wants to talk to me anymore."

"Then you are clearly blind as a bat. If he looks over here one more time, I'm having him arrested for eye-stalking."

"Oh, shut up."

"No, you shut up. No, don't. Go talk to him."

"I am fine just where I am."

I bent over to pick up a dead inner tube. I could feel Teddy Mac staring at me. "Well, I am bored to tears talking to you," he finally said. "I feel the need for a little change." Teddy Mac beelined for the section of beach that Zara and Luke were currently working on. "Zara, baby!"

"Oh come on, Teddy Mac!" I called after him, desperate.

He completely ignored me, that jerk, and bounded right up to Zara. "I have not had the opportunity to truly make your acquaintance. Let's switch partners and dish like schoolgirls, why don't we? Luke, you're okay to work with Jane for a while, aren't you?"

And before anyone could say no, Teddy Mac had reconfigured the whole scenario so that Luke and I were alone together at Bienville Point, the part of the beach where the shoreline meanders north and turns a corner. Here the gulf turns into the bay, and the terrain changes dramatically. The sandy beach narrows down to a quarter of its size. There are more trees. Beach grasses. Marshy areas. Small inlets with cattails and other water grasses where birds frolic and turtles play. It's beautiful.

Luke and I walked along in silence. Finally, I couldn't take it any longer. "So what have you been up to?"

"What have I been up to? Let me see. Interesting question. Since when? Since the last time I saw you five years ago? Or the other day when I saw you at church?"

Well, that took care of that question. I guess he did see me that day, after all.

"Let's try the last five years."

"Okay. I ate my Wheaties on a regular basis and grew about fifteen inches, put on the corresponding weight. Still at OMS, going to be a senior this year. My grades are pretty decent. Probably applying to Alabama, Vanderbilt, maybe Tulane. Captain of the soccer team. President of the French club. Started a band with Lancer and a couple of guys. Our influences are the Smiths, the Cure, Dead Can Dance, the Allman Brothers, the Eagles, Jack Johnson, and Metallica. There. Happy?"

No. Not at all. The résumé listing actually managed to sound pretty ugly. Not so charming. What was I supposed to say to that? Here's what I did say: "What's that noise?"

"Yeah, that's what people usually say about the band, but we think it works."

"That's not what I meant. There's a weird sound. Over there."

Luke cocked his head to one side and we both listened. There was a thwacking sound, a wet *thump, thump, thwack* coming from the marshy inlet a few yards ahead of us. "An alligator?" he suggested.

"Sounds more like fluttering?"

We made for the inlet, parted the marsh grasses, and found the source of the sound. And I'll tell you, it took my breath away. Immediately. There before us, perched on—no, in—the water, flapping its wings in a valiant attempt to get airborne, was a bird. An oil-soaked, blackened, incapacitated bird, who could not fly because its wings were covered, DRIPPING with oil.

"That's a brown pelican," said Luke.

"He must have been diving near the spill," I replied. "He has so much oil on him!"

The pelican strained to extend his broad brown wings again and feebly flapped them but to no avail. He was sinking deeper.

"Oh my God, he's going to drown," Luke said.

"We have to save him!" I cried.

Without missing a beat, Luke and I launched into emergency mode.

"I'll call Officer Meeks!"

"I'll try to grab him!"

I sprinted over to our other teammates and yelled, "Teddy Mac! Run and get Officer Meeks! Tell him to come quick! We found a bird!"

"A Bird? OMG!" Teddy Mac took off running back toward headquarters, and I careened back to the marsh to find that Luke had waded into the water and was trying to pick up the bird with his hands. It was so not working.

"Luke, we're not supposed to touch them!" The pelican lunged at Luke with his long, formidable beak. "And you're making him more anxious!"

"But he's going to drown!" It certainly looked that way. The poor thing could barely keep itself afloat.

"I know, but there's got to be a better way." I scanned the

area. "How about that?" I pointed at a plank on the small bluff above the marsh. It was about one foot wide and ten feet long, probably something that had come off somebody's fishing shack or pier during one of last year's hurricanes. "Maybe we try to get it underneath him and get him to walk onto it?"

"Good idea." Together we dragged the board over and floated it out into the water. That was the easy part. The hard part was trying to maneuver it underwater and under the bird. We had no control from ten feet away and the resistance created by the water made it almost impossible to lever the board with any sort of direction or power.

"We need more traction," I said.

Luke waded slowly back into the water, careful not to upset the bird. He stopped at about the middle of the plank, and from there guided it under the bird's feet. "Come on, boy, we have a little life raft for you here. Hop on," he said.

I held fast to my end of the plank, trying not to let it make any sudden motions or splashes. "Just find your feet, Peli, just put your feet down."

"You don't have to struggle so much."

"We're here. We got you."

Luke and I both held our breath and then, miraculously, the pelican felt the board under its feet. Stopped flapping. Took a few heavy steps forward before taking a well-deserved rest. We sighed in relief. Without saying a word, Luke and I worked together to draw the plank onto the sand. When the bird-end of the board made it to land, Luke and I gently laid it to rest and stared at the oil-soaked creature.

"Ack!" it cried, glaring plaintively at us.

"Ack is right," I said back. I had to turn away from the sight. This helpless, unlucky animal. The victim of such unjust circumstances far beyond its control. It killed me.

Luke shook his head in anger. "This makes me so mad. It's just not right, Jane. It's just not right."

I was about to reply, but then Teddy Mac showed up with Officer Meeks, who was carrying a cage. Right behind him came everybody else: Team In-Crowd, Team Redheaded Stepchildren, our Facebook and Twitter recruits. We quickly explained what happened, then Luke stalked off, obviously furious.

I wanted to ask him what exactly wasn't right: the bird, the oil, or me?

Chapter Thirteen

"Wait, y'all, there it is!"

"It's on, everybody!"

"Y'all, come watch this!"

It was a few hours and a few beers later, and the fund-raiser had morphed into a party and relocated to Lancer's family's bay house. We all rushed to gather round the TV in the family room to watch CNN and see Luke talk about rescuing the bird.

"Woo-hoo! Looking good on the TV, Church-Vegas!"

"Check it out! Reverend Luke on the national news!"

The rest of the day had turned out to be crazy and not just because Luke totally walked away from me after what I thought was a pretty intense bonding experience. As Mallory repeated every time she opened her mouth, it was a day that would go down in Magnolia Maid history. After Officer Meeks contained the pelican in the cage and took it off to the Bird Sanctuary for cleanup, we all returned to the task at hand, finishing garbage patrol.

Both teams were pretty much neck and neck, and by the time each group got to their last segment, the situation was hectic. Everybody rushed around and ran into each other trying to get every last piece of trash so that we could race for the finish line. Teddy Mac and I fought to pick up the same Coke can. Zara and Luke and Brandi Lyn and JoeJoe went bonkers on a stack of paper plates someone had just dropped there.

"Get it! Get it!"

We thought we were done when someone yelled, "There's one more plastic bag!"

"Where?"

"Over there!"

Luke grabbed it and we took off for the midpoint where Mr. Walter had set up shop so that he could be the judge. At that same moment, Ashley and her team were running for it. Racing, running, pummeling. It was so, so close . . . .

"Slide!" cried Luke.

We dove into the sand, headfirst toward the finish line . . .

. . . and beat Team In-Crowd by an inch!

The Redheaded Stepchildren went wild.

So did Mr. Walter. After we counted up all the pre-event donations we got from individuals and corporations, the cash in the beach bucket, and the pledges that came through

Twitter and Facebook, the final tally on the donations was well over fifteen thousand dollars. It was more than any Court had ever raised in a single day in the history of the organization! We had made enough to donate a big portion of our funds to the Alabama Bay Watch to assist with further cleanup *and* pay for travel to the Rose Bowl, to New York, to Disney World for Easter. Plus, we all agreed that it felt good to make a difference. The thing that made Mr. Walter's lid flip with excitement, though, was that we had made the news. And not just the local with Maven Rice. It turned out that a CNN correspondent had been in the area during the bird rescue, and had interviewed us for the story. Since this was the first oil-soaked bird found in Alabama, it was a big deal.

Later, I overheard Mr. Walter call the president of the chamber of commerce and brag. "Billy, we got us some good national PR today, we sure did! You shoulda seen these girls out there. Best belles we've ever had!"

To celebrate our massive accomplishments, Lancer had invited everyone over to his parents' unchaperoned bay house. Everybody went, even Brandi Lyn, JoeJoe, and their crowd. Apparently, cleaning the beach together had been a great equalizer. There was one exception—Teddy Mac. He excused himself, claiming Lacey Wilkes had called and begged him to swing by the pharmacy on his way home to pick up her anxiety meds because she was getting a case of the melancholies.

Anyway, we all agreed that instead of making good on the bet with Picklefish Pizza, we would stop at the Piggly Wiggly and stock up on burgers and hot dogs and beer. We had been drinking, eating, and making merry ever since, waiting for the piece to air on CNN.

Now on the television, Officer Meeks was talking about how the brown pelican must have dived into an oil slick that was now only two miles off the Bienville Beach coastline. "It's a real shame, too," he said. "The brown pelican had just gotten off the endangered list when the spill happened. I'm sure he'll be back on it any day now."

Hearing that dark reality brought the mood crashing down. Saddened, I raised my glass. "To Peli," I said. "To surviving your cleaning and making it back into the wild."

Bottles and glasses clinked all around me. "To Peli!" "To survival!" "To the wild!"

"Oh, here comes Jane!" Mallory yelled.

I covered my face in mock horror. "Ugh. I hate seeing myself on-screen." We watched as I muddled through an explanation of what the Magnolia Maids were and what we had been doing down there that day.

Ashley sighed. "Don't worry, Jane. You'll get better at speaking in public. Maybe you should take some classes." The funny thing is, I think she was actually being sincere for a change.

As soon as the newscast was over, Mallory leapt to her feet. "Y'all, we haven't been Maids for a month and we're already on national TV! Nobody's ever done that!" Mallory raised her beer bottle. "To the most successful day ever in the history of the Magnolia Maids!"

"Hear, hear!"

"To Alabama's best belles!"

"Bienville's finest!"

Everyone toasted and with that, the party officially kicked into rager gear. Jules whipped out his MacBook and went DJ ninja on the joint, pumping everything from Gnarls Barkley to Franz Ferdinand through the house. Ashley and Mallory organized a beer pong game around the coffee table. Caroline repaired to the loft to read a trashy Danielle Steele novel. Brandi Lyn, jacked up on a billion Diet Cokes, turned out to be quite the dart player and challenged anyone who came within five feet of her to a game. JoeJoe had had himself a couple of beers and joined forces with the Lancer posse to design a MoonPie-eating contest that wasn't just about how many you could eat, but how many could you eat before you puked. Guys are so creative when they're drunk.

Meanwhile, I stuck close to Zara all night and watched the boys flock around her like bees to a flower. They peppered her with a billion questions: Where was she from? How did she like Bienville? Had she ever been to Mardi Gras? She played along, answering their questions between bouts of texting with someone not there.

Normally, I would have been curious about those texts, and it might have looked like I was listening to Bienville boys ask Zara about her football-playing cousins, but really I was lost in thought.

Luke and I trying to save that poor pelican, well, it had felt like old times. Like the time we rescued a bag of kittens that had been tossed in a ditch near the park. Or the time we picked Luke's little sister up off the sidewalk after she took a rough tumble off her bike and landed on some broken glass and needed stitches.

It kind of felt like a bonding experience, a homecoming of sorts, yet here we were back to avoiding each other. Or at least pretending to. In reality, I was watching his every move. Who he was talking to. What he was doing. How many beers he drank (three). I started wondering why exactly Luke seemed so angry with me. I just couldn't figure it out. I mean, it had been five years, and the last time we had seen each other wasn't exactly a good time. So I could understand discomfort, awkwardness. But anger?

I contemplated this as I sucked down my frozen margarita with a straw, managing not to get freezer head. Then I made my decision. There was only one way to find out. "So help me God."

I didn't realize I had said it out loud until I noticed Zara gave me a strange look.

"Everything okay?" she asked.

"Yeah, sure, no. Send in reinforcements if I'm not back in ten." I set off for the porch, where I knew Luke was currently playing Ping-Pong with his old friend Henry. I could feel Zara's concerned eyes follow me every inch of the way.

Out on the porch, the Henry/Luke Ping-Pong match was in full swing. I sidled up to the table and spooked Luke in the middle of a volley.

"Jesus, Jane! What is up with you?"

I raced Henry to the ball, grabbing it before he could. "Beat it. Luke and I need to talk."

Henry glanced at Luke; Luke nodded. "Catch you later."

The second Henry was gone, I whirled on Luke. "So you knew I was in town, but you didn't think about swinging by the house?"

"And say what? How come you never returned any of my phone calls?"

"For starters."

"That's all water under the bridge, Jane. History."

"Oh, really? Then what was that stalker drive-by last week?"

"I don't know what you're talking about."

"You, your daddy's Mercedes, cruising a whopping negative five miles per hour down my street as you stared up at my bedroom?"

"Must have been somebody else."

I jerked my head out toward the yard, where his dad's Mercedes was parked. "So someone must have stolen your car then, because, swear on a stack of King James Bibles, I saw it coming down my street."

He sighed. "Fine, Jane, maybe you're right. I did drive by, and I probably will again because it's on the way to places I go." He thought for a minute. "And, for your information, it just so happens that I dropped something in the floorboard. I had to slow down to pick it up."

"What?"

"What?"

"What did you drop?"

"I don't know." He shrugged. "My iPod."

"Your iPod?"

"And, anyway, what's up with coming to my church?"

"It was a Magnolia Maid thing," I lied.

We stood glaring at each other eye to eye, except we weren't exactly. When last we had stood face-to-face, we were the same height. Now, here he was, towering a foot above me. And flaring his nostrils.

"I just don't understand," I said. "Why are you mad?"

"I'm not mad about anything."

"Yes you are. Why?"

He looked out to sea. Thought for a second. Finally turned back to me. "Okay. Here goes. After that day, after your father went ballistic, I felt so bad about your getting in trouble. I tried to get in touch with you. Your father, your grandmother, they made it real clear that *you* didn't want to see *me* anymore. You would rather go to boarding school than talk to me, and every holiday you were back in town you were 'too busy' to see me. So now you're back for good and you want to act like everything's normal and no problemo here? Sorry. No can do."

While Luke was talking, my jaw got closer and closer to the floor. "Wait, what? No! They said I didn't want to see you? That's not how it happened."

"Yeah, right! If that's not how it happened, then why didn't you ever e-mail me? Why didn't you call?" He lowered his voice. "Why didn't you come to the door when I came over and cried on your grandmother's doorstep?"

It's true. He had once cried on Grandmother's doorstep while I silently watched from the staircase. Remembering that nearly killed me. "Luke, please, you've got to believe me, I . . ."

Before I could get out my side of the story, though, Luke's glance moved beyond my shoulder and his eyes lit up. "Hey, babe, it's about time you got here." I turned to see a girl step onto the porch, a tall, skinny brunette with long hair and Bambi eyes. Luke breezed by me to plant a kiss on her lips, and I realized that this was one Luke fantasy that had never even occurred to me: ex-beau has new love. Makes out with her in front of you.

Oh, the horror.

I don't know how long I had to endure that moist, succulent sucking going on right before my very eyes before Mallory and Ashley stumbled onto the porch, their arms wrapped drunkenly around each other.

"Hey-ey!" Ashley said. "Mallory's looking for Katherine and I'm looking for Jimmy. Y'all seen them?"

Never in the history of the universe had a distraction been so welcome. "Nope. Not lately."

Mallory's vision cleared enough to notice Luke and his girl. "Hey, Luke. Hey, Posey. Y'all seen Jimmy or Katherine?"

Luke shrugged nonchalantly, but I tell you what, there was something odd, very odd about the way he responded. "Maybe they went for more beer," he said.

My weirdness radar kicked on.

"But there's still tons in the fridge!" Mallory exclaimed.

Wait, did I detect something strange going on with her, too?

"I know! I bet they're on the beach," Mallory decided.

Ashley rolled her eyes. "Now why would they be on the beach?"

Luke jumped on her bandwagon. "Yeah, why would they be on the beach? The party's going on up here!"

"I don't know, silly, but let's go check!" Mallory tossed open the screen door and half carried Ashley down the stairs.

And that's when a, shall we say, worried expression settled on Luke's face. He whipped out his phone and sent a text.

I lit myself a cigarette and played it supercool. "Look, Luke, I realize there's all this awkwardness surrounding a thing that happened, ohhhhh, five years ago, but suck it up and tell me what's going on here."

"Maybe they got lost," offered Posey. "Oh, I remember you! You're Jane! The one who's mother . . ."

I blew a smoke ring in her face that sent her coughing and scurrying inside for a glass of water. "Nice to see you, Posey," I called after her.

Luke snapped his phone shut and grabbed a Ping-Pong paddle. "I don't know what you're talking about. Wanna play?"

I arched an eyebrow at Luke and said nothing, which by the way, is a very powerful tool for getting someone's attention. Most human beings do not like silence, and they work to fill it, which is exactly what Luke did after a few moments of silent acting like nothing is going on.

"You shouldn't smoke," Luke said.

"I also shouldn't talk to strangers, but that doesn't stop me. So. Jim, Katherine, subject at hand?"

He motioned for me to follow him around the side of the house to another porch, which I did. "They took a walk on the beach," he whispered.

My radar was confirmed. Ashley's beloved Jimmy had gone for a "walk on the beach" with her darling BFF Katherine. Everyone knew what that meant.

"How long?"

"About an hour or so."

"No, I mean how long have they been uh, seeing each other?"

"I'd say at least three weeks."

So that's what Mallory had been talking about during our "fun with makeup" mystery conversation. It was *Ashley* who was being cheated on. "Oh no. Ashley loves that guy," I said.

Luke nodded. "I can't believe he's such an idiot to sneak off with Katherine when she's here."

I shot him a look.

"Or anytime. He should just break up with her if he's not happy."

"And with one of her BFFs, too. So not right." Granted there was no—and I mean zero—love lost between me and Bienvillite Supreme Mary Ashley LaFleur. But she didn't deserve this. I felt bad—about to throw up, food poisoning, vomit bad. What kind of friend was Katherine to do that to Ashley? I knew what it was like to lose someone you loved. To have someone hurt you. To have your worldview turned upside down and peed on. And I knew that if Ashley found Jim and Kat together, acting all lovey-dovey, it would crush her. I didn't want to see it, and frankly, no one deserved that sort of public smack-down.

Ashley simply had to get out of there.

"Thanks, Luke," I said, and quickly headed down the stairs to get the wheels of exit in motion. I didn't have a plan, didn't even know how I could enact a plan, but I was on a mission. I headed toward the beach and found Ashley and Mallory stumbling down the boardwalk toward the bay. "Hey, y'all, what's going on? I'm thinking we need to get this party dancing! Jules is rocking it, have you heard?"

"I'm too tired," said Ashley. "And a little sunburned."

"And a little tipsy," Mallory added. "We just want to find Jimmy and go home."

"Oh, who cares about him? Let's dance. Seriously. Let's have a Magnolia Maid celebratory dance!" I managed to insert myself between Mallory and Ashley and maneuver them back in the direction of the house.

But it was too late.

Twinkling giggles and a low laugh floated up from the beach.

At the end of the boardwalk emerged the very image I had tried to prevent Ashley from seeing: Katherine, hair a mess, lipstick smeared, and James, button-down shirt distinctly mis-buttoned, their arms around each other. . . .

"Katherine? Jimmy? What . . . What's . . . ?" Ashley's voice faltered.

Katherine and Jimmy froze.

You know that look on the gazelle's face on those Discovery Channel documentaries when it's just noticed that there's a cheetah on the scene? That was the look on Katherine's face. "Oh my God, Ashley. I thought you were playing quarters. But you're . . . not, are you?" Her sentence turned up in a question mark of desperation.

James at least had the decency to appear ashamed. "Ashley, look."

Oh, this was going to be painful.

Even under the influence of a six-pack, Ashley quickly put the puzzle pieces together. "Y'all are fooling around behind my back, aren't you?"

James and Katherine stepped away from each other and stuttered out some pathetic attempts at explanations. "Well . . ."

"You see . . ."

Ashley glanced at Mallory. "Did you know about this?"

"Me?" Mallory fluttered. "No! It's terrible. I'm as shocked as you are!"

Then we heard barks of laughter. From the back porch. That's right. Lancer and his drunk bastard friends had somehow gotten wind that a "situation was in progress," and their drunken selves were lined up along the porch railing watching.

"Ooooh, Jimmy's busted!" cried Jules.

"Jimmy, you man-whore!" shouted Ashley's cousin Henry.

"It's like that song 'Torn Between Two Lovers!'" shouted Lancer. "You should feel like a fool!"

Oh, great. These guys were spoiling for a show, dying for fuel for tomorrow's gossip mill, and Ashley was about to be it.

"Ashley," I said. "Let's get out of here. Y'all should talk when you have more privacy. Mallory, go find the other girls and tell them we're leaving." I grabbed Ashley's arm and led her toward the front of the house, which unfortunately required passing the peanut gallery. "Show's over, boys," I called. "Go eat something and throw it up."

"Aw, Jane, you're no fun," Lancer called.

"Yep, that's me. 'No fun Jane.'"

Meanwhile, Katherine was charging after us. "Asssshhh-ley, wait! I hate myself, simply hate myself!" Katherine cried. "I'll make it up to you, I will. Just tell me how!"

Ashley whirled on her. "Shut your filthy mouth! You knew I was here! You wanted me to see you with him."

"No I didn't! You're my friend!"

"Was. Were. I was your friend. You were my friend."

"I was going to break it off with him, I swear!"

"That explains the giggles and the hand-holding as you came up the beach." I couldn't help myself. It just slipped out.

Ashley's head bobbed up and down with agreement. "You were wrapped around him like Spanish moss on an oak tree! Why, Katherine? What is it, that you're jealous? You know I did everything I could to get you and Courtney on the Magnolia Court! It's not my fault what happened."

By this time, Mallory had returned with Zara, Caroline,

Brandi Lyn, and JoeJoe. Clearly, she had given them the 411 because JoeJoe brought his fighting words. "Who's done you wrong, darlin'?" he said to Ashley. "You need me to beat him up?"

Speaking of the devil, Jimmy chose that moment to make an appearance.

"This the guy?" JoeJoe sized up Jimmy. "'Cause I can take him easy."

Ashley wiped away her tears. "Well, thank you, JoeJoe. I appreciate it, but I think I'm good."

"You just let me know. Any sister Maid of Brandi Lyn's is a sister Maid of mine."

Brandi Lyn swooned and wrapped her arms around her boy. "Aw, baby, aren't you the sweetest?"

Meanwhile, Ashley gathered herself together, cocked her chin up in the air, and sniffed. "Katherine, you've put a real dent in my beautiful relationship, and for that I hope you rot in hell." She turned to Jimmy. "As for you, James. I'm very mad right now, but we'll get through this. Call me tomorrow and we'll discuss. Maids, can we go?"

"Absolutely."

"Let's get out of here." We rallied around Ashley and headed down the driveway. We almost made it to our cars when we heard a voice behind us.

"No!" James stood behind us, holding a fresh can of beer.

Ashley furrowed her brow. "No, what?"

"No, we don't have a beautiful relationship. No, I'm not calling you tomorrow, Old Mother Ashley."

Ashley blinked. Blinked again. "James, are you making fun of me?"

"I sure am, Old Mother Ashley. Did you know that's what the guys call you? Because you're just like my mother, calling me 'James' when I've been a bad boy. And I have been a bad boy, haven't I, honey?"

Ashley looked so pained, it was hard to watch. "Jimmy, why are you doing this?"

"Because I'm sick. I'm sick of the way you call me up and tell me what to wear so I won't clash with your outfit. I'm sick of the way you won't drink Sunny Delight if that's all they have—that you have to have orange juice or your cosmo just doesn't taste right. Ordering me around like a slave all day to pick up your trash. You criticize my driving, make me go to Sunday dinner at your grandmother's. You gossip with my mother! It's like we're married or something!"

"Well, we will be one day. Won't we?"

A long, endless pause hung in the air, filled only by the sound of crickets chirping and drunk Old Bienvillites spilling out onto the back porch to watch the rest of the show. James took a look at Ashley. Glanced over his shoulder at his buddies. Eyed Katherine, who now was being consoled in the arms of Courtney. He had an audience. And he was milking it for all it was worth.

He chugged the rest of his beer in one giant swig. "No, Ashley, we're not going to be married. You and me, we're over. Call my mother and gossip about that."

Chapter Fourteen

"Song!" we all called out.

Mallory nodded, counted on her fingers, then held up nine of them.

"Nine words!"

She drew a squiggly shape in the air.

"Question mark!"

"A question!"

"A song in the form of a question!"

Mallory clapped enthusiastically and indicated that she was going to act out the second word, which would be one syllable that sounded like . . . she held up two fingers.

"Two."

"Sounds like two."

"Boo, coo, do, e-oo, foo."

"You."

While Mallory jumped with joy that I had gotten the second word right, I didn't even look up from filing my fingernails. It's not that hard to figure out when it's totally obvious that e-oo and foo are in no way shape or form words.

Oh, ho-hum-hummedy-hum-hum-hum. Here it was Tuesday night in B'ville, and I could have been doing an *Ugly Betty* marathon out at Hawkleigh with Teddy Mac and Lacey Wilkes, but nooooooooooo. Instead I, along with all my Magnolia sisters, was being held hostage in the home of Mizz Upton and her lovely daughter Caroline and being forced to play charades at gunpoint.

Okay, that's an exaggeration, we weren't being held at gunpoint. But have you ever seen a good Southern home? We're big believers in the old right to bear arms, just in case the Yankees ever get it in their minds to invade again. So a lot of us keep weapons around the house: ancient swords and Revolutionary War–era muskets as decoration on the walls, rifles for hunting and pistols "just in case." That was the situation at the Upton house. So we girls could have been held at gunpoint, if Mizz Upton had gotten it into her head that she wanted to do so. Let's just say we were held in the "spirit of gunpoint."

On Monday, after our great success with the fund-raiser, Mizz Upton admitted that we had done well but that we had a serious problem on our hands. She was horrified at all the talk running around town about how we didn't have a queen yet. It was a major issue. Big humiliation. So even though, yes, she was proud of us for raising so much money and getting on local and national news, we needed to shape up and fast. "Maids, we're having an intervention here," she said. "In my fifteen years of being involved with the Magnolia Maid Organization, it has never been in such a disastrous state mere days in advance of the Boysenthorp debut. You must elect yourselves a queen. You must—and I mean this—learn to work as a team."

I raised my hand. "Mizz Upton, with all due respect, we worked really well as a team on Saturday." Little did she know that it was more than just the fund-raiser. That we had also rallied around Ashley after Jimmy humiliated her with that oh-so-public dumping, that we had gotten her the hell out of Lancer's party as fast as we could, that our designated driver, Brandi Lyn, had driven straight to Ashley's house and we had poured her into bed before she really knew what hit her.

"I couldn't agree more," said Mallory. In fact, there were nods around the room. Ashley was catatonic, which was only to be expected, but the rest of us were in agreement at least.

"Well, that is good news, but we do still have a deadlock. Personally, I would prefer that Mr. Hill and I go ahead and take care of selecting the queen ourselves," said Mizz Upton. "But he insists that we follow the bylaws and give you until the day of the debut. So listen to what I've got planned."

A slumber party. She had planned a freaking slumber party. Instead of having our final dress fitting with Miss Dinah Mae at the chamber of commerce where we usually met for rehearsals, we were to report at five o'clock on Wednesday to Mizz Upton's house for a rollicking evening of dress-fitting, fun and games, and female bonding. She put Caroline in charge of coming up with games to play and bonding activities. If we didn't come out of the situation a happier, tighter group who could sort out the queen situation for ourselves, then she would break the tie for us on Saturday, which would be a dreadful first. "This is your last chance, girls, and I do mean last. Be responsible and make a choice."

So we'd had our potluck dinner party for which Mizz Upton required each of us to contribute a homemade dish (Ashley's famous crab casserole, Caroline's cheesy chicken rice casserole, Zara's grandmother's corn and okra casserole, Brandi Lyn's ham hock and green bean casserole, Mallory's broccoli casserole, and my sausage and collard greens casserole). We'd listened to two guest speakers—former queens, a couple of enthusiastic Old Bienvillites named Mary Megan and Haleigh—tell us how magical and mind-blowing our year of Magnolia Maid-ing was going to be. How you should never eat in your dress because last year Julie Danville had to get a whole new bodice after a run-in with the prize-winning chili sauce at the Memphis Barbecue Festival. And how you should never wear your hoopskirt in the car because it might pop open and limit your vision and cause you to crash like what happened with Amber Davis about five years ago.

But nobody, I mean not one of us, was in the mood. I take that back. Mallory was chipper as ever, but the rest of us were in our own little worlds: Ashley was still reeling from the breakup with Jimmy. Zara was more reserved than ever, and she kept glancing over at me and lifting her eyebrows to the top of her head in a show of "Can you believe this crap?" Caroline, tasked with the job of leading us through our little bonding activities, mustered up as much pep as she could, but she snuck off to read *Pirate Romance of the High Seas* or some such every chance she got. Even Brandi Lyn's sparkly self seemed to have taken the night off. She kept looking off into the distance and sighing. When I asked her if she was okay, she slapped on a smile, and said, "Oh yes, of course. I've just been putting in a lot of hours at Karl's recently and am so tired, that's all." As for me, I was mourning the death of Luke. Well, the death of any potential relationship/ friendship with Luke. Which was pretty obvious after his aggressive make-out session at the party. That guy wanted nothing to do with me.

So we were stuck in Mizz Upton's basement rec room with the blues, and only thirteen hours left to go.

The third word of Mallory's question of a song rhymed with something that vaguely looked like a fish, or at least that was the expression that she put on her face.

With a bored sigh, Ashley rattled through the alphabet, combining letters with "ish." "Bish, cish, dish, eish, fish, gish, hish . . ."

"Wish."

"Yes, yes, yes!" Mallory jumped up and down.

"It's that Pussycat Dolls song, 'Don't Cha W—'" Ashley guessed.

"That's it, that's it!" Delighted, Mallory broke into the

song and a well-choreographed series of "drop it like it's hot" and gyrations. "Come on, Ash, remember?"

"That is so fourth grade, Mal. Give it a rest."

"Well, it's still hot. I don't care what you say." She was deflated, though, and plopped down onto her sleeping bag. "We could at least try to make this fun, y'all."

"I'm afraid I'm never going to have fun again." Ashley sulked over to the corner.

The doorbell rang. Miss Dinah Mae had arrived.

We trudged up to the living room a bunch of sad sacks, and to my immense surprise, it took all of thirty-seven seconds for that vibe to change. The dresses were here! The dresses! Giant pastel-colored antebellum dresses with flounces and ruffles and bodices and corsets. I was a little freaked out by the whole thing, but they were a sight to behold, so much heavy fabric in giant cloth bags the color of our dresses that it took three of Miss Dinah Mae's grandsons to lug it all in. Ashley dropped her catatonic state in a millisecond as she and Mallory grabbed their bags and started yanking out yard after yard of taffeta ruffles. "Careful, Maids!" called Mizz Upton. "Wait till I explain how to put it all on!"

"Oh, don't worry, we know!" Ashley replied, and she and Mallory commenced shimmying into everything that came out of their bags. Mizz Upton teared up with joy at the sight.

Meanwhile, I was pulling enough fabric from my pink bag to make a dozen prom dresses. "What is all this stuff?" I exclaimed.

Mizz Upton stifled a glare and launched into a lecture on

the proper order of Magnolia Maid enrobing: hoopskirt, slip, full skirt, apron, cummerbund. In layman's terms:

1. Put on a corset. Like the kind that Keira Knightley wears in *Pirates of the Caribbean* (the first and most awesome one) when she faints and plummets into the sea while wearing the gold medallion that raises the Black Pearl and the zombie pirates. Put one on and then stand still while someone else pulls the laces so tight that the stays suck your ribs in and take your breath away.

2. Cover said torture device—I mean corset—with a beautiful frilly bodice and wait for someone else to button all twenty of the mother-of-pearl buttons up the back.

3. Take a hula hoop. You know, one of those unbendable plastic circles that you gyrate around your waist like some reject from a sixties beach blanket show? The kind with Sally Field in it. She's the mom on *Brothers and Sisters*? Well, she used to play a surfer girl named Gidget. Seriously. Gidget. Look it up.

So take a hula hoop. Attach it to a slightly smaller hula hoop with some white muslin. Attach that slightly smaller hula hoop to a slightly smaller than that hula hoop with some muslin, and so on and so on, until one thin hoop rests about six inches beyond your thighs and one spreads out about five feet in diameter around your feet. Lay this contraption on the floor, then step into the center and draw it up to your waist—"The natural waist!" Mizz Upton barked, but she was excited, very excited. "These are not hip-huggers, Maids! I insist that they sit on your natural waistline."

4. Put on the slip: it's partially a slip, with white organza from waist to knee, but the bottom layer is the colorful lower ruffle of the dress.

5. Shimmy into the full skirt: this consists of the middle layers of ruffles, anywhere from two layers to, I don't know, ten? Ashley and Mallory went with more the merrier on the ruffle front, which meant they now resembled giant wedding cakes. Me, I just had two.

6. Place your apron over the skirt—no, not an apron for cooking, but the top layer of skirt. It covers the midsection, from waist to upper thigh.

7. Circle your waist with the cummerbund: this is the three-inch-wide sateen belt that hides all four of the waistbands of the various skirts (and the pantaloons, but we didn't even have those yet). Fluff out the giant bow on the back of the cummerbund.

8. Adorn yourself with all the accessories: the parasols that match the dresses, the frilly bonnets that tie in a wide bow under the chin, the dainty lace gauntlets that slip over the hands to protect them from exposure.

9. Then pretend like you can still breathe with all those layers forcing your stomach in. And don't even bother trying to walk!

While Ashley and Mallory were twirling and curtsying as if they had been doing this every day of their lives, I could barely move an inch.

I raised my hand. "Mizz Upton, I'm stuck! This thing weighs a ton!"

"No, Jane, your dress has only two ruffles, so it weighs only about thirty-five pounds."

Mallory agreed. "Ours are closer to fifty!"

"Lucky you," I said, and turned back to Mizz Upton. "And they're hot! If I have a heatstroke, who do I get to sue?"

Mizz Upton shook her head. "Fortunately, you've signed all sorts of waivers and so has your grandmother."

Mallory glided by. "Don't worry, you'll get used to it. And my cousin Lucinda says the bruises go away. Eventually."

"Bruises? What bruises?"

Zara dragged me over to a giant mirror on the wall so that we could check ourselves out. We totally looked like we had stepped out of the 1850s into Tara. It was scary. Zara whispered to me. "Am I a traitor to my race for putting this on?"

"Probably," I answered. "But I won't tell anybody."

Meanwhile, Brandi Lyn had pulled on the hoopskirt she made herself and was giggling up a storm. "Oh my, I feel so Scarlett!"

"Scarlett's dead, Brandi," I called out to her.

"Not in spirit!" she chirped. "Well, hello, Rhett, you devil, you."

"Rhett's dead, too, Brandi Lyn." Brandi Lyn reclined into

a seat, and she would have looked quite elegant, too, if the hoopskirt had not popped right out in front of her, revealing everything she had on underneath. Great. You can't even sit down in these things.

"That is NOT how you do it." Mizz Upton loomed over Brandi Lyn, scowling down at her. "And where is the rest of your dress?"

"Oh, um, I, I'm almost done. It's looking beautiful! I mean, not as good as what Miss Dinah Mae does, but I'm proud of it!"

"Bring your dress to the next rehearsal. They have to be Magnolia-approved before the debut next week."

"Yes, ma'am." Brandi Lyn nodded vigorously, and Mizz Upton moved on.

Miss Dinah Mae clapped her hands. "All right, you girls hush and line up and let me check you. I'm tired and I want these dresses done so I can go home and watch *Dancing with the Stars*."

We were all so busy with this final inspection that I don't think anyone noticed at first what happened when Mizz Upton finally walked over to Caroline. All I know is that when I looked up, Mizz Upton had pulled the hoopskirt out of the bag and thrown it on the floor and said, "See what you can do with this." Caroline was eying the thing as if it were a viper on the verge of biting her. Now, y'all, I have to say, I am not good at spatial relationships (just ask any one of the math teachers who has tried to get me to answer a geometry question right) but even I could tell that the circumference of the natural waistline did not match the circumference of the waist it was intended to fit.

Mizz Upton pursed her lips. Tension hovered in the air. It was official: the mood-killer was in the house. "What are you waiting for, honey?" Now, to most Americans and other speakers of the English language, *are* is a one-syllable word. In that moment, however, Martha Ellen Upton drew it out into about sixteen syllables, in a way that only the older class of Bienville Prepster Supreme can. So it sounded like this: "ahhhhhhhhh-er." "What ahhhhhhhhh-er you waiting for, honey?" Had you seen the words on the page, you probably would have thought that she was encouraging her daughter to get a move on. "What are you waiting for?" would have just meant "Hurry up, honey, we need to get busy."

But Mizz Upton had laced so much ugly through that sentence that it permeated every molecule of air in the room. Mallory halted mid-twirl. Brandi Lyn stopped her sitting practice. Ashley quit admiring herself in the mirror. Zara paused mid–inner conflict, and I ceased bitching about the bruises I'd just learned we'd all get from carrying the weight of the skirts on our hips.

"Try it on, Caroline," commanded Mizz Upton.

Poor Caroline, she now had a full audience. She stepped one foot into the circle. Then the other. Then she bent over and started drawing the hoopskirt up her body, interminably slowly.

Until it got stuck at her hips. And she couldn't button it.

Ashley stifled a giggle. Mallory looked away politely.

Zara and Brandi Lyn and I traded "WTF?" glances. Miss Dinah Mae clucked her tongue, and Mizz Upton narrowed her eyes. She brought herself up to her full height and said, "Disgraceful."

Caroline, stupid hoopskirt stuck around her waist, shambled out of the room as fast as she could.

"Caroline, it's not your fault your mother's a complete and total bitch!" I yelled through the door separating the rec room from the laundry room. After her mother's horribly humiliating comments, Caroline had run downstairs and locked herself inside. Zara and I ran after her, or at least tried to, but we got hung up at the door with our multi-layered hoopskirted dresses. Seriously, we couldn't wedge ourselves through the door in those things! "You have to bank up," Mallory called out, instructing us on how to pull the various hoops up and collapse the fabric so that we could walk through the door, but Zara and I were in such a clumsy hurry, we ended up pulling them to our shoulders on one side and scurrying through.

Caroline sobbed through the transom. "Yes it is. She's always telling me, watch my weight, don't eat this, don't eat that."

Zara sighed. "That was just plain mean what she did to you back there."

"I deserved it." Caroline wailed even louder. "I've gained too much weight since Miss Dinah Mae took my measurements!"

"Caroline, I told you to go on a diet, didn't I?" Ashley glided into the room, properly banking her skirts before she did so. She kicked up the bottom ring of her hoopskirt with her left foot, grabbed it with her left hand, pulled the bottom layers up to her waist, then reached down and did the same thing on the right side. She pulled the hoops in toward her body, which made it look like she was wearing a sky blue kayak around her waist, and sailed gracefully through the door.

Zara and I exchanged glances. "Well, at least somebody knows how to work this thing." I hit Ashley on the arm. "But seriously, Ashley, stop being mean."

Zara glared at her. "If you aren't going to help, just mind your own business."

"I'm not trying to be mean. It's a cold, hard fact. If you eat too much, you can't fit into your skirt."

Then Ashley rooted through her purse, whipped a flask out, and downed a sip. No lie!

Zara and I gaped. "What the hell are you doing?" I screeched.

"Taking the edge off. It got tense up there."

"Well, give it here." I ripped the flask out of her hands.

I took a swig. Vodka and cranberry juice. Nice.

"Jane!"

"So rude, not offering it to anybody else. Zara?" I handed the flask to her and she got in on the action.

Brandi Lyn arrived at that moment, still wearing her hoopskirt, making an attempt to bank it properly. "What's that smell? Ohh! Are y'all drinking?"

Ashley offered her the flask. "Want some?"

To my immense surprise, Brandi Lyn did. She had a big swig and sputtered up a storm. Then she called to Caroline over the transom. "Caroline, I can fix your waistline! It's not hard. I can put in a small panel. Or I can extend the loops for the buttons with elastic. It'll work!"

"Really?" Caroline's weak voice came fluttering back.

"Really."

"Come on out, Caroline. Let us help. We can fix this."

"I don't know."

At that moment, Mallory glided in, but she wasn't the sweet, fun-loving puppy dog we all knew and loved. She was *raging*. "All right. I have had it. This is supposed to be the greatest day of our lives."

Brandi Lyn looked confused. "Isn't that supposed to be our wedding day?"

Mallory ignored Brandi Lyn. She was on a roll. "I have waited twelve years to wear this dress! Twelve years to serve our fine city as a Magnolia Maid! And, so help me God, I am not going to let all y'all ruin it with your bad moods and your bad attitudes! Give me that." She grabbed Ashley's flask and chugged from it. She handed it back. "It's almost empty. Now, listen up. Caroline, you come out of that laundry room right now. Everybody else, go sit your butts down and let's figure out what we have to do to make this work. Everybody hear me?"

You should have seen the glances flying between me, Zara, Brandi Lyn, and Ashley. "Go, Mallory."

"I didn't know you had it in you."

"Who would have guessed?"

"Look who's got her bloomers in a bunch."

Suddenly self-conscious, Mallory giggled. "Well, I'm fired up, and when I'm fired up, I speak up."

"Nice job."

"Come on, Caroline," Mallory called over the transom. "Will you please come out?"

"I just want to know . . . y'all won't laugh at me?"

"We're here, aren't we?" I said. "Of course we're not going to laugh at you."

"Ashley?"

All eyes turned to Ashley. She sighed. "Caroline, I like to pride myself on always telling the truth, but I guess sometimes the truth hurts and I could be more respectful of other people's feelings."

I raised an eyebrow. "Are we actually calling that an apology?"

"Trying!" Ashley groaned. "I'm sorry, Caroline. I really am!"

The door unlocked and a tear-covered Caroline appeared in the doorway. Ashley offered her the flask. She drained it of the last drop. "Thank you. Why are y'all being so nice to me?"

We stood there for a moment, contemplating. And there it was, happening. The very bonding that Mizz Upton had been exhorting us to create for three weeks straight. All the board games and charades in the world could not have achieved what witnessing the Armageddon of Ashley's love and Caroline's humiliation had. Nothing brings people together like tragedy. I mean *nothing*.

"Because we're Magnolia Maid sisters," Ashley stated. "We're a team."

It turns out Team Magnolia Maid, without even talking about it, was definitely on the same page regarding something else—getting a party started. Back in the rec room, I dove into my duffel bag and pulled out a bottle of tequila that Teddy Mac had donated to the cause, courtesy of his mother's well-stocked bar. "You're going to need this," he'd said. Ashley yanked out a liter of vodka, Mallory pulled out Grand Marnier, Zara brought out a bottle of champagne, and even Caroline revealed a bottle of Boone's Farm. Brandi Lyn accompanied Caroline to the kitchen for ice, limes, cranberry juice, and every supply necessary for good cosmopolitans, and within fifteen minutes we had set up a bar as fine as any tailgating party the South has ever known.

Then we sat down to talk. Or tried to. Nobody had bothered to change out of their dresses, so we were all hoopskirted up. It was a disaster. Balancing our drinks, Zara and I carefully sat down on the couch, only to have our skirts fly right over our heads, just like Brandi Lyn had done earlier. We howled with laughter. And did it again just for fun.

"Are you kidding me?" I yelled. "Are we not even going to be able to sit down in these things?"

"No, you can," replied Mallory. "I'll show you. Move."

I jumped out of the way. Okay, that's an exaggeration. There's no jumping when you're wearing thirty-five pounds' worth of skirts. One side at a time, Mallory kicked up the lower rung of her skirt and grabbed it. Then she shimmied her butt up to the couch, lifted the back of the skirt, plopped it over the back of the couch, and sat. "See, the skirts fly over your head if you sit on the hoop. If you move the hoop out of the way, and don't sit on it, you'll be fine."

"That's like a ten-step process to sit down. And you look ridiculous backing your butt up to the couch like that, by the way."

Zara asked, "How do you know all this, Mallory?"

"Told you. Twelve years I've been waiting. In the meantime I've been practicing in my cousin Lucinda's hoops."

"There is an easier way to sit," added Ashley.

"Oh yeah, show them, Ash!"

"You just cross your ankles and kind of flutter to the ground." Ashley demonstrated, ending up in a flurry of flounces and ruffles as her skirts and hoops collapsed all around her.

That did look easy. "Aha! That's what I'm doing."

So we moved the furniture out of the way and we all "fluttered" to the ground in a circle, ending up looking like a bowl of pastel sherbets.

Finally, the talking began. Ashley started. "I thought Jimmy and I would be together forever," she said.

"I'm sorry, Ashley," Caroline said. "I thought y'all were

the perfect match, what with your fathers being in the same law firm and everything."

A tear came to Ashley's eye. "I did, too. I thought everything was set. We'd finish high school, go to college, get engaged senior year. Get married the next summer. I wanted to have my first baby by the time I was twenty-four."

Wow. "Isn't that young?" I asked.

"Not around here," said Brandi Lyn. "Anyway, it's good to have a life plan."

"I had it *all* planned," continued Ashley. "We even got a room reserved at the Riverview for next Saturday after our Boysenthorp debut for, well, you know . . ."

Mallory gasped. "What?! You didn't tell me that!"

"He said he couldn't wait to get a certain dress up over my head."

I grinned. "I will say this, that's more original than doing it after prom."

"I guess he just couldn't wait for me." More tears came to Ashley's eyes. Poor thing.

I had to ask something, though. "Out of curiosity, Ashley, how did Jimmy feel about your whole life plan?"

"Well, he didn't know about all of it. I mean, we'd talk about where we'd live if we ever got married, but mostly it was something our mothers talked about. That I talked about with them. They just loved the idea of us as a couple."

"Hmmph," I said, sounding like Grandmother. "It sounds more to me like y'all didn't have much choice."

"Yeah, like it was something that your parents expected you to do," said Zara.

"But you loved him, right, Ashley?" asked Caroline.

"Yes, of course I did! I mean . . ." Ashley trailed off.

As Ashley sank into her own head, Mallory turned to Zara. "So what's your problem?"

Zara sighed. "Ugh. My controlling, freak-show father is ruining my life!"

"Sounds familiar," said I.

"He went through my phone."

"Oh no."

"This can't be good."

"I hate it when my parents do that."

"What did he find?"

"Texts. Lots of them. Between me and this boy."

Mallory leaned closer. "Who?"

Zara went conspicuously silent. Totally buttoned up.

"I know!" I said. "It's that guy from the pictures!" I turned to the other girls. "Y'all, I have seen this specimen and he is indeed hottie pa-tottie! Tell, Z, tell!"

"Well," Zara demurred. "It is kind of scandalous, you guys."

"We love scandal!" Mallory cried.

"That's why my father is about to kill me."

"Now I'm interested," Ashley said. We all leaned forward toward the front edge of our dresses.

Zara suppressed a grin. "Well . . . he was a teacher at my school." We all shrieked. A teacher? How taboo-licious!

"Well, he isn't really a teacher, he's a teaching assistant and he's only three years older than me, so it's not that terrible, but still. Daddy is livid." She explained that the specimen's name was Charlie, and he was a student at Georgetown University and he had been the darkroom monitor for her photography class. They had hit it off during the long hours Zara spent developing film and printing pictures, which had turned into having coffee, which had turned into hanging out at his dorm room on a Friday night, which had turned into them dating until her parents had viciously moved her here to Bienville.

"It must be so hard for you!"

"Do you miss him?"

"Every single day. What can I say? He's my muse."

"Awwwww."

"You have a muse?"

"I've never known anyone who had a muse before."

"The thing is, I was supposed to go to DC in a couple of weeks, to see my friends, so Charlie and I started texting, and . . ." Deep breath in. "He invited me to stay with him."

"To stay with him!"

"Here comes the scandal!"

". . . and my dad read all those texts and now he's making me cancel the trip."

"That's so sad!"

"You poor thing!"

"He was threatening to call my old school and get him fired, but Momma talked him down off that ladder."

227

"Ugh, this is terrible."

Zara grimaced. "And I have no idea when I'll see him again. If ever."

Mallory turned to Ashley. "We can make that happen, right, Ash?"

Ashley came out of her funk. "Of course, when we go to DC."

"We'll sneak you out!" Cool, more sneaking around! I raised my glass in the air.

"To sneaking Zara out to see a cute boy!"

"To cute boys!"

"Of which Jimmy is no longer one!"

"Hear, hear!"

We toasted, clinked glasses amidst Mallory screaming, "Don't spill! No spilling on the dress!"

"We need more drinks!"

Mallory jumped up. "I'll get them!" And she bustled back to our bar and fired up her cocktail shaker to make another round of cosmopolitans.

Zara leveled a look at me. "You know what else we need? We need to know what's going on between Jane and Luscious Luke Churchville!"

"Yes we do!" Mallory sang from the bar.

"No we don't!" I sang back to her.

Zara was not giving up. "Come on. Everybody on our team at the fund-raiser noticed that something was going on. I have never seen so much eye ping-pong in my life. Glance here. Glance there. Glance everywhere."

"Ha-ha. I never knew you were so funny, Z."

Ashley jumped on Zara's bandwagon. "And I saw y'all out there on the porch at Lancer's the other night. It looked like some awfully personal words were being exchanged."

"I saw that, too!" Caroline giggled.

"Tell us."

"It won't kill you!"

Oh yes it will, I thought. I had never told anyone the story. Ever. My heart was beating so fast as every eye in the room pounced on me, demanding I tear down the brick wall, pull out the box with Luke's name on it, and open it for all to see. It felt like I was in front of a firing squad, a pastel-colored, cosmo-tipsy, sweetly concerned firing squad. I tried to put them off. "Oh, it's such a long story."

"We have time."

"We have about ten more hours between now and breakfast."

"Please, Jane," said Caroline. "We really want to know."

Something burst inside me. My heart? The dam holding back the waters? Whatever it was, I found myself spouting out everything about everything, from Disney World to Daddy and back again. I told the truth, the whole truth, and nothing but the truth. Every blow, every moment, every detail from five years ago to just last Saturday night. When I was done, the room was totally silent.

"Jane?" Caroline spoke tentatively after a few moments. "I . . . Was that your first kiss?"

I nodded, then in a fit of "Oh my God, I just revealed

way too much!" I awkwardly wriggled my way to standing and rushed over to the bar to make myself another cosmo.

As I returned, I couldn't help but notice that Ashley was staring at me, mouth open as if she wanted to speak. "What, do you want to make fun of me now?" I snapped.

"No. Not at all." She shook her head. "I'm just really sorry for you, Jane."

"You're sorry?"

"Yeah, your family life, I can't imagine how hard it is not to have a mother. Or your father around. To live with your elderly grandmother. It's just not normal."

"Okay. That sounds kind of terrible the way you said that, but I think you actually mean well."

"I do!"

"You've had such a hard life, Jane," Mallory said.

"Harder than anyone else's here, I bet," said Brandi Lyn of all people.

I shrugged. "I don't know. I think everyone has a hard life, one way or another."

Everyone nodded at that one. We sat quietly for a moment.

Finally, Zara broke the silence. "What are you going to do about Luke?"

"What is there to do? It's a done deal. He hates me."

"Do you still like him?"

I thought about it a minute. "How can I? I don't know him. He's a memory. I have no idea who he is now. And he obviously hates me."

"No he doesn't."

"I don't believe that."

I grimaced. "And he's with Mosey or Posey or whatever her name is."

Mallory and Ashley exchanged glances. "I don't think so," said Mallory.

"They may have hooked up at a party or something," Ashley added.

"But if they were really dating, we'd know."

"Yeah, this is Bienville. We'd totally know."

Meanwhile, Caroline was mulling the whole thing over and coming up with a different take. "Jane, I bet he still likes you."

Huh?! "I doubt it."

"No, seriously. I bet he was really hurt by what happened back then and now that you're back in town, he really wants to see you. That's the kind of thing that happens in romance novels ALL the time. There's a misunderstanding, feelings get hurt."

"But because he's a boy"—Ashley switched into total shrink mode—"and boys are notorious for being emotional morons, he lashed out."

"But secretly underneath it all he still loves you."

I nearly snorted my cosmo up my nose. If I had learned one thing it was that my life was definitely not a romance novel. "Yeah, right. Nice fantasy."

Mallory grabbed my hand. "We could talk to him if you want."

"NO!" I barked like a rabid dog. "Absolutely not, no way, no how!"

"Okay, okay. Calm down."

"I'm serious, Mallory, Ashley. I just want to put the whole thing behind me."

"Are you sure?"

"Yes, I'm sure! Leave it alone. Please. Let me forget about him." Clearly, it was time to change the subject. "Anyway, Brandi Lyn," I said, "what's going on with you? I thought you didn't drink anything stronger than Diet Coke? And you've had like, what? Three cosmos already."

She giggled. "Oh, I'm just real tired, that's all. I've just been working hard at the Shack to make extra money and then at night on the dress."

But out of the blue, her entire face transformed. Her easy smile slid away and her lower lip started trembling. She burst into sobs. "I'm sorry, y'all, it's just, I'm so, feeling so emotional. These stories are so sad! Ashley, what Jimmy did to you . . . I would just die if JoeJoe ever acted that way toward me! Zara, the fact that you can't be with the boy you love . . . And Jane, you poor thing! I just feel for you so much!"

It was as contagious as a yawn, her weeping.

Caroline burst into tears.

Then Mallory burst into tears.

Ashley was the next to go. At first she was calm, thanking Brandi Lyn for her sympathy, but once she got going it wasn't long before she was hiccuping and hyperventilating.

"He was my whole life! I don't know how to carry on!" she exclaimed over and over again, as if she were straight out of some Shania Twain song (not that I'm dissing Shania Twain here because I'm not).

Mary, Mother of Meltdowns! What a big, blubbering pastel mess. The scene on the Bienville Civic Center stage four and a half weeks ago was nothing compared to this. This was a sixty-tissues-per-girl-meltdown mess.

Zara and I looked at each other, at first in this "Oh, Lord, can you believe the drama kind of way," but then I couldn't help it, I felt a tear quiver in my eye, and I saw Zara's lips start trembling.

Under such conditions, it should come as no surprise that the histrionics level rose faster than a flood during a category five hurricane. One Maid threw out an idea and then another one picked up on it and we spiraled ourselves into a frenzy.

First it was:

"Boys are dumb!"

"Boys ARE dumb!"

"Boys are SO dumb!"

Then it shifted to:

"Jimmy is such a jerk for breaking up with Ashley in front of everybody!"

"We should have let JoeJoe beat him up!"

"Do you think he still will?"

"Oh yes, he and my brothers would totally do it! You want me to call them?"

"Kind of!"

"No, y'all are talking crazy talk!"

Then it spiraled in this direction:

"Jane, you need to straighten things out with Luke! Tell him the truth!"

"I told y'all, he doesn't care! Although we did save a bird together."

"You saved a bird *together*!"

"Together!"

"That has to mean something, right?"

"Oh, it definitely means something!"

"He still likes you."

"Soooo obvious!"

I shook my head. "No, y'all, it's not." But then I got to thinking. And trust me on this, nothing good comes from thinking after downing three cocktails and interacting with a sixty-Kleenex meltdown. "But you know what *is* obvious? Luke owes me an apology. How dare he make out with some girl right in front of me?"

"Yeah!"

"You are soooo right!"

I turned to Ashley. "And furthermore, how dare Jimmy dump you so publicly? Doesn't he have any manners? Doesn't anyone have any manners anymore?"

"Yeah, Jimmy owes you an apology, Ashley!"

"Luke owes Jane an apology!"

And that's when I got the idea that changed everything. "We should go find them right now and get this taken care of."

"Yeah."

"Yes, ma'am."

"You said it!"

"I wish we knew where they were."

"Shoot. Too bad we don't."

"I know where they are." All eyes flew to Caroline.

"My cousin Jules told me. They're playing pool at his house tonight. Jimmy, Luke, Lancer, all of them."

It took about sixty seconds for that to sink in. Then there was a mad scramble of hoops and ruffles and flounces as we all, as one, waddled to our feet.

Off we went, six sweet little Magnolia Maids, into the night to seek vigilante boy justice, secure in our beautiful newfound friendship.

If only it had lasted.

Chapter Fifteen

"Maybe we shouldn't be driving anywhere," Caroline cautioned.

We were busily fixing our makeup before we went to confront the boys—after all, you have to look supercute while seeking vigilante boy justice—when Caroline made this salient point.

"I'll be right back!" Ashley exclaimed. She bustled out to her car and returned a few moments later with a small handheld device with a tube attached to it.

"What's that?" I asked.

"A Breathalyzer!" she rhapsodized. "Daddy got it for me for Christmas so that I would call him if I ever got too drunk to drive." We eyed it with a combination of shock and awe.

Finally, I articulated what everyone was thinking. "Isn't your dad totally and completely encouraging you to be irresponsible and drink?"

"Jane! He knows I'm going to drink anyway! Might as well make sure I'm doing it responsibly."

I thought about that for a moment, then shrugged. "Okay, it's genius!"

Zara could not believe it. "My daddy would never ever ever consider doing that, not in a million years!"

Ashley passed around the Breathalyzer to see who was sober enough to drive. One by one we inhaled into the device, and a number would flash on the screen telling us our blood alcohol level. Ashley went first and giggled. "Oopsy! I guess it's not me who's driving!" She passed the Breathalyzer to Mallory.

"I am so drunk," Mallory slurred before she even blew. "Look how drunk I am!" she bragged as she flashed her score around.

Brandi Lyn, the lightweight in the crowd, blew a low-ish number, but just looking at her you could tell she was wobbling on her feet. Caroline and I were in the fair to middling range, not quite designated driver material. But Zara won our contest, blowing a very respectable low number. Clearly, she had not been knocking them back like the rest of us.

Ashley raised her hand in victory. "And we have a designated driver!"

"What can I say? I just like to sip," replied Zara.

"Well, you are cut off now, young lady!" said I. "You and only you are responsible for the fate of Bienville's finest feminine specimens!"

We waddled out of the house and decided to take Ashley's SUV, since it had the best chance of accommodating us plus our tons of taffeta.

"How are you supposed to get into a car in one of these things?" I asked. Ever tried to step *up* into an Escalade in a thirty-five-pound dress? Not so easy.

Mallory and Ashley frowned. "Well, that's the thing," said Mallory. "You're not supposed to."

Ashley nodded. "Yeah, you're supposed to carry your skirts in the bag and put them on when you arrive at your appearance."

"Should we go in and change?" asked Brandi Lyn. She just had on the hoopskirt, not the additional heavy layers, but that was still going to be an issue.

Now if we'd been smart, we would have taken all of this as a sign. We would have gone back inside, put ourselves to bed, and forgotten the whole thing.

But instead, I said, "Nooooo! We're Magnolia Maids!"

Ashley got on board. "Yeah! Let's do this!"

I got an idea. "I know!" I cried. "Y'all come push me in!"

Brandi Lyn and Mallory followed me around to the front passenger seat. I grabbed on to the handles in the Escalade. They put their hands on my butt.

"One! Two! Three!" They gave a giant heave as I pulled with all my might, and I soared into the SUV, landing face-first in the leather of the driver's seat. "Yay!" I cried.

"Yay!" everyone else cried.

"Okay, Zara, you come around to the driver's seat and I'll pull you in."

We pushed and pulled each other into the Escalade, ruffles, flounces, hoops, and bonnets flying everywhere. Getting into the car was one thing. Getting those hoops corralled was another. They were popping all over the place. There just wasn't enough room for anyone to settle down into a seat properly. Mallory kept yelling, "Try to collapse them! And don't spill!" Yes, somebody had thought it was a good idea to bring along our liquor for the drive to Jules's house. Again, not the world's best idea.

When we finally got underway, I whipped out my iPhone and took a picture. I burst into laughter when I saw the results. "Oh my God! We don't even look like normal humans! We look like tiny heads floating on a sea of dresses!"

"Let me see! Let me see!" I passed the phone back and everybody started posing for the camera.

When we reached a stoplight, Mallory yelled, "Zara, Jane, turn around! Let me get your picture." Zara put the emergency brake on and shifted in her seat. We leaned our bonnets toward each other and mugged like runway models. Beautiful!

The light turned green and Zara put her foot on the gas. We resumed our drive down Country Club Road, and all was well until Zara's skirt suddenly flew up behind her and knocked her bonnet over her eyes!

"Oh no, I can't see!" she yelled. The car swerved back and

forth across the road as she fought off the lace and taffeta covering her face.

We screamed in terror.

"Ahhhhh!"

"Oh my God! Oh my God!"

"We're gonna die!"

"Oh my God, we're gonna die!"

"Lord, please don't let us die, please don't let us die, please don't let us die!"

"Jane, take the steering wheel!" Zara cried.

I darted forward to grab it, but I was tipsy, remember, so we were still careening a bit out of control. And I guess my sudden move forward must have loosened *my* hoopskirt, because out of nowhere it flew in my face, so I couldn't see, either! I panicked, shouting, "Help! Help!" I jerked the wheel by accident and all of a sudden the Escalade jumped the curb. "Zara, stop the car! Now!" I yelled.

Zara slammed on the brakes, or tried to. "I can't! My skirt's caught under the pedal!"

"Kick it out of the way!" I yelled.

"I'm trying!" But that clearly wasn't working.

"Stand on the brake then!"

Miraculously, Zara was able to lift herself straight and press all her weight on the brake pedal, and finally we screeched to a swerving, gut-wrenching halt.

We froze in stunned silence. After a moment, Brandi Lyn lifted her eyes to heaven. "Oh, most benevolent God," she said with a slur. "Thank you, thank you, thank you for letting us live."

"Amen," we Maids replied in unison.

Alas, that's when we heard the sound of the siren.

It began normally enough, our pull-over. We flipped out, of course, when we realized the siren and the lights were for us, because a) we were all drunk as hell (except Zara), b) the SUV had jumped a curb at Le Moyne Park and come to a stop terribly close to the duck pond, and c) there was enough liquor in the car to service a Mardi Gras float. Everyone rushed to stash the bottles under seats, in the glove compartment, in the way backseat with Brandi Lyn. As the cop approached the driver's-side window, Mallory grabbed the cocktail shaker out of Ashley's hands and frantically searched for the lid. "Where is it? Where is it?" With mere seconds to spare before the officer arrived, I told her to shove the cocktail shaker between her feet and keep still.

"What about the smell?"

"Put something over it!"

"What?"

"I don't know, your skirt!"

As the officer got closer and closer, Brandi Lyn suddenly retched. "Y'all? I'm feeling a little . . . queasy."

"Just keep it together," I said. "We'll be out of this in no time."

By the time the knock of authority sounded on the driver's-side window, we had composed ourselves into the cheeriest group of Magnolia Maids anybody ever saw in their life. "Hello, Officer," we chimed as he leaned down to ask Zara for her license and registration. Officer Unfriendly was clearly not playing along with our perky little game—he frowned when he saw that Zara had to ask Ashley where the registration was. He frowned again when he saw that her driver's license was from DC. "You're not from around here, are you, young lady?"

"No, sir. My family moved here a few months ago."

"You realize that you're supposed to update your license within ten days of change of address?"

"Uh, no, sir. I did not."

"I could give you a citation right now."

"I apologize, sir, I'll take care of it first thing Monday morning."

"You do that." He stared at her, his eyes laser beams burning through her skin. Then he aimed his spotlight into the car, highlighting us one by one.

"Hi, Officer," I said when his light got to me. "We are Bienville's new Magnolia Court. You've heard of us, right?" He didn't look too excited, but at least he nodded. "Well, we're just coming home from our very first Magnolia Court event, and well, we've been having some wardrobe malfunctions." I explained what had happened with my and Zara's skirts and how we had ended up jumping the curb into the park. "But we're fine. Everybody's okay." I gave him my brightest Southern belle smile. "Except for having to wear these super-awkward outfits."

"Y'all, I'm gonna throw up!" Brandi Lyn clawed to get out of the back of the Escalade. "Somebody help me out of here!"

Great. Perfect timing for ruining my cover story. I attempted to bat my eyelashes at the officer. "Poor Brandi Lyn, she hasn't been feeling so good tonight."

"Y'all! Help!"

I jumped out of the front seat and ran to the back and ripped open the door . . . just in time to receive the bountiful gift of Brandi Lyn's vomit all over my bodice. "Ewww!" I screamed.

"Oh, Jane, I'm sorry, so sorry!" And she puked again, but this time only on my skirt. Thank God.

Officer Unfriendly beamed his light back on Zara. "Get out of the car, please." Officer Unfriendly made Zara do the walking test, the one where you have to follow a straight line, then hold your arms out and touch your nose. She passed it with flying colors, thank goodness. Meanwhile, Caroline found a beach towel in the backseat and handed it to me so I could dab the vomit off my chest.

"Okay, young lady," Officer Unfriendly said to Zara as she got back in the car. "Get this vehicle cranked and turned around."

Mallory gasped. "Oh no! You're taking us to jail!"

He shook his head. "No. Suspicious and ridiculous as this situation is, I'm gonna let you girls off." He raised a threatening eyebrow. "This time."

The sighs of relief in the Escalade were so enormous, our sea of dresses ebbed and flowed like a taffeta tidal wave.

The biggest sigh of all came from Caroline. "Thank you, Officer! God bless you, Officer!"

"But," he continued, "I'm gonna make sure you get home without any more incidents. So get this vehicle cranked and let's go."

"Yes, sir! Thank you, sir!" Zara started the engine, and our night probably would have ended there, except . . .

"Wait, follow us home?" I gave the officer a super-fake smile. "Actually, Officer, that won't be necessary."

He leaned down and scowled at me.

"Jane, please." Zara shook her head.

"No, Zara, there's no need for him to follow us."

"Jane, forget about it. Let's just go back to Mizz Upton's and call it a night."

But in my mind we'd done nothing wrong. "But we're fine, Zara. We don't need a police escort."

Zara's eyes pleaded with me to shut up. "The nice officer is just making sure we get home safely. So let's let him."

"But we have to finish our mission for the day," Ashley called from the middle of the backseat. "Excuse me, Officer! We have something we have to do."

"You'll do it tomorrow, then," Officer Unfriendly replied. "You girls are a menace to society driving around in those dresses, and I want you home where you belong NOW. Before you jump any more curbs. Or worse."

But that Ashley, she wasn't having it. She leaned across

244

Mallory to yell out the driver's-side window, "But Officer, we have official Magnolia Maid business! If my uncle, the sponsor of the program, the head of the chamber of commerce, hears about you stopping us, you are going to be officially in trouble!"

Oh no. It was so obvious that the "do you know who I am routine" was pissing off the officer. But the thing that really threw him over the edge was that she leaned over to wag her finger at him, getting into Mallory's face, so Mallory jumped back, which caused her to kick over the cocktail shaker and send its contents streaming across the Escalade's floor. Within seconds, the air reeked of vodka and Grand Marnier, and Officer Unfriendly's nostrils came to serious attention.

"No, young lady," he said. "*You* are officially in trouble. Everybody out of the car. We're going downtown."

Chapter Sixteen

I think it's pretty safe to say that the Bienville County Jail had never seen anything like the sight of six little Magnolia Maids, in varying stages of Magnolia dress, trudging in to the county jail. *Swish, swish, swish.* The officers at the front desk stared, the good citizens filing reports gawked, the folks bailing out their loved ones gaped. Bonnets are very useful, it turns out, for covering your face when you're doing the most humiliating walk of shame ever.

As we were escorted into Cell Block 3, two "ladies of the evening," who had been picked up earlier in the red-light district, greeted us from the next cell over.

"What the hell?" asked Lady One, eyeing our ridiculous getups. "Y'all come through some time travel machine or something? Which a' you is Scarlett?"

Lady Two shook her head. "Uh-uh-uh," she uttered, looking at Zara. "Girl, what you doing wearing that plantation dress? Shoot."

Thank God they put us in our own cell.

Having had a few run-ins like this before, I knew our situation wasn't as bad as it could have been. I tried to cheer up my completely down, suddenly sober crowd. "At least they didn't book us."

No one responded.

"Seriously, y'all. They didn't take our mug shots, didn't fingerprint us. We should be happy."

"Shooooot," drawled Lady Two from the other cell. "She right. Y'all fine, long's they don't fingerprint you."

Caroline spoke from the corner of our cell. "It doesn't matter. My mother's still going to kill me."

"She's going to kill all of us," added Mallory. "There's never been a Maid arrested before! Not even during the civil rights marches of the sixties!"

"Look on the bright side. We'll definitely go down in history, then." I snorted. Gallows humor.

Mallory looked like she was going to burst into tears. "It's not funny!" she cried.

"Oh my God, my scholarship! Sorry, Lord." Brandi Lyn's hand flew to her chest and she looked heavenward in apology. "No one gives scholarships to girls who have been arrested! How am I going to pay for college?"

I heaved a sigh. "Clearly, you girls haven't been in trouble much. Let me break it down for you. The City of Bienville can't afford to have the pristine Magnolia Maid name sullied. They can't afford to let this go on our permanent record. It would be a humiliation to them.

They're gonna let us go with a hand slap, I will bet you money."

"I'd bet on that," called Lady Two from the next cell. "Bunch a' white girls ain't gonna have no problems getting their sorry selves out a' trouble. Hey, sugar, you wanna spare a smoke?" Of course I handed her a cigarette. We were going to need allies if we were going to be in jail long.

Zara glared at me. "Excuse me, Miss America's Most Wanted," she spat. "But do you have a crystal ball hidden underneath that antebellum dress forecasting the outcome of this situation? I'm sorry, but I think the rest of us are a little worried here."

"Worried? Who's worried?" I asked.

"I am." Mallory furrowed her brow.

"Me!" Brandi Lyn raised her hand.

Caroline scratched at her arm. "I have hives."

"Can I ask you something?" Zara asked.

I shrugged. Might as well.

"Did you even think about me? About how I felt? Or any of us? Because if you had, you might have thought about how terrified I was. I nearly wrecked back there! And then when I heard that siren. I was the one driving the car! I was shaking to death! All I wanted to do was get out of there and go home and then he was gonna let us and you had to go and pick a fight!"

"What do you mean pick a fight?" I spluttered. "I was just saying we didn't need an escort! Ashley's the one who pissed him off!"

"Well, I would expect that from Miss Name-Dropper-Holier-Than-Thou over there, but you? I thought you had more sense than to pick a fight with a cop! But then that's your specialty, isn't it? Picking fights."

I rolled my eyes. "Oh, please. I don't pick fights."

"That's all you do."

"No I don't."

"Well, you kinda do."

I swiveled around to find Brandi Lyn actually agreeing with Zara. "What? How?"

"Well, remember how you wouldn't let me quit when Mizz Upton said I should? And then you declared war on her? That's kind of picking a fight, isn't it?"

Caroline nodded. "And you tried to get me to change my queen vote to Brandi Lyn as part of your ongoing fight with Ashley."

"You get into a fight with Ashley every chance you get," said Mallory.

"Except tonight," replied Zara. "When the two of you actually joined forces to insist we go find those lame boys!"

"Zara, I . . ." I went silent. I was what? Sorry? Tipsy? Annoyed? Misunderstood? Some combination of all the above?

"You done it now, girl!" cackled Lady One from the next cell. "Gone crazy after boys! You should be ashamed of yo'self." She pointed at my silver earrings. "You wanna let me have those earrings? They sure is pretty!"

I shook my head. "You know what, you guys? That's not

fair! How can you say I'm just all about picking fights? I have worked really hard for the Magnolia Maids! I spearheaded the fund-raiser idea. And I've been there for you all personally, too! Brandi Lyn, I got you that makeover, and Caroline, I tried to cheer you up about your mother, and Mallory, well, I gave you advice on how to deal with the Ashley/Jimmy/Katherine situation. I think y'all should be a little more appreciative of me!"

Somewhere in the middle of that, Ashley's mouth hit the floor. "What? Jane, you gave Mallory advice?" She whirled on Mallory. "You knew? And you asked Jane about it? You told me you had no idea!"

Uh-oh.

"Well, I . . . I . . . I . . . ," Mallory stammered.

"You kept that information from me? And let me suffer the worst humiliation of my life?"

"I wanted to tell you, I really did!"

"How could you not?"

"I was scared."

"Scared? Of what?" Ashley screamed, sounding scary.

Mallory shrunk back against the wall. "I love you to death, Ash, but you're always so . . . Everything's such a big deal with you."

"What do you mean 'everything's such a big deal' with me?" Ashley screeched, making a big deal of everything. Mallory zipped her lip. But it was too late. The lid to Pandora's box was off and Ashley was not, I repeat *not*, backing down. Mallory soon found herself tearfully confessing that there was indeed some truth to what James had said that night on the bay. Everything always had to go Ashley's way and the fits she threw when it didn't were known the whole state over. Ashley denied it, of course, saying that Mallory was overreacting, which spurred Mallory on to a dissection of the history of Ashley's demands starting with part 1: The Ken and Barbie Years, through to part 7: Birth of a Magnolia Maid.

Mallory's venting was like lice in kindergarten—contagious. While she built up steam with each installment of the Ashley Must Have Her Way Show, Zara laid into me even more for not backing down and letting her handle the cop situation as she saw fit.

Brandi Lyn tried to play diplomat. "Y'all! Stop it! We're supposed to be sisters in Magnolia Maid love!"

Everyone groaned.

"If we were ever sisters, it's all over now!" Ashley retorted.

"Y'all, hush!" Caroline begged. "We're going to get in even more trouble!"

"How?" Zara replied. "We're already in prison! What else can they do to us?"

At that moment, Mallory shouted, "AND I already had a dress picked out for tryouts when you e-mailed us saying we had to coordinate and that pink was *your* color! *I* wanted to wear pink! But nooooooo, Ashley had to get her way and wear pink!"

Oh, wow. Had Ashley really sent that memo straight out of my devious imagination? Of course she had.

Then, above the chaos, a little voice wailed. "I have to quit the Magnolia Maids!"

Girl by girl, we all turned to the source of the cry: Brandi Lyn.

"What?"

"Huh?"

"Why?"

Through tablespoons of tears, Brandi Lyn blubbered out that making the dress herself had turned into a disaster of epic proportion. "Have y'all ever tried to sew on taffeta?"

We all shook our heads. Not a one of us knew how to sew.

"It's impossible! First, it was taking forever, and what with all the extra hours I've been putting in at the Krawfish Shack to pay for the fabric, I simply could not find the time to work on it! But then I was up late sewing the other night, and I was half asleep and I made a mistake and made a mess of the ruffles on the skirt, and, and ruined yards and yards of fabric." She started gasping for air. "And I'll have to start all over again and buy new material, but there's no way I can afford it. So I'm going to have to quit!"

"So that's why you've been throwing back the cosmos all evening," I said.

"I'm sorry, y'all," wept Brandi Lyn. "I'm so sorry. Caroline, you'll have to take my place."

Caroline leapt off the jail bench. "No, what? No!" She swayed precariously.

"Oh, don't faint, Caroline. We've already done that once."

Brandi Lyn and I rushed to her side and helped her sit back down.

"You can't quit, Brandi Lyn! I can't be a Magnolia Maid!"

"You can! You're beautiful! You'll be great!" Brandi Lyn tried to keep a brave face, but her lip was trembling like a California earthquake.

"I'll faint. I'll fall down!" Caroline's arms and chest turned red and blotchy. Poor thing, now she really did have hives! "I'll look like a whale in the dress!"

"We all will," I said, not very helpfully.

"People will laugh at me. My mother will yell at me. Oh my God, my mother." She didn't even have to go into detail on that one. We knew what she meant. "Please. Please, y'all. You can't let Brandi Lyn quit. I'm begging you."

That's about the time old Walter Murray Hill walked in.

Chapter Seventeen

We all live with expectations, whether we realize and acknowledge them or not. Our expectations define the way that we think our world should be, the way things should go. Some expectations are obvious. When you walk into a restaurant, you expect someone to serve you a plate of food. When you go to school, you expect to be bored out of your mind (I mean, learn something). You go to a shoe store, you expect them to sell shoes, not handguns.

So when you get dragged into the Bienville County Jail for drinking under age, what do you expect from the authority figure who shows up to bail your behind out? An endless lecture and punishment up the wazoo. And if you're a Magnolia Maid, you expect to be kicked off the Court, then sent home for more punishment from your God-fearing, authority-respecting Southern parents.

Me, I was convinced we were going to be fine, but the girls were terrified. The minute Uncle Walter showed up, Ashley dropped the catfight and switched into full damage-control mode. "Oh, Uncle Walter, I don't know why that officer stopped us!" "Yes, we did each have a little teeny-weenie drink but all those big bottles must have been Daddy's, I don't know where they came from! I'm so worried that Zara's in trouble, Uncle Walter. Please say it isn't so!" Of course, she was trying to cover her own butt, but she was at least covering everyone else's in the process.

Mallory also went into hysterics mode when Uncle Walter came in. She was so panicked about losing the opportunity to wear her antebellum dress and represent Bienville that she wept uncontrollably as we were escorted into an investigation room. "Please don't kick us off the Maids. Please don't take this away from us! I'll just die if you take this away from us! Just die!"

The rest of us remained quiet.

There were only four chairs in the interrogation room (just like in the one Kyra Sedgwick uses to interview people of interest on *The Closer*—God bless her and her totally fake Georgia accent). Walter Murray Hill gestured for us all to take a seat, and everyone did except me and Zara. We repaired to opposite corners, like prizefighters waiting for the bell to announce the first round.

Standing at the head of the table, Walter Murray Hill loomed above us. "Girls. Maids," he corrected himself. "This is a night that will go down in Magnolia Maid history."

"I knew it!" weeped Mallory. "No Maid has ever been arrested before. We're the first ones. It's a travesty!"

"It is true that this is the first time I have ever in my life gotten out of my bed in the middle of the night to bail a bevy of Magnolia Maids out of jail. I have on more than one occasion bailed out my sons and their wayward friends, but you girls." He shook his head. "I thought y'all had more sense than this, okay." One by one, we hung our heads in shame.

Walter Murray Hill sighed deeply. "Maids, I knew changing up the Court was going to be hard. Many of my acquaintances and colleagues told me time and again that the way things were was fine. 'Walter, why go rocking the boat, okay,' they said. 'Let's run things the way we always have.' To those people I have said, Bienville's ready. We can do it. Let's leave the past behind. Move into the future."

Mr. Walter paused and looked us each in the eye. "But I may have made a mistake here, okay. I did not take into consideration how hard this was going to be on you all. Ashley, Mallory, your expectations about what this year was going to look like were not met, and you've had a hard time bonding with the other girls."

They nodded, though their agreement lacked the fervor and anger of their initial reaction at the pageant all those weeks ago.

"Zara." Walter Murray Hill turned to her. "You being a newcomer to town, and Jane, your having been away so long, well, it's affected your ability to fit in. Brandi Lyn, I sure am sorry to hear about your money situation. That's a real issue, it sure is, and I didn't take that into account when

I approved you. Caroline, I know it's not easy for you, what with your mother being the sponsor." He sighed again. "I kept thinking, though, this group of girls, they're interesting. Modern. They're going to be able to do a lot for us here in Bienville. You proved that right with the fund-raiser, that's for sure. And I thought with time you'd all be able to pull it together. But what happened tonight . . ." He closed his eyes. "Tells me I made a mistake. A big one. Do you have any idea how many rules in the handbook you just broke?"

I raised my hand. "Four. Drinking while wearing the dress, driving while wearing the dress, wearing the dress on an outing not approved by the organization, getting arrested while wearing the dress."

"That is correct, Jane. And one of those is a crime. Do you have any idea what I've just had to do to convince the police not to book you? Mizz Upton was right. This is the most unfit group of Maids I have ever encountered. Which is why I'm considering disbanding the organization for the year."

Boy, when he said that, you could have heard a hoopskirt drop, it was so quiet. We were all a little shocked by Walter Murray Hill's announcement. This was so much more serious than what I had seen coming.

And we may have been completely and totally mad at each other, but there ain't nothing like a group of Magnolia Maids on the verge of being disbanded. No way were we going to let this end now.

"No, Mr. Walter, please don't!"

"We'll never do anything like this again!"

"I know we're difficult, Mr. Walter, but we can do this!"

"We are modern!"

"The fund-raiser is only the beginning of what we are capable of!"

"We can live up to your expectations!"

"Are you kidding? We can surpass them!"

We were such a whirling dervish of ferocious persuasion, Walter Murray Hill couldn't keep up with us. He held his hands out to shut us up. "I hear you! I hear you! I want to give you all another chance. I want this to work, too. But there are going to be some ground rules, okay." He cleared his throat. "Number one. I do not—repeat DO NOT—want Martha Ellen Upton to hear word one about this. I do NOT want it in the gossip columns. I've talked to the boys out there about making sure this thing stays private, and they've agreed. You girls do your part and keep your mouths shut. Don't tell a soul. I mean anyone. Not your parents, your siblings, your friends, your boyfriends. The first phone call I get with somebody asking about Magnolia Maids being hauled to jail, I will disband you. Do you understand?"

We couldn't yell "Yes, sir!" fast enough. This was really good news, and we all knew it. The fact that Mr. Walter was powerful enough to control the small-town gossip mill was going to make life a whole lot easier.

"Number two. You girls are going to sponsor an alcohol-education course for teens as one of your charity events, and you're going to actually take the class yourselves." Oh, I had to hand it to Mr. Walter. Make it look like we were helping the community, when we were really saving ourselves from a future as lushes? Genius.

"Number three. I need you to elect a queen by Saturday, okay. Number four. If anything else happens like this again . . ."

"We know," said Ashley.

"We'll be the first Court in history to be disbanded," said Mallory.

"Exactly. Now don't you ever let me catch you here again."

As he escorted us out of the police station, Walter Murray Hill chuckled. "You know, Maids," he said. "You girls have spark and passion. You remind me of the first girl who ever asked me when was I going to integrate the Court."

"Really?" Mallory leapt on this information like a rooster on a hen. "A Maid asked you to integrate? I never knew that!"

"A queen, as a matter of fact. She said, 'Mr. Walter, how can we say that we truly represent the city of Bienville, which is a wonderfully diverse place, if we only have wealthy white girls on the Court? It's just not right, Mr. Walter,' she told me." Melancholy invaded his words as he shook his head. "I've heard her voice in my head every one of the twenty-five years it's taken me to get up the gumption to do it."

"Who was she?" Mallory asked. "The maid who asked you?"

Walter Murray Hill put his hand on my shoulder and looked me in the eye. "Cecilia Fontaine. Jane's mom."

Chapter Eighteen

Unlike Uncle Walter, I still couldn't hear my mother's voice. All these weeks of cruising around B'ville asking her questions, trying to integrate her into my life as Grandmother suggested, and I still couldn't hear her.

By the time I turned nine, the ALS had started to work its decaying ways on the muscles of her vocal cords. At first, it sounded like she was slurring, and we'd laugh that *oops! She must have had one too many glasses of champagne!* But as the disease stole more and more power from the neurons in her throat, Mom's words came out as grunts and groans struggling to shape themselves into comprehensible sentences. Sadly, more and more often, our ears were incapable of making sense of them. Along came the DynaVox, and Mom would spend endless spans of time typing her thoughts into a mini-laptop that would then read them in a computer-generated voice. "Dyna," we called her, and she eventually became the only way Mom could communicate. So what did the real voice of the fully capable woman my mother had once been sound like? I couldn't remember. Was it screechy and high-pitched? Or low and breathy? Did she call my name quickly—"Jane!"? Or did she sing it out into two syllables, "Jay-ayne"? How did she construct a sentence? Did she ramble on? Or was she efficient and precise with her word choice? At least I remembered her laugh. That never changed, no matter how much her speech deteriorated. It kicked off as a bell tinkling, but if something was really funny, Mom's laugh turned into a train rumbling high-speed off the tracks into sweet chaos. Even after she couldn't speak, that woman could laugh, and she loved to hear me laugh. She called my laugh "her sweet nectar." Cheesy, I know, but I liked it.

I wonder what she'd say about my laugh now that it's all hoarse and croaky from the cigarettes? Ugh.

And what would she say about the train wreck that was my own personal Magnolia Maid experience? Ugh times two.

I wish I could describe the final days of rehearsals as full of forgiveness and friendship, love, peace, and happiness. But the damage had been done. Regardless of our passionate plea that Mr. Walter not disband the Court, we had fallen apart. Chatterbox Brandi Lyn had resigned and it was like we had all received a memo that no one was to talk to or look at anyone else. Ashley wasn't speaking to Mallory, Brandi Lyn wasn't talking to anybody because well, she wasn't there, Zara wasn't talking to me, and Caroline was so terrified she just wasn't talking, period. She was a walking zombie, and who could blame her? Mizz Upton had ramped herself up into a frenzy way beyond her normal freak-show level. On the one hand, she was delighted that she had gotten one of her so-called undesirables off the Court. On the other, she worried like a madwoman about how the debut was going to come off since Caroline wasn't "Magnolia-ready." She constantly fretted about all the potato chip–eating and romance novel–reading Caroline had engaged in instead of participating in training. Mizz Upton took every opportunity to remind her of all this, and let me tell you, that's such an effective way to inspire someone to greatness. Tear them down as much as possible so they'll feel really crappy about themselves, then they'll rise to fabulous heights. Riiiiiiiiiggggghhhhtttt. Whatever. Never fear, she used the same tactic on the rest of us as well. "When are you Maids going to understand that you simply are not ready for the responsibilities that lie before you!" Had we perfected our banking up? No! Did we have our curtsies down? NO, no, NO! Did we have any idea how to do the flight formation correctly? NO because we didn't have a queen yet.

I tried to talk to Zara, but she wasn't having it. Oh, she wallpapered a veneer of detached politeness/ polite detachment, however you want to put it, onto her countenance, but she made a point of escaping over to the other side of the room as soon as she could extricate herself. *Fine, be that way, Zara,* I thought.

So, yeah, since nobody was talking to anybody at re-

hearsal, and I didn't feel much like talking to anybody anyway, B'ville had turned into a ghost town again. I had a lot
of time on my hands, so I ran. I got addicted to *Glee*, which I
watched while carefully sponging Brandi Lyn's vomit off my
dress with dish soap. I started to look forward to Cosmo's
visit and prepared for his arrival by trolling the Internet
for everything I could find on international business and
shipping. After all, we'd need *something* to talk about
over long, leisurely dinners at the Petroleum Club. And
I roamed around Grandmother's creakingly empty house
trying to recollect my dead mother's voice and thinking
about Walter Murray Hill's midnight revelation that it was
she who pushed the idea of integrating the Magnolia Maids
to begin with. Of course it had been Cecilia. Cecilia at seventeen had been blessed and perfect. Everybody loved her.
She never did a thing wrong, had a completely normal life
with two adoring parents. If she were alive, Daddy would
never have left town, I never would have been kicked out
of my own life and packed off to boarding schools or developed a bad attitude. Certainly, I would never have gotten a tattoo. No, I would have been sweet and wonderful
and loving and kind and adored and adoring of others in
return. I would have lived in a beautiful pink castle with a
cute little pink lapdog and driven a little pink convertible
and come in singing "The Hills Are Alive with the Sound
of Muuuuuuu-sic!" every day after school and would have
just *adored* life! Cecilia and Cosmo and I would have gone
on family vacations together to Paris and eaten croissants

on the Seine and waxed eloquent about how *fabulous* our family life was!

Ewwwwww. Enough of that. But I did ponder over and over the question what would Cecilia do if she were in this situation?

I would have given anything to hear the answer.

A few days after the jail incident and about a week before our Boysenthorp debut, I was sitting out on the back porch furtively puffing on cigarettes and pondering the whole scenario once again. Zara's words were starting to infest my thought process. Was I personally responsible for this mess? Had I really overstepped my bounds? Hmmm. Okay, so maybe I did go a *little* crazy. Maybe I could have controlled my mouth a little better. Looked at the whole situation more clearly. Decided to keep my bear-sized trap shut given the fact that everyone in the car was tipsy. Maybe I *had* made a mistake.

And if Walter Murray Hill hadn't come down to the police station and thrown some of his high-class Old Bienville weight around, we might have been booked and gone to court and had to have done community service of a most un-Magnolia Maid variety. Me, I was accustomed to such getting in trouble and to paying the consequences—it had been my way of life for years—but the rest of the girls, they didn't have the criminal element gene anywhere near their DNA. No wonder the whole thing bothered them. Maybe I *was* to blame!

In the middle of the sinking ship of my unwelcome self-realization, the doorbell rang. I threw open the front door to find Ashley standing there.

Ashley?!

I glanced out to the street to see her Escalade, recovered from impoundment, parked at the curb. So she wasn't a hallucination, but still. All I could do was gape at the apparition before me until she rolled her eyes and scolded, "Jane!!! The proper thing to do is to invite me in and offer me a sweet tea."

Shockingly, I did exactly what she said and a few minutes later we were out back on the porch. Grandmother had left for her Genealogical Society meeting, so I lit up another cigarette. "What are you doing here?" I asked Ashley.

"Well, don't get too excited! It's only because I have no one else to talk to that I'm here."

"Still freezing out the Mal-ster?"

"Yes. And I'm certainly not talking to Katherine. And Courtney, well, she's as big a part of it as anybody else." Ashley took a sip of her sweet tea. "You know the worst thing? We all live at Bienville Place. There are only four houses, Jane, and three of them contain people I never want to see again in my life!" Agitated, she grabbed for one of my cigarettes.

I raised an eyebrow. "Ashley, you smoke?"

"Sometimes." She lit up, took two puffs, coughed up a storm, stubbed out the cigarette. "Ugh! How can you do this?"

"Practice. Self-hatred. Love of the nasty."

Ashley jumped up and started pacing. "And I can't go anywhere without seeing someone who was at Lancer's the other night! Everybody in our circle, even the people who weren't there, knows what happened. They're all talking about me, I just know it!" She whirled in my direction. "Do you have any idea what that feels like?"

I laughed. "Uh, yeah. Happens to me every day."

Ashley glared at me. "Thanks, Jane, the last thing I need right now is your sarcasm." She slammed her sweet tea on the table and jumped up to leave.

I grabbed her arm. "Wait, I'm not being sarcastic!" I said. "In all seriousness, Ashley, it happens every day. Some old blue hair, or some middle-aged friend of my mother will see me out and tell me I'm the spitting image of Cecilia and how kind and generous and fabulous she was and how sad it is that I'm left here without parents. That's what they say to my face. And I know what they say behind my back is even worse because Mizz Upton told me."

Ashley's head rocked into a slow nod. "That's true. People do talk about you. *I* talked about you. . . . Oh my God!" Her eyes fell to her sandals, in something that kind of appeared to be . . . shame? "Oh, Jane. I am so sorry. I just didn't think."

"It's okay." I shrugged. "Gossip. It's Bienville's favorite pastime."

Ashley sighed and sat back down. "I don't see how you stand being talked about so much. I saw Andrew Lancer at the Stop and Pump the other day, and you know what he did? He turned and acted like he didn't see me. Like he didn't see me! We've been friends since the sandbox, Jane! How could he?"

I sympathized. "Or what about this? Has this happened? Where someone comes up to you and acts all friendly, 'How are you doing? How have you been?' But the whole time you just know they're thinking 'Wait till I call so-and-so and tell her what's going on!'"

Ashley gasped. "Oh my God, that happened yesterday! I ran into Missy Milliner at Dillard's, you know her, right?" I shook my head. "She's Katherine's first cousin on her mother's side, so of course she's heard about everything. It was so obvious she was pumping me for information!" Ashley looked relieved. "Jane, you totally get it!"

"I told you I live it," said I. "By the way, what's the news on our jail time? Has it gotten out?"

"No. I think Uncle Walter really squashed it."

"We should write him a thank-you note. 'Dear Mr. Walter, thank you for saving our butts and keeping jail time off our permanent records.'"

Ashley laughed, and so did I. Wow, laughing with Ashley. One for the history books, as Mallory would say.

"There's something I've been wondering, Jane," Ashley said. "That night, down at the bay, you tried to save me, didn't you?"

I looked away.

"Because I've been thinking about it," she continued. "And I remember it was you who pushed so hard for us have a dance party. Then to leave. You knew what was happening and you tried to get me out of there, didn't you?"

Finally, I nodded.

"Why did you do that for me? After I was so horrible to you? Why?"

I shrugged. "Oh, you know, that party was boring anyway. All those drunk bastards running around with their Ping-Pong paddles and their beer bongs. It was time to go."

Ashley leveled a no-nonsense "I am not letting you get away with that answer" look at me.

"Okay, fine," I confessed. "I just didn't think anyone deserved that kind of humiliation. Not even you."

"Wow. Thanks, Jane."

"You're welcome." Ashley reached for another cigarette but I knocked her hand away. "Ashley! You don't smoke!"

"I can't help it. I'm just so nervous." Her fingers tapped incessantly on the arms of Grandmother's antique wooden rocking chairs. "It's funny, Jane. I've been thinking about what you and Zara said the other night, about Jimmy. About how it sounded like I was just doing what everybody, what my mother, expected."

"Really?"

"I'm starting to wonder if I ever really liked him, I mean for me. Or if it was just for her." She sighed. "But still, I don't think I can do this, Jane. I can't go out in public and be the laughingstock of the young set." All the breath in her body exploded out in an even deeper sigh. "I have to quit."

"Quit what? *The Magnolia Maids?*" I leapt out of my chair. "What! No, no, no. You can't quit, too!"

She burst out laughing. "Wait. *You* are trying to get *me* not to quit?"

"Seriously, Ashley, you can't skulk around town hiding from everyone until you go off to college! You have to make your next public appearance a huge triumphant splash! You have to put on your beached-whale dress and twirl your parasol and go out there and show everyone that you're just fine. In fact, you're perfect. In fact, Ashley part two, now that that cretin James is out of your life, is more than perfect. You're better than ever."

A slow grin crept across Ashley's face. "Oh my God, Jane, that's good advice!"

"I know. I'm the expert at picking fights and throwing things in people's faces." I flashed a grin that could only be described as rueful.

She grinned back. "That's true, you are."

I chose my next words carefully, knowing full well I was going out on a limb. "But Ashley, I don't mean to sound mean, but you really are a controlling, demanding princess. You do have a knack for making life hell for people." I braced myself for a furious response.

But I am happy to say that Ashley didn't shake me off at all. "I am starting to realize that," she replied. "Except I prefer to use the word *belle*. Controlling, demanding belle." She winked, which totally made me giggle, which got her started giggling and before I knew it, we were giggling together. Our giggles turned into belly laughs, and our belly laughs led us over the invisible threshold of enmity into friendship. Had my own worst enemy just turned out to be a friend? Dear Lord! Sorry, Brandi Lyn.

When the laughing stopped, Ashley wiped away her tears and said, "No, I'm realizing that maybe it's time to let some things go. That maybe I don't have to control *everything*. Just some things."

"Awww, progress. So nice to see."

"Let's say I do stay on with the Magnolias. This thing is a *mess*. How in the world are we going to get it together?"

"I know. Every day I sit here and ask myself what Cecilia would do."

"Cecilia?"

"My mom! The most perfect Magnolia Maid ever? You may have heard of her?" I sighed. "She'd know how to pacify everybody's hurt feelings, how to save Caroline from her worst nightmare ever, scrounge up some dress for Brandi Lyn. . . ."

And that's when it hit me. Sweet Maids a-Milking! Of course! The answer was right in front of me! I flew out of my chair and yanked Ashley out of her seat so fast, sweet tea exploded out of her glass and onto the tile floor.

We didn't even stop to clean it up.

Chapter Nineteen

Master plans require finesse, elegance, allowances for contingencies, and just for fun, the element of surprise. During my tenure as mischief maker numero uno at my various boarding schools, I developed quite a facility for masterminding the most demanding plans. However, unlike those, Operation Return to Magnolia was about making things go right. Not wrong. *Right.* At a public event. With oh, say, a thousand people in attendance. The stakes were as high as that poker game in *Casino Royale*, the one with superhottie Mr. Daniel Craig. Every step of the plan had to come off without a hitch. In the hours following the unexpected solidification of our friendship, Ashley and I designed the foolproof plan, and it went something like this:

Step one: the makeups after the breakups. We piled into Ashley's Escalade and swung by Mallory's so that the healing could begin. Mallory burst into tears when she answered the door and saw Ashley. She blubbered on and on about how sorry she was and she didn't mean it about Ashley being such a difficult person and would she ever forgive her? Ashley countered, "No, you're right, I was a bitch." That dried Mallory's tears in like a millisecond. You should have seen the way she looked at Ashley, as if she had suddenly been inhabited by aliens. "Really? You . . . *agree* with me?" Ashley admitted that we both had decided to turn over a new leaf. We outlined our master plan and, in a fit of hysterical delight, Mallory got on board.

Step two: My making up with Zara, was a lot more complicated. We piled back into the Escalade, and drove out to the country club where Zara's cousin Chinay let us in and told us we'd find her out by the tennis court. Zara was out there banging the crap out of tennis balls flying at her at eighty mph, courtesy of the latest in tennis-ball-serving technology. To say she was stunned to see the three of us parade onto her court would be putting it mildly. Five tennis balls in a row whizzed by her head, hitting the wall behind her before she gathered herself up and resumed lobbing the balls back across the net. I have to hand it to Zara. She's no Williams sister but she could hit that ball for sure. Ashley and Mallory shot the breeze with her for a few minutes, commenting on how lovely her home was and how lucky she was to have a tennis court, she must just love that. Zara grunted out polite comments in between hits, but it was clear she wasn't really thrilled to have us there. Me, I stood watching each ball shoot out of the machine, vaguely listening to this conversation go down until Ashley announced we were here on a mission.

"Go ahead, Jane," said Ashley. "Tell her."

"Tell me what?" Zara didn't even glance my way.

I cleared my throat. "Well. Um. I've been thinking about what you said. And you're right. I'm the one who pushed things so that we got in trouble. And if I had kept my mouth shut, we would have gone home and gone to bed and slept like little angels."

Zara slammed another ball over the net. Was it my imagination or was she banging on those balls even harder than when we arrived?

"And?" prompted Ashley.

"And that even though I am often convinced that I am the all-knowing mistress of the universe, I should respect your feelings about how to handle situations that apply to you."

"And?"

"And I'm going to try to keep my mouth a little more closed and try to be a little more civil in my approach to discord."

"And?"

Oh shoot. Here came the hard part. I became riveted by the top of the tennis net blowing in Bienville's perky summer wind.

"Jane?" Ashley prompted.

I sighed. "Fine. I'm sorry."

Zara stopped hitting the ball. Put down her racket.

Turned off the machine. "Okay, I accept. And thank you. But why did it take all three of you to come over here for one of you to apologize?" So we told her our master plan, she agreed it was genius, and we quickly bundled ourselves back into the Escalade.

Next step: Caroline.

Mizz Upton nearly had a fit when she saw us all on her front porch. "I am as delighted I can be that you girls are finally getting along! Isn't it wonderful? And are we electing a queen today?"

"No, not today," said Ashley.

"But soon," I added.

Mizz Upton sent us upstairs looking for Caroline. Really, all we wanted was Caroline's stamp of approval before we went any further. We were pretty sure she'd give it to us, but no one expected her to burst into tears of joy. She cried and cried and thanked us profusely then hopped in the car and off we went in pursuit of step four: Brandi Lyn.

I called Brandi Lyn's house, and her mother told us that she was working but she sure would love for us to visit! So we all drove out to the Bienville Causeway, that long thin strip of land that traverses the Bienville Bay. It's a survivor, that strip of land. Like Brandi Lyn. It's lived through so many hurricanes and tropical storms, people say it's blessed. Well, except for the hollow shells of a dozen former motels and restaurants that were beaten into submission by 150 mph winds and thirty-foot waves. But not Karl's! The original Karl (I think it's Karl IV who runs the place now) opened up a fried seafood stand back in the forties, then added a dining room off one side here, another off that side there, as the place grew more popular with each passing decade. When the hurricanes got bad, one of the Karls hired a couple of cranes and lifted the whole ramshackle sprawl of a place up on stilts not one, not two, but *three* stories high. You've got a great view—almost out to the Gulf of Mexico—once you take a seat at your table, but it is a major pain in the butt to get up there just to get your eat on. Believe it or not, there's no elevator.

Brandi Lyn went into hysterics when she saw us. "I cannot believe that y'all have taken the time to come and see me! It is so sweet! I've been missing you all week and here you are! Come and sit! Here! Have the best picnic table in the joint! And a basket of Karl's World Famous Puppies and Poppers—a delicious combination of hush puppies and jalapeño poppers (they're hot but not *tooooooooo* hot)—on me!"

As we dove into Puppies and Poppers and brown plastic tumblers of Diet Coke, I got down to business. "Brandi Lyn," I said, "we need you. And we have decided, as a group, that we are not letting you quit."

"Oh, y'all are so cute! I am such a lucky girl! But you know I can't afford it."

"Yes you can." And I laid out the next stages of the master plan.

When I was done, Brandi Lyn chewed on her lip. "I don't know, Jane. That's still a thousand dollars, easy, I bet!"

Ashley shrugged. "We're going to pay for it."

"You are?" Brandi Lyn couldn't hide her surprise.

"I know I fought against you," Ashley said. "But you're an asset to the Magnolia Maid community and we need you."

We all nodded our agreement.

"But it's too much!" Brandi Lyn protested. "I can't ask that of y'all!"

"I'd withdraw a thousand dollars of my own money right this very second if I didn't have to be a Magnolia Maid," Caroline said, nodding vigorously.

Brandi Lyn burst into tears of joy. Sweet Willows a-Weeping, we were a crying bunch today. Brandi Lyn got another waitress to cover the rest of her shift, and we headed off into the hot, hot humidity to activate steps five through five thousand of the master plan.

It was going to be an action-packed couple of days.

It almost worked. The flurry of activity and excitement I had generated by figuring out the answer to the question, "What would Cecilia do?" had almost gotten my mind off Luke.

Almost.

But not quite.

Every so often—okay, every five seconds or so—my encounters with Luke would pop into my head. And I'm not sure which was more harrowing, reliving the "he has a girlfriend" moment that made things suck, the "saving the bird" moment when things seemed awesome, or the ancient "busted by Cosmo" moment that served as the beginning of the end. All I knew was that I was NOT looking forward to seeing him again.

Unless it involved him crawling back to me with a dozen roses in his mouth, apologizing and begging me to forgive him.

As if there were a snowball's chance in high humidity of that.

Chapter Twenty

"Where are they?" Caroline asked, her voice just loud enough to carry across the Boysenthorp Manor ladies' parlor where we were all dressing in anticipation of our impending grand debut.

"Shhhhhh!" I whispered, jerking my head in the direction of her mother. Mizz Upton was a nervous Nelly fluttering between Mallory and Ashley, making sure their dresses were fitting right. "Sure, Caroline, I'll fix your bow for you!" I announced cheerfully, acting like I was snapping her bow on the back of her dress. "Let me put a little extra fluff in that." I leaned close to Caroline's ear and lowered my voice. "They'll be here, don't worry."

If truth be told, though, I was a little worried, too. We had decided to proceed according to Mizz Upton's game plan, meaning that we had dragged Caroline, dress and all, down to Boysenthorp Gardens and insisted that she act as if she were going to make her debut with us. The idea behind this was that the less notice we gave Mizz Upton of the changes we were making in the lineup, the less time she would have to create reasons to prevent Brandi Lyn from coming out with us. But Caroline was right to be worried. Brandi Lyn was supposed to have arrived ten minutes ago with Teddy Mac Trenton and Lacey Wilkes Hawkes. Where were they?

I whipped out my iPhone and dialed Brandi Lyn. "Where are you?" I whispered.

Brandi Lyn's voice was shaking with nerves. "Something happened with the hem! I don't know!"

"But you're on your way, right?"

"We-ell, no, not quite yet."

"Brandi Lyn!" I screeched, then caught myself as Mizz Upton turned in my direction. I waved excitedly to Mizz Upton. "It's Brandi Lyn calling to wish us good luck." The Bobbed Monster gave a curt nod and left to inspect the Grand Verandah where we would be presented. "Brandi Lyn, the ceremony starts in thirty minutes. You have to get out here and get yourself dressed. Tell Miss Dinah Mae she has to stop."

Brandi Lyn sighed. "I know, but I hate to hurry her. . . ."

"Brandi Lyn, just do it! She can fix the hem later!" I hung up before she could argue. The girls surrounded me, concerned.

Caroline gave me the most pained look ever.

"It will be fine. They'll be here." But not one of them looked reassured.

"I'm just so nervous. Aren't y'all nervous?" Mallory

attempted to slip her gauntlet—this totally pointless concoction of lace—over her fingers. Again and again, she couldn't get the elastic over her middle finger.

"Terribly." Zara nodded, picking at her ruffles.

"About to come out of my skin," said Ashley, swaying back and forth to redistribute the weight of her dress.

"Me too," I admitted. "With this Brandi Lyn thing and my dad coming, I'm about to die."

"When's he gonna get here?" asked Zara.

"Soon, I guess. He flew into New Orleans, so he's driving over." I thought for a moment. "Come on, y'all, we cannot let this get to us. I know! Let's do a dress check. Mallory, you want to kick it off?"

She halfheartedly agreed, leading us through the insane list of items we were supposed to have on our bodies. "Let's, uh, start with the bottom then," said Mallory. "Pantaloons?" We lifted our skirts to check for the bloomers with giant pockets that we had to wear under the dress. Magnolia Maids aren't allowed to carry purses, so this is where we hid our lipstick, cell phones, car keys, etc.

"Check."

"Check."

"Check."

It was precisely at the moment that I had my skirts lifted to my stomach and I was about to say "check" when a male voice unexpectedly intruded into our lair. "Uh, Jane?"

Thrilled, I whirled around. "Cos—Dad?" But it wasn't Cosmo who stood in the threshold.

It was *Luke*.

"Hi," he said, all tentative. Looking oh-so-handsome in dress pants and a jacket.

I was astonished. "Uh, hi, Luke. You know, um . . . the dandies are all congregating down on the lawn. There should be some seats reserved in the first row."

"Yeah, I know. They're all down there. Except Teddy Mac."

"He's on his way."

"Good, good. And you know Ashley's cousin Henry took James's place."

"Yeah. Seems like a good choice."

"Sure." Luke's gaze traveled over to the other Maids, who were all staring at us like we were the live version of a reality show. "Um . . . can we go somewhere a little more private?"

"Okay." He led me out to the small verandah right outside the ladies' parlor and took a seat in a rocking chair, motioning for me to sit as well. I shook my head. "Sorry, I haven't mastered the art of sitting in the four circles of hell, I mean, hoops, yet."

"Oh sure." He jumped back up. He plunged his hands into his pockets and shrugged his shoulders high around his ears. And then we just stood there.

And stood there.

And stood there.

Finally, we both broke the silence: "You see—"

"What did you—"

"You first," he said.

"Me? You're the one who wanted to talk."

"Right. Okay, I admit it. I did drive by your house that night. And not because it's the shortcut to Dauphin. I've driven by a thousand times since I heard you got back to town."

Ohhhhhhhh. Intriguing. "Well, why didn't you . . . ?"

"I wanted to stop in. I just didn't know what to say."

"And probably your girlfriend wouldn't like it?"

His brow furrowed. "My girlfriend?"

"Posey or Mosey or whatever her name is. The one you called 'babe.'"

Looking embarrassed, he plunged his hands deeper into his pockets. "Yeah, that. She's just a friend. I know I kissed her but . . . it didn't mean anything. I was, well, nervous."

Well, well, well, this was shaping up to be interesting indeed.

"The thing is, Jane, I thought if you really cared about me, you would have made an effort to get in touch with me."

Okay, it was time to clear the air. "But, Luke, I couldn't! I was in so much trouble back then! My father . . ."

"I know."

"You know?" He knew?

"Ashley made a big effort to track me down and tell me."

"Ashley? Darn it! Remind me to kick her butt later."

"Nope, you can't!" I heard Ashley call through the window of the ladies' parlor. "I did you a favor!"

I poked my head through the window and parted the curtains to find Ashley, Mallory, Caroline, and Zara standing right there. "What are you doing?" I asked.

"Nothing," sang Mallory.

"This is sooooo romantic!" cooed Caroline.

"Do you think he's going to apologize?" whispered Zara.

"Leave me alone! Take your sneakifying little ears and go away!" I dropped the curtains and turned back to Luke. Inside, there was a kerfuffle of ruffles and ribbons as the girls maneuvered themselves to the other side of the parlor. I sighed. "Sorry, Luke. What were you saying?"

"I don't know. That ever since I heard you were back in town, I've been a little out of my mind."

A tiny smile started to explore the corners of my mouth. "Out of your mind how, exactly?"

"I tried to ignore it, tried to write you off, to convince myself that you weren't worth it. But I couldn't stop thinking of you. Why do you think I agreed to be Zara's dandy?"

"Because Lancer and Jules and James were doing it?"

"No. Because of you."

Because of me. *Because of me!* Well, well. I was so surprised, I began exhibiting manners unbecoming a Magnolia Maid. Gaping being the main one.

"I never forgot you, Jane. Every girl I've ever been out with, I've compared to you. I know we were only twelve, I know it's been five years since we've seen each other, but still. I've been out with a dozen girls since then, and I can't help it. I can't get you out of my mind."

From the ladies' parlor came a long, drawn-out "awwwwwwww." Obviously the girls were still eavesdropping but my tongue was too tied to do anything about it.

283

"Well?" he finally said. "I just poured my heart out to you here, Jane. Want to get back to me?"

I handed him my parasol. "Hold this." I turned my back to him and moved aside the extra-wide strap that Miss Dinah Mae had sewn into my bodice. "See that?"

"Wow. Your grandmother let you get a tattoo?"

"Not really. See what it's of?"

"Yeah, Cart . . ." His voice trailed off. "Cartman? You got a tattoo of Cartman? Why?" I just gave him a look. "Because of me? You got a tattoo of *Cartman* because of *me*?"

I *really* couldn't look at him now. "I never forgot you, either, Luke. Don't think my heart wasn't broken, too. It was. You were my best friend."

I swear I heard another "awwwwwwww" from inside but I was beyond caring at this point. This was just between him and me.

"So what do we do now?" he asked.

"I don't know." I wished I could stop feeling so incredibly awkward and nervous. "What do you want to do?"

"I don't know. Go on a date?" Luke suggested.

"A date? I can do that."

"Next Saturday?"

"I think I'm available."

He nodded. "Okay. We're going on a date. Pick you up at seven." Luke lifted my lace-clad hand and bowed over it. "Until then, my lady." A smile broke out on his face and swam its way over to mine. He headed for the grand staircase that led to the Great Boysenthorp Lawn.

"Hey, wait!" I called after him. "You know where I live?"

He tossed a grin over his shoulder. "Yeah. I drive by there all the time!"

I couldn't help beaming as I made my way back to the ladies' parlor and was immediately *swarmed* by the girls.

"That . . ."

". . . was the . . ."

". . . most romantic . . ."

" . . . thing . . ."

"Ever!"

"I knew Luke Churchville would come through!" screamed Mallory. "I knew it, I knew it, I knew it!" The girls jumped up and down. Well, as much as you can jump up and down in a fifty-pound dress.

"Y'all, please!" I beseeched. "Calm down! It's just one date." But if that was the case, then why was my heart beating a billion times a second?

"Just one date?" Ashley scoffed.

"Yeah," I said. "Let's just see how it goes."

Caroline rolled her eyes. "It's obvious where it's going to go."

I stifled a laugh. Then my phone vibrated in my pantaloons. I pulled it out and read a text. "Brandi Lyn's here, y'all, we've got to move!"

Zara and I scurried through the fussy public rooms of Boysenthorp Manor—well, as fast as two girls who have to collapse their hoopskirts in order to get through door frames can scurry—searching for Mizz Upton. We found her and Walter Murray Hill in the music room dispensing last-minute orders to the string quartet that would be playing background music during our appearance.

"Mizz Upton! Mizz Upton!" I called.

"Maids!" She hurried over to me and Zara. "What are you doing out here? No one's supposed to see you until you go onstage!" She dragged us away from the musicians to a side room where Zara and I held her hostage with a series of really dumb questions about the details of the proceedings. She was so annoyed—"Haven't we gone over this a dozen times?"—that she didn't even notice a fully made-up Brandi Lyn dash across the verandah and into the ladies' parlor, Teddy Mac Trenton and Lacey Wilkes Hawkes trailing behind with garment bags.

A few minutes later, Mizz Upton was done with our ridiculousness. "If you don't know it now, I can't help you. It's almost showtime." She bustled into the ladies' parlor. "Maids, it's . . ." Her voice trailed off.

Standing before her was Brandi Lyn, completely bedecked in full Magnolia Maid regalia. "What the . . . ?" the Bobbed Monster started then stopped. She was clearly at a loss for words.

Frankly, so was I.

Because the answer to the question "what would Cecilia do?" turned out to be simple: she would have done anything within her power to fix the situation, even if it meant giving someone the dress off her very own dress stand. The dress that had allowed Brandi Lyn back into the fold, that Lacey

Wilkes Hawkes had bribed her favorite dry cleaner to touch up to perfection and, stat!, that Miss Dinah Mae had been nipping and tucking up to the very last second, wasn't brand-new. It was the dress my grandmother had pulled out of the attic, the dress I had tried on.

Cecilia's dress.

So in my mind, it wasn't Brandi Lyn who appeared before my eyes. It was my mother. For a moment, it was Cecilia, at seventeen, curtsying, twirling, laughing, showing off her ribbons and ruffles. It was Cecilia who rushed over and threw her arms around me. It was Cecilia who squeezed me tight and hugged me as if her life depended on it.

Mizz Upton stood straight as a board. "Would. Someone. Please. Explain. To me. What. Is going on?" she said through clenched teeth.

We all exchanged glances. "Caroline?" I prompted.

Caroline stepped forward. Paused. A pause so long that it made me fear she wouldn't be able to say what she had said she wanted to say. She fished a piece of paper out of her bodice. Licked her lips. Breathed. "'Mother,'" she said, "'I know that this is going to disappoint you, and for that I am very, very sorry.'"

Mizz Upton stared at her daughter. "What are you doing?"

Caroline faltered.

"Come on, Caroline, you can do it," said Ashley.

Caroline started to read. "'Dear Mother, I don't want to be a Magnolia Maid. I respect the organization, and your tireless work for it, but I never wanted to try out, and I don't think, no, I'm certain that I never want to wear this dress. I feel very uncomfortable in the public eye and resent your attempts to thrust me into it.'" She gestured to Brandi Lyn. "'Thanks to the generosity of the Fontaine Ventouras and Hawkes families, and all my sister Maids, Brandi Lyn Corey is now able to take her rightfully earned place on the Court. I speak for all of the girls here . . .'"

We all nodded agreement.

"'. . . when I say that we all would like for you to respect that she is the fifth Maid as the judges initially decreed. I will agree to serve as alternate. But it is my sincere hope that I never have to fulfill those duties. Thank you, and I'm sorry.'"

As Caroline finished reading the letter, dear Lord (sorry, Brandi Lyn!), the silence was deafening. Caroline folded up the paper and placed it back in her bodice. She looked relaxed for the first time since I had known her, especially when we all gathered behind her and presented a united front.

Mizz Upton looked like she was about to faint. She yelled toward the verandah. "Walter?! Please get in here? Walter!"

Mr. Walter came running in, and Mizz Upton yammered up a storm about how she wasn't sure that Brandi Lyn could come back after resigning. And was she allowed to wear a dress from a bygone Maid? It wasn't in the bylaws, she'd have to check with the Jaycees, Maids were required to commission their own dresses, etc. But old Walter Murray Hill took one look at the perfection that was Brandi Lyn in that dress, saw Caroline hanging back, looking relieved, and he clapped Mizz

Upton on the back and declared, "Why, Martha Ellen! The dress has tradition, okay. Just like the Magnolia Maids! And as long as Miss Caroline is fine with it—"

Caroline nodded emphatically from the corner.

"—then we are good to go! Let's do this!" he announced. That Mr. Walter. What a good man. "T-minus ten minutes and counting," he said.

So . . . ten minutes to go and I decided to peak outside at our audience. It looked like a billion people were crowded on the Great Lawn of Boysenthorp Gardens. Okay, slight exaggeration. More like one thousand. But that was a lot, considering how small B'ville usually felt! I scanned the crowd, searching for Cosmo. It was impossible to find anyone, though. Except Grandmother, who, all of a sudden, was standing right in front of me.

"Jane, sweet pea, can I speak to you for a moment?" she asked.

I followed her onto the verandah, the very site of my recent victory with Luke. "No problem, but make it quick, I was just looking for . . ." I trailed off. Oh no. I looked at her and I knew. I just knew. "He's not coming, is he?"

She shook her head. "He's got a big . . ."

". . . convention in the Bahamas or deal to make in Norway or . . ." I stopped. I was tired. My sarcasm tank had run out. I felt empty.

"I'm so sorry," Grandmother said.

I shook myself. "It's okay. It's better really. Today has been so hectic anyway, you wouldn't believe all the drama we've

289

had, and . . ." I trailed off as the wave of disappointment washed over me.

Grandmother produced a handkerchief, lace, of course, from her handbag to dab away a tear that had formed at the corner of my eye.

I laughed. At least made a pathetic attempt to. "Yeah, wouldn't want to ruin all this makeup Mizz Upton had us put on."

A sad smile tweaked Grandmother's lips. "He'll be there for you one day, Jane. I think he's gone so often because it's easier for him not to remember. He's haunted."

"But I miss her, too, Grandmama. I loved her, too. Why can't we miss her and love her together?"

Grandmother sighed. "Honey, sometimes it doesn't work that way. There's no telling how people are going to react to things. Sometimes they push away from each other when they should be circling in."

I knew what she meant.

I shrugged. I wanted to believe her. Wanted to believe that one day he would come back to me. That I would be enough. But I wasn't so sure.

I looked at Grandmother and felt a surge of love. For her, I would be hopeful. "I guess I just have to accept it, don't I?"

Grandmother smiled for real and gave me a quick kiss on the forehead. "That's my girl. Now. This is supposed to be one of the most memorable days in a Magnolia Maid's year. You get back in there and have the time of your life! Okay?"

It was Grandmother. How could I possibly say no?

Chapter Twenty-one

When I returned to the ladies' parlor, Zara could tell something was off.

"Everything okay?" she asked.

I shrugged and whispered, "My dad." She squeezed my hand in solidarity.

And Great Day in the Morning, y'all, but you could have knocked me over with the tiniest of feathers if you had even hinted at what transpired next.

Walter Murray Hill announced that it was time for the final vote for queen. He handed out white slips of paper and instructed us each to write down the name of the Maid we thought should be queen. In the event of another tie, God forbid, he and Mizz Upton would make the final call. After all, we couldn't make a debut without a queen! I scribbled *Brandi Lyn* on my white slip and handed it back. I saw Ashley giving Mallory and Caroline the eye and thought, oh great. Ashley's *still* twisting arms into voting for her. After everything we'd done together this week. Puh-leez. Zara and Brandi Lyn breezily jotted down their votes. I smiled at them. They smiled back.

Walter Murray and Mizz Upton huddled together to tally the votes, and to my great delight, Mizz Upton looked greener and greener with every opening of a slip of paper.

"It's about time y'all agreed on something," she muttered. But she was disgusted. I could tell. Why else would her Estée Lauder Maraschino–colored lips be scrunched up like a lemon? I took it as good news—someone from Ashley's team had finally woken up, smelled the magnolias, and decided to vote for Brandi Lyn.

Walter Murray Hill, however, maintained an inscrutable expression until the very last slip of paper was opened, and then a grin wider than the Grand Canyon split his face. "Congratulations, Maids, we have a new queen." He turned to us girls, and I must admit, his excitement was contagious!

We all gathered around him and joined hands like a bunch of beauty-pageant finalists.

"It is my supreme pleasure to announce that the young lady who will be our primary ambassadress of the city of Bienville, the leader of her sister Magnolia Maids, the queen of the Magnolia Court . . . is Miss Ashley Jane Fontaine Ventouras!"

Miss Ashley Jane Fontaine Ventouras. The name reverberated in my head. *Miss Ashley Jane Fontaine Ventouras. Miss Ashley Jane . . .*

"Oh my God!" I screeched. "That's me!"

There's a whole chapter in the *Magnolia Court Orientation Handbook* titled "Manners Befitting a Maid Upon Revelation That She Is Queen of the Court." It goes something like this, with a few flourishes for dramatic purposes:

1. DO smile humbly and thank your Magnolia sisters for having faith in you and selecting you as their leader.

2. DO NOT gasp with shock, widen your eyes in surprise, then berate your sisters for being out of their minds. Magnolia Maids are supposed to be hostesses extraordinaire, and having an inherent ability to repress and ignore any and all elephants in the room is a requirement of gracious Southern living.

3. DO take your place at the head of the flight formation and prepare to lead your flock out to the clamoring crowd gathered under the oaks of Boysenthorp Gardens.

4. DO NOT remain frozen solid, actively shoving bile back down your throat as you ponder what part of "I'm the rebel in the group" those Magnolia sisters of yours did not understand.

Guess who violated number 1, committed number 2, was incapable of performing number 3, and absolutely one hundred percent enacted number 4?

Me.

"No, no, no, you didn't mean me." My eyes pleaded with Mr. Walter to make it all go away.

"I sure did, Jane." He squeezed my arm. "And I think it's a fine choice for the year we're getting ready to have. Now. Y'all get in formation and let's go meet the good people of Bienville, okay!"

The string quartet launched into some ode to summer, and Mr. Walter headed out the French doors to the Grand Verandah. A moment later, a microphone kicked on and we heard Mr. Walter welcome the crowd and begin his opening speech.

Meanwhile, I was as frozen as Caroline had been when she heard her name announced as alternate. I felt milliseconds away from pulling a Brandi Lyn and fainting. Seeing my condition, the girls rallied around to prop me up and fan me with the three-hundred-dollar fans Miss Dinah Mae had made for us. I glared at them all. "How could you? What were you all thinking?"

"You take care of us, Jane," said Brandi Lyn.

"You solve our problems," said Mallory.

"You care about our feelings," said Caroline.

"You have an admirable sense of justice," said Zara.

"But I pick fights! I get you into trouble!" I whirled on Ashley. "You agreed to this?"

"It was my idea."

"You've lost your mind. I thought you wanted to be queen."

Ashley shrugged. "What with my recent heartbreak and not-so-private humiliation, I've had enough of being in the public eye for a while."

"Well, what about Brandi Lyn? Remember? Weren't we going to vote for her?"

"That's sweet, Jane," Brandi Lyn said. "But we all agreed. You're our true leader."

Off in the distance, I could hear Mr. Walter working the crowd. It was happening. The debut presentation had actually started.

Mizz Upton butted her way through Brandi Lyn and Mallory. "Jane, what in the world is going on here? You're supposed to be out there in two seconds! Do we need a doctor?"

"No." I am sure it did look that way. I would have fallen on my ruffle-encased behind if Ashley and Zara had not been holding me up.

"What then? Are you refusing to be the queen? It is a rather"—her evil eye traveled angrily around the circle—"unusual choice. If you aren't feeling up to it, we can recall the decision and Walter Murray Hill and I can choose." Anticipation dripped from every one of Mizz Upton's words. Once again, she was dying for me to resign.

And frankly, this was one of Mizz Upton's ideas that actually sounded appealing. As Brandi Lyn would have put it, being queen was so not in my five-year plan. I was no queen. I was the anti-queen. What were the girls thinking?

I searched the beautiful bright faces all around me: Zara. Mallory. Ashley. Caroline. Brandi Lyn. I glanced out the window at the gorgeous Bienville summer day and once again wondered . . . what would Cecilia do now?

Brandi Lyn, wearing my mother's dress, squeezed my hand. "Please, Jane," she said. "We need you."

Suddenly, I knew the answer.

I aimed one last petrified glance at the girls, painted a glittering smile onto my face, and addressed the firing squad of Mizz Upton. "Actually, ma'am. I believe that if the girls want me, we should follow tradition and honor our legally held election." I nodded at the Maids. "Get into position, Maids!"

"But this is a terrible idea!" Mizz Upton sniffed. "This can't possibly work!"

Ignoring her, the girls lined up behind me. Brandi Lyn and Ashley on one side, Zara and Mallory on the other, Caroline, many happy steps behind.

"It's going to work just fine," I said. "Ready, girls? One, two . . ."

On three, we all stepped forward in perfect unison with our right feet. The French doors to the Grand Verandah magically swung open and we floated as one outside to greet the mass of cheering Bienvillites.

And it was at that moment that I finally heard it. The voice that had eluded me for nine years. It was only eight tiny little words, but I felt them in my heart, just like Grandmother said I would.

Welcome back, Jane, said my mother with warmth and hope, love and joy, reassurance and affection. *I'm so glad you're home.*

Acknowledgments

I couldn't write a novel about the power of friendship without giving a shout-out to my family and to all my friends who encouraged its writing from the very beginning, especially Gail Lerner, Gina Neff, Karyn Kusama, Lisa Brown, and Daniel Handler.

Many thanks to Hedgebrook and the Elizabeth George Foundation for supporting the writing and research of the project and to the many good people who launched the finished book into the world: particularly my crackerjack agent Meredith Kaffel, who found it a home with the fabulous Regina Griffin at Egmont USA, and Molly McGuire, the most insightful, cheerful editor a girl could ask for.

A curtsy to the City of Mobile, Alabama, and its beautiful Azalea Trail Maids for inspiring the world of the story. Special thanks to the Boutwell family for their kind hospitality, especially to Emily for aiding and abetting my research. I am grateful to the Azalea Trail Maid alumnae who so enthusiastically shared their experiences on the Trail and explained the ins and outs of the hoopskirt: Dr. Be Phetsinorath, Meridy Jones, Leslie Foster Gaston, Katie Patterson, Anna Flock, and Alexandra Twilley.

Last but not least, this book would not exist were it not for Susan Boutwell Cannon. Thanks for being the one person I could talk to back then, and for being the one person who truly understands it all now.